MAGIC MAN CHARLIE

THE DRAGON MAGE BOOK 4

SCOTT BARON

"In the World through which I travel, I am endlessly creating myself."

— Frantz Fanon

CHAPTER ONE

The crackling flash of light came and went in an instant, briefly illuminating the darkness of space at the edge of Earth's atmosphere. This was disconcerting in and of itself. More so was the unexpected appearance of a spaceship in a place where none had been just moments before.

And it was plummeting toward Earth.

"What do you mean it came out of nowhere?" Captain Mendez exclaimed into her comms as she banked her ship hard, heading for the new, unidentified blip on her screen.

"Exactly that, Captain," the tactical monitoring AI replied. "There was an unusual anomaly across my scans, followed by the appearance of what seems to be a ship."

"So it came in via a warp jump, then," she stated with confidence.

"No, Captain, it did not. That's the unusual thing. There was no warp signature at all. I'm afraid this was something else. Something I've never seen before."

Mendez didn't like the sound of that. The monitoring satellite array surrounding the bright blue orb had been put in place by the greatest combined minds of the human, AI, and alien residents of the planet. For something to just pop in like that, leaving them all scratching their heads as to what it might be, was not how the system was supposed to work.

But that was why Captain Mendez, and others like her, still flew sorties despite the planet being at peace. Having experienced enough war and death at the hands of alien invaders, Earth's residents knew how quickly calm could become chaos. Working hand in hand with the many great AI minds helping run the planet, they'd kept a watchful eye over the globe. And it had been a quiet watch.

But that had all just changed.

"Contact in twenty seconds," the calm voice of the AI said over Mendez's comms.

"Copy that. I should have visual in––hang on, there it is. I see something."

She squinted her eyes at the display screen. The tiny, glowing orange speck was still too small to make out properly, but as it grew rapidly on her monitor, she could see that it was definitely not a meteor, and the debris field of derelict ships previously circling the globe had been salvaged and removed from orbit years ago.

This object was new, and it was man-made. Or alien-made, perhaps. None of that mattered. What did matter was, regardless of whoever had built it, the craft was coming down, and fast.

"Trajectory?" she asked the powerful tactical mind monitoring the situation as it unfolded.

"Given the speed and angle of descent, it appears to be heading toward the eastern portion of the Atlantic. A water landing is imminent."

Martinez zoomed her optics in for a closer look as she sped toward the target, getting the first glimpse of the superheated craft blazing through the sky. It was definitely a ship, and decent sized, though the model was unfamiliar.

"Unidentified craft, power up your engines, level out your

2

descent, and identify yourself," she transmitted on all open frequencies.

No reply.

"Unidentified craft, I repeat, engage your engines, level out your descent, and identify yourself," she said, activating her weapons systems. "You have been target-locked. Failure to comply will result in forcible downing of your craft."

The pilot of the mystery ship either didn't hear her or didn't care. The craft continued its blazing descent. Its hull was beginning to cool as it reached lower altitudes, the visual distortion from the heat thrown off resolving enough for Martinez to get a better look. What she saw stunned her.

"You've got to be kidding me," she gasped into her comms in utter shock. "Uh, you're not going to believe this."

"I've received your vid feed," the AI replied. "Please confirm. Do another pass and acquire a second set of images."

"Roger that," she said, banking the ship for a second go-around. She also turned off her weapons, putting them in standby mode. There was no way she was shooting that ship down if she could avoid it. Not if it was what she thought it was.

Martinez eased in line for a second run and set her recording instruments to high resolution. The ship came into focus once more.

"There you are. But how in the world did you get here?" she mused.

As if it could hear her, the craft abruptly shifted course, dropping sharply from its original trajectory.

"What happened?" the AI asked. "My readings show an altered angle of descent."

"Affirmative. It just changed course. Still no engine readings, however."

"I see the same on my readouts. Was there an external reaction of some sort?" the confused AI asked. "How did it shift course?"

"I don't know. Hang on, I'm diving for a better look."

"I copy you. Given this development, support craft have been scrambled and will reach your position in two minutes."

"In two minutes this thing is going to be a smoking crater. It's not on a water landing trajectory anymore. It's heading toward—" She realized where they were. "Shit. It's going to crash into London."

The AI, being an incredibly powerful computing mind, already knew this, naturally, and had reached out to Vic, the resident city-sized AI overseeing the area. He, in turn, had activated the surface-to-air defenses for the slowly rebuilding city. Vic didn't want to blow the craft out of the sky, but if he had to, he would.

Captain Mendez was gaining quickly, her monitors filling with the image of the impossible spaceship. She adjusted the resolution and transmitted backups of what she was seeing to their tactical relay hub. From there, it would be shared with the conglomerate of the planet's AI minds.

Sure, she had been briefed on what to do in incredible circumstances, but she'd never thought something so outrageous as this could ever happen. Not on her watch. But there it was, right in front of her. A ship that simply *couldn't* be there. She'd studied it in her history lessons, as anyone in flight school had. A cautionary tale about man's overconfidence and folly.

The craft abruptly shifted course, again with no sign of engine activity.

"Shit, where's it going?"

She rolled her ship, locking her cameras on it once again.

"Now it's heading *away* from London," she said. "It's tracking west. Are you seeing this?"

"Yes. Images are coming in clear."

"So, you know that ship," she said. It wasn't a question.

"We *all* know that ship, Captain. But this is just not possible."

She couldn't believe the words that were about to come out of her mouth. "I know," she replied. "But it's the *Asbrú*."

"It would appear so."

"But that's impossible," Mendez said.

"As I already said."

The AI paused to consider its options. For a quantum mind as powerful as it was, that was saying something. Finally, it sent a priority notification to the western coast of the United States. "I believe we had best contact the newcomers," the AI said. "Follow the ship, and stay nearby until a support team arrives. I've just sent notice to Charlie Gault."

CHAPTER TWO

The small trail of smashed trees and rutted earth marked the arrival site of the long-lost ship. Charlie's old ship. A ship he had left in a broken heap on a distant planet in a distant galaxy many, many years ago. And now it was home, somehow.

The *Asbrú* had come in hot, its heat shielding glowing orange as it glided to Earth, its engines stone-cold. *That* was the thing giving Captain Mendez an uneasy feeling as she circled the site of its landing. The ship *should* have crashed into the ocean. It *should* have broken up on impact. But here it was, intact and unscathed.

Something had directed it––made it shift course. But from her vantage point, she was certain its engines had most certainly not powered up during its descent. But somehow it *had* changed direction, and though its landing was a rather hard one, it was nowhere near what one would call a crash. The whole thing just didn't make sense, and a low rumble of unease spread through her gut as she surveyed the scene.

Mendez flew another low pass, looping around the entire landing site, transmitting a non-stop stream of information back to the AIs and their human counterparts who were monitoring the situation in real-time. Whatever was going on, the big brains would figure it out. She hoped so, at least.

The *Asbrú* had finally come to rest in a remote part of Wales, not far from the great limestone caverns near the coast. Why it had chosen that particular area, she couldn't tell, but at least it wasn't an inhabited one. Much of the world was that way these days.

After the alien invasion and ensuing Great War––which was really more of a slaughter than a war, to be fair––the planet was sparsely populated, at best. Even with civilization slowly regaining a foothold, most had clustered around the major cities of the world. The rest of the planet was void of people.

As such, and given the remote location where the ship had come down, the risk of civilian injury was minimal. And with a major, rebuilt hub relatively nearby in London, a ground team had been hastily assembled and was already on the move, heading to Wales as fast as they were able.

Unfortunately, most of the AI-powered ships that had made rebuilding and global transit so easy after the war were currently off on a massive exploration mission, seeking out other habitable systems, while also hoping to make contact with new alien species.

Mankind was very much not alone, and *this* time, they wanted to be the ones to make first contact. But that meant ships capable of communication––learning the basics of an alien language as only a machine could––were required for the task.

The AIs had been happy to embark on the mission, enjoying the opportunity to explore, along with their human and Chithiid crews. The tall, four-armed aliens were fully integrated into Earth society at this point, and to venture forth without them wasn't even a remote option.

But those crews were the lucky ones, setting off on an

adventure into the vast unknown, while the rest of the population would go about their usual routines, no space voyages or adventures lined up for them. Just the boring, daily routines they'd all come to call life.

That is, until a strange ship burned a trail through the morning sky and landed in Wales, of all places.

Volunteers leapt at the opportunity. This was something different. This was exciting. This was more than just rebuilding cities and infrastructure. This was an actual adventure.

The men and women selected from the hastily assembled group would travel quickly to the landing site and secure the ship and form a perimeter, as instructed. While Captain Mendez had confirmed the location and status of the craft, they still lacked more vital information as to its threat level. For that, however, they had already put other tools into action.

Vic, the London AI, sent a survey drone, its sensor array repurposed specifically for the task at hand to ensure there was no imminent risk from the *Asbrú*, such as a radiologic or chemical leak. So far, all appeared normal.

The team had deployed quickly, making relatively good time, while the AI minds of the world, as well as those of the fleet orbiting the planet and residing on the Dark Side moon base reviewed what little data they had and formulated a plan.

"Seems well and proper crashed," Duncan Hughes, the sturdy man selected to head the team, transmitted to Vic.

"Thank you, Duncan. Have your team secure the perimeter, and do please report any unusual observations," the massive AI said.

"Will do, Vic," he replied as he and his team walked around the ship. "Hey, Vic. It looks like there's a door here, right close to ground level."

"Do not enter the ship. We're discussing this situation with Cal. He has a team in Los Angeles that will be deployed to your location shortly."

Duncan was a little put out. They were already there and had done a good job of the task assigned them thus far. It seemed only fair that they should be the ones to make history, not some bloke from halfway around the world who wasn't even there yet.

Cal and Vic knew that, human nature being what it was, it was only natural they would want to go poking around inside. Which was why Cal decided to step into the discussion—with Vic's blessing, of course.

The enormously powerful AI running Los Angeles didn't want to step on any toes, even if computers didn't technically have them. Fortunately, his fame for his role in retaking the planet during the final days of the war made him something of an AI celebrity.

"Gentlemen, women, and non-binaries, this is Cal. You should know that we are all extremely grateful for your hasty arrival at the landing site. Most impressive. And now that you are there, I would like to reiterate what Vic has requested. Please, do not approach or enter the ship. It is an unusual situation we are in, so just wait until my people get there. Is that clear?" Cal transmitted to the team.

By expressly forbidding them from entering or even approaching the ship, he hoped to avoid any regrettable mishaps. They would have one shot at this, and they did not want well-intentioned—but inexperienced—volunteers to taint any evidence they might find.

"We'll be careful. Copy that," Duncan replied, though he didn't sound terribly happy about it. It was the first bit of excitement any of them had seen in ages, and now they were on babysitting duty for a spaceship full of cool goodies and who knew what else.

"Cal, how long until you can have your team here?" Vic asked his counterpart.

"It's still night here, so rousing them may take a little time," he

9

replied. *"However, we do have a new AI ship at our disposal. Eddie is his name. He just passed his final flight checks last week. I'll deploy him for transit detail. The team should be geared up and on its way to you within no more than a few hours."*

"Fantastic. I look forward to assisting the newcomers. I'm sure they'll be thrilled to return to my shores."

CHAPTER THREE

All was quiet along the Malibu coast, and the newcomers, having recently arrived from their freak time jump from medieval times, were enjoying the comforts of modern beach living.

Charlie and Leila had gladly taken one of the long-vacant homes along the bluffs as their new residence, as had Bawb and Hunze. The Great War had obliterated the population, but the construction had been designed to last, and last it had. With a simple cleanup and some basic repairs, habitability of the oceanfront estate was restored in short order.

But not all of them wanted beachfront life. Rika had been a city girl growing up and found living in one of the gleaming towers downtown far more her style, even if the city was no longer a bustling metropolis. This also placed her in closer proximity to Cal's command hub, as well as the underground fight club locals used to blow off steam, which she'd stumbled upon while exploring late one night.

It had been a satisfying discovery, and one she planned on revisiting in the future.

The comms alert chirping in the dark roused Charlie from a

deep sleep, sending him lurching for his nightstand, his konus on one arm and pistol in the other hand before he even realized he had grabbed them. Leila, however, woke without the violent start of her king.

"What is it?" she asked, rubbing her eyes groggily.

"I don't know," he replied. "Who the hell calls at three in the morning? Or is it three at night? At this hour, I don't even know if it's really late, or really early."

"Charlie. The comms."

"Oh, right," he said, looking at the caller ID and slapping open the line. "Do you know what time it is, Cal?"

"Of course, Charlie. I'm a computer. Keeping track of time for me is like breathing is for you."

"It was rhetorical," he said with a sigh.

"I know," Cal replied. *"And it is eleven a.m."*

"No, it isn't."

"It is in Wales."

That got his attention. Hearing the name of the place his recently freed dragon friend had been trapped in a limestone cavern for a few thousand years gave him goosebumps.

"Why Wales? What's happened, Cal?" he asked, still groggy but suddenly less so.

"Something...unexpected."

Charlie groaned. "Oh, come on. It's only been a week since we arrived in LA. And we've just traveled a few thousand years through time, into our future, no less. Whatever it is, can't it wait until morning?"

"The Asbrú *just landed in Wales."*

Now Charlie was wide awake.

"That's impossible."

"I would tend to agree with that assessment, yet here we are, discussing the impossible, it seems."

Charlie was already getting dressed, a full load of adrenaline flushing through his body. Leila, mirroring his urgency, was likewise reaching for her clothes.

The *Asbrú,* the ship that had started it all. It couldn't be in Wales. It had crash-landed in a desert wasteland on a planet in a distant galaxy, and Charlie would know. He'd built the damn thing, his whole life changed in an instant when it was sucked through a wormhole and spat out in a place where magic, not technology, powered civilization.

The only other survivor was their second-in-command and mech pilot, Rika Gaspari. But she had been taken. Captured by a group of slave traders, her brain had been permanently damaged as they tried to force her into compliance. Charlie had thought her gone forever. Until he encountered her at the end of an opposing sword a few thousand years in the past, and back on their homeworld, no less.

It had been a surprise courtesy of Malalia Maktan, his former nemesis's equally cruel daughter. Rika had been tracked down, bought as a slave, and made into a weapon. And all to hurt Charlie.

Malalia was nothing, if not vindictive.

Charlie had defeated his former friend in combat, taking her captive. Then he and his friends managed to overpower Malalia, but only barely, sending her back to her home galaxy, while they remained on Earth, accidentally throwing themselves far into the future. A future nearly a thousand years farther than Charlie and Rika's own timeline.

And the Rika they'd brought back with them was not the woman he'd known. She was something different now.

But, in a way, she was herself again. At least, personality-wise. She still lacked the memories stolen from her when her mind was tampered with, but she had replaced them with combatives and magic knowledge, forced into her head by her captor. And, more importantly, now that she'd been healed properly, she was Charlie's ally once more.

"Cal, you've told the others, I assume?"

"I will contact them momentarily. I wanted to speak with you first."

"Appreciated. But I guess it's time to get 'em all up and going." He turned, appreciating the sight of Leila dressing as much as he enjoyed the opposite.

How the hell did I get so lucky? he mused.

The greatest benefit of all the ordeals he had endured was his girlfriend. His *queen*, and quite literally at that. Leila, along with the rest of their unlikely band of rebel adventurers, were his friends, and in a much deeper and substantial way than any he'd had in his former life, before being sucked down a wormhole. Hell, he was even blood-bound to a magic-wielding dragon.

"I'll tell Ara," he said.

"Thank you. I was unable to find her on my scans."

"She's *very* good at not being seen when she doesn't want to be."

Despite her considerable size, it was a fair assessment. Also true was that while she was mostly okay, she was still having a bit of a hard time regaining her former high spirits. Being trapped in a cave for a few thousand years had done a number on her, and while she was more than fully recovered physically, it was the residual emotional distress that worried Charlie.

She'd get over it, in time, but for now, they had all agreed to give her however much space she needed to deal with it.

Doctor McClain, the local head-shrinker, had been more than a little startled when the massive dragon had accepted the suggestion she speak with her, but she, and the other resident therapist, a tranquil, almond-eyed woman with silver hair named Fatima, had taken Ara under their proverbial wings, helping her deal with the residual survivor's trauma. It was an unusual arrangement, to say the least.

The two women had also taken on another new patient, this one quite human.

Rika had passed the physical assessments with flying colors. She was the picture of perfect health, largely due to her contact with the healing Balamar waters, which helped heal and restore her mind as well as her body. But psychologically, she was dealing with issues that healthy brain tissue alone would not mend.

Her life had been stripped from her, and while snippets remained, she had a great many gaping holes. Holes that would never return. Fortunately, her friendship with Charlie had reformed, and the pair trained together once more, as they'd done in the old days, only now they formed new memories rather than reminiscing about old ones.

And now they would all be flying back to the UK, the same place they'd just spent a considerable amount of time, albeit a few thousand years in the past.

"Bring your weapons," Charlie called out to Leila. "No idea what we'll find there."

"One step ahead of you," she replied merrily, a shining konus already on her wrist.

"Ya see? This is why I love you," he said with a contented grin. "Now, come on, Ripley's almost certainly awake. We can have her and Eddie give us a ride," he said of their teenage friend and neighbor.

Her parents had long ago staked claim to one of the largest estates in the area, simply based on the size of the kitchen it boasted. And they'd welcomed the newcomers with open arms, and a lot of home-cooked meals.

"Does that girl ever sleep?" Leila joked.

"She's a teenager, so the answer is no. At least not at this hour."

Leila laughed brightly. "A valid observation."

The pair quickly gathered up the rest of their things and headed for the door.

"Where's Baloo?" Charlie asked.

"Probably out stalking another deer," Leila replied.

It was one of the enormous wolf-like animal's favorite games, stalking and chasing deer, which were incredibly plentiful in the overgrown hills of Malibu. Typically, he would just pursue them for fun, but every so often, he'd take one down, feasting happily, while not even putting a dent in the deer population. It was a good thing, too, because as huge as he'd grown, feeding him would have been quite a chore, otherwise.

"No time to track him down. We'll just let him be. You ready?"

"Yes. Let's go find Ripley."

CHAPTER FOUR

Bawb lay peacefully in the warmth of the bed, sharing the soft covers with Hunze, watching her with quiet wonder as she slept. This was all so new to him. To her as well, really, though for far different reasons than the assassin's.

As for Bawb, he had never stayed in one place for any length of time, which was simply part of the life of a Wampeh Ghalian. No routines. No weaknesses. No attachments. But that all changed when he unexpectedly took the golden-haired woman under his protection.

It had started as a simple matter of keeping the innocent safe, while simultaneously denying the Council of Twenty her magic-storing hair, grown for nearly three decades. Or so he had told himself. But in retrospect, there had always been *something* between them, from the very first moment their eyes locked when he saved her from a burning Council ship.

She had only been freed from her life of slavery a short time when Bawb and his friends faced off against their powerful enemy. The resulting mix of spells and magic flung them so very far away from all she had ever known, stranding them on ancient Earth. But despite the challenge suddenly confronting them, Hunze had flourished in her new reality.

Free life saw her blossom, her fears melting away in the warmth of her new family's friendship. She learned to bake, learned to garden, and ultimately, learned to love. And it was from that love that she willingly gave half of her hair––filled with decades of power channeled into it since her youth––to Bawb as he faced his most challenging foe yet.

And he had succeeded––with the help of their friends, of course. But in her eyes, Bawb had become a transcendent being, evolving from a silent and stoic guardian to a man worthy of the gift she had given. Worthy of her love.

And now they lived together in an unexpected state of grace, the most unlikely of couples in either galaxy. A sweet, loving former slave and a deadly vampire assassin with more blood on his hands and in his stomach than entire armies had shed. Surprisingly, they settled into domestic life quite easily.

For Hunze, part of it might have been the clime of their new home. Unlike the UK, where they had first arrived and settled in, this new place––Malibu, on the shores of Southern California––was a world of warmth and wonder. And with that warmth came an abundance of sunshine, every ray of which soaked into Hunze's golden hair, charging it with even more power, which slowly continued to grow.

She found it an amusing new pastime, devising hairstyles, now that a full half of her hair was gone from her head, carefully shorn, and safely tucked away for her love to use when the need arose. A powerful tool at his disposal should the need for it arise again.

The thing Hunze had noticed immediately was that the sheer weight of it had been such a constant for so many years that she felt almost buoyant minus its weight. The steely muscles of her neck and back, long accustomed to supporting the burden of all that golden mass, were suddenly getting a break. Their first break ever, really.

Everything was easier now, and though the close-shorn hair on the sides and back of her head was beginning to grow out, nourished by the sun, she wasn't sure if she wanted it to. But there was time. For now, she was simply living a contented life in this new and amazing place. And with Bawb's strength to rely on, she had never felt safer.

Next to her in bed, Bawb felt that now-familiar warmth in his chest as he looked upon her sleeping profile.

So, this is love, he mused, his heart swelling with unfamiliar emotion. *It is no longer an abstract. I now understand why men are willing to die for it.*

The comms chirped out, demanding his attention.

"At this hour?" he grumbled.

He had quickly learned to operate this realm's communications systems, as well as a host of other amazing devices, though he still preferred his magical ones out of habit.

"Yes?" he said.

"Hello, Bawb. I apologize for waking you—"

"I was not asleep, Cal."

"Then I apologize for disturbing your evening," Cal corrected. *"In any case, there has been an incident abroad. Wales, to be exact. We are preparing to do a scene survey. Given the potential danger, I thought it would be best if you joined your friends for this outing."*

He looked at Hunze, now groggily smiling up at him from their bed. *No more danger for you,* he thought. *You'll be safe here.*

The pale man rose to his feet. "I will be at your command center straightaway."

"Excellent. Find Ripley. She is giving the others a ride."

"I will. We shall speak again shortly," he said, shutting off the comms and getting dressed.

"Bawb, what's going on?" Hunze asked.

"I am requested, it would seem."

Hunze moved to rise, but he gently put his hand on her shoulder. "No, Hunze. You sleep. This should not take long." He leaned in and kissed her gently, that twinge in his chest rising to greet him again.

"Don't be too long," she said, something more than just affection sparking behind her eyes.

"I'll be back before you miss me," he replied, then stepped out of their bedroom.

Bawb geared up quickly, donning a few of his usual weapons, then casting a dozen layers of increasingly deadly booby-trap spells as he left their home. They would not harm Hunze, but if anyone not in their immediate circle of friends came calling, they would be in for a *very* nasty surprise.

Satisfied at her safety, Bawb walked out toward the roadway, calling Ripley on her comms. "I'm at the intersection. Cal says you're giving us a lift?"

The dark shape of the ship sitting in a long-abandoned home's yard presented itself as its door opened, spilling out light. A teenage girl leapt down the short steps in exuberant greeting.

"Heya, Bob! Been waiting for ya. The others are already on board. You ready to do cool stuff?"

Teenagers, Bawb sighed. Her energy was boundless.

"Let us depart, then," he said, following her into the belly of the ship. "And hello to you as well, Eddie."

"Hi, Bob," the ship replied. "Just a quick stop at Command, then we'll jump into orbit for a minute and make the hop over to the UK. Sound good?"

"Of course," he said as he nodded a greeting to his friends and took a seat.

"Everyone is aboard, Ripley," Eddie called out.

"Great," she said. "Next stop, Uncle Cal's place."

CHAPTER FIVE

Eddie the talking ship flew low over the sleeping city of Los Angeles.

Charlie had befriended a dragon, fought aliens, and become king of a land a few thousand years in his past, but *this* was still throwing him. An actual, functional, *smack-talking* AI. Things really *had* changed in the future.

The passengers watched the city drift by beneath them as they headed toward the lights of Downtown. They could make out the lines of some of the streets and roadways below, but the absence of the dense population they'd been designed for had left them eerily vacant, like the city itself, save for the small groups slowly repopulating the area.

With no need for streetlights, the plague of light pollution that had been such a concern prior to the Great War had been unintentionally eliminated. A happy byproduct of the global near-extinction. Energy conservation was no longer an issue either, the solar collectors and fusion plants all producing far more power than was needed for the minuscule number of survivors.

The result was a silent, eerie landscape where man-made

structures reflected hints of their shapes in the ambient moonlight. And there, in the middle of it, roughly fifteen miles from the coast, stood the illuminated towers of the city center. And beneath those was the global loop tube hub Cal had chosen to serve as his command center.

"Hey, you guys. Hang on. We're gonna do a rooftop landing on one of the lower buildings," Eddie said over his internal speakers.

"Uh, isn't the place we're going *below* ground?" Charlie asked.

"Shh! Let him do it," Ripley hissed. "He only barely passed that part of his flight check and needs the practice."

"Shut up, Rip. I did not *barely* pass. I was just having a bad day," the AI shot back. "And I totally aced my space flights and re-entry trials, if you remember."

"Of course I do, Eddie. I was there, remember?"

"Well, duh. But with that little meat brain of yours, I never know what you'll forget," he said, the snark in his artificial voice clear as a bell.

"Oh my God, you two are insufferable," Charlie groaned. "In my time, AIs were supposed to be the promise of objective geniuses helping better mankind. Instead, we've got a moody teenager with wings."

Bawb allowed a slight grin to crack his otherwise stoic façade.

"It's not my fault," Ripley cracked. "I have no idea where he picked that up."

"Sure thing, kid. But if you two are quite done with your oh-so-clever banter, could we *please* land a bit closer to where we're actually going? My long-lost ship just rather impossibly popped up in Wales after crashing a bazillion miles away hundreds of years ago. I think a sense of urgency is appropriate."

"Fine," Eddie grumbled, setting down in the empty street outside an accessway to the loop tube network. "Here you are."

Ripley followed them down the lift into the tube terminus, where a handful of humans and a small group of tall, four-armed Chithiid were working to repair one of the tube platforms. One of the men had a replacement leg, the metal showing at the cuff of his pants. An older woman sported a shiny artificial hand.

The younger workers, however, appeared to be one hundred percent organic, born and raised on the planet. A lone cyborg was working among them. He had a living flesh covering and looked entirely human, but a subtle "offness" in his movement cued Charlie in to his true nature.

"Hey, guys, we're meeting up here," Rika called down from a small balcony overlooking the terminus, having arrived there before the others. One of the benefits of living so close.

They bounded up the short flight of stairs and stepped into the corridor that looped around to the command center access door. Had they come from the other side, they'd have just taken the lift straight to that hallway's landing, but Eddie's sense of direction was either off, or he just didn't care.

Charlie greeted Rika with a warm hug, though it still felt a tiny bit odd. She had been trying to kill him just a few weeks prior, after all. But with her mind her own once again, she and Charlie had struck up a renewed friendship.

To Rika's surprise, Leila stepped in and hugged her as well. It wasn't a particularly warm embrace, but she appreciated the effort all the same.

Bawb, on the other hand, merely nodded his greeting, while Ripley bounced over to one of the low couches and flopped into its plush embrace.

"Hey, Uncle Cal. What's the word?" Ripley asked.

"Hello, Ripley. Thank you for ferrying the others here on such short notice."

"No worries."

"Well, let's get right to it, then. Several hours ago, an

unidentified object appeared just at the edge of Earth's atmosphere and began a rapid re-entry. We dispatched a ship to obtain visual confirmation and engage if necessary. What the pilot saw was an ancient craft, apparently flying with no visible source of power."

"Hang on, are you saying it was *gliding* in? We tried that once, and tore up the belly of the ship when we landed as a result. She's not really designed for it."

"And with that, we get to the unusual part of the incident."

"Wait. The *Asbrú* showing up out of nowhere isn't the unusual part?" Rika said.

"Normally, it would be. However, when our ship approached it, the Asbrú *changed course."*

"So someone was performing evasive maneuvers," Rika noted. "Pretty standard procedure, really."

"But the engines were still cold. In fact, they were not once engaged during the entire descent, including both instances of directional change, as well as the landing, which, admittedly, was a bit rough."

Charlie and Rika shared a look. If the ship wasn't flying under its own power, then there was only one thing that could be at play.

"Shit. They magicked our ship," Charlie said. "There's not much of a way to fly it like that, but I suppose maybe fail-safe spells used to help ease down a crashing ship could have done the trick. But shit, this is magic. And on an old Earth ship. We need to get there, ASAP."

"Agreed," Bawb said. "If we have magic-wielding opposition, time is of the essence."

"A small team was dispatched to maintain a perimeter a short while ago, and I'm confident—"

A blinding, green flash filled the room as the Magus stone hanging from Leila's neck blasted forth its emerald light.

"What just happened?" Ripley gasped, rubbing her eyes.

"Yeah, what was that, Leila?"

"I don't know why it did that," was all she could manage as the pendant returned to its normal, dormant state.

"Oh, no," the AI said.

"What is it, Cal?" Rika asked.

"Vic, my counterpart AI in London, has lost contact with his team. Stand by."

A long silence hung in the air. AIs could, when not slowing things down to talk to humans, communicate and transfer huge amounts of data in nanoseconds. And still, the silence continued.

"This is not good," Ripley said, rising from the couch. "Uncle Cal? What's going on?"

"What exactly was aboard your ship, Charlie?" Cal finally asked. *"Any experimental devices we don't know about from the historical records?"*

"Why?"

"Because the fools in Wales boarded it, despite my express orders to the contrary. A drone just transmitted the recordings from the event."

"What event?"

"A few moments after they entered the ship, there was a flash, causing them all to freeze in place."

An alarmed look flashed on Bawb's normally placid face. "Likely a version of a *verata* spell," he said. "A magical booby trap. This does not bode well."

"I'm afraid it gets worse. Far, far worse."

"What do you mean, Cal?"

"It wasn't just the team at the Asbrú who were frozen in place. The same thing happened globally."

"What do you mean? I don't understand," Ripley said.

"All global AIs just conducted an emergency survey. Every living thing, and even many lesser machines, have frozen in place. It would appear the occupants of this room are the only people on the planet who escaped its effect."

25

CHAPTER SIX

It was a shitshow.

Leila had been in a state of utter shock as she and the others rushed outside. And Bawb was the closest Charlie had ever seen to outright losing it, which in his case meant calm, and quiet, with a buzzing air of danger around him. But also a barely restrained tension that was almost tangible.

"I must get to Hunze," he said, the muscles in his jaw flexing slightly.

"I know, man. Just give us a minute to——"

"*Now*, Charlie," the Wampeh said, the pain in his eyes clear to his friend no matter how he tried to conceal it.

"Okay. We'll be in the air in a minute." He turned to their stunned teenage pilot. "Rip, when we get on board, have Eddie tie us in to Cal remotely as we fly."

They hurried from the command center, Bawb a blur of crackling anxiety as he raced ahead. The five of them quickly retraced their path to where the ship was waiting to whisk them away, passing the work crew on their way. It was the first proof that what Cal had said was true. All of them were frozen in place. All but the cyborg, who was desperately looking around, confused. Charlie would have explained to the poor tin man, but there wasn't time.

"Ara, can you hear me?" Charlie silently reached out for his friend.

"Yes. I assume you've seen what just happened."

"Yeah, and it's global."

"How did you escape the spell?" the dragon asked.

"Leila. Her Magus stone gave off some sort of massive, glowing light. Everyone in the room was spared."

"Then that particular Magus stone is far more powerful than any of us would have imagined. Only a handful have been rumored to that capacity, which makes me wonder, who exactly was Leila's mother? From what family might she have been forced into slavery?"

"Good question. But we've got bigger problems at the moment."

"Indeed. But at least you're all safe, correct?"

"No. Hunze wasn't with us. And Baloo was out doing his thing when we were called in, so we left him to it. We're rushing back to Bawb's place right now."

"Then two of our number have almost certainly fallen victim as well."

"I know. But I think he's holding out some hope that the Magus stone protected her too."

"Not from that distance," Ara said with a sigh. *"And I'm sure he knows that."*

"I know. But he's in love. For the Geist, that's really saying something, ya know?"

"I do."

"This all started at the Asbrú.*"*

"Your ship? But it was a wreck in the Balamar Wastelands. I saw it with my own eyes. And that was some time ago."

"I know, Ara. But someone salvaged it and sent it here. That's what triggered this spell."

She was silent a long moment. *"The sheer amount of power required to cast a spell of this magnitude, it's staggering, Charlie, let*

27

alone the power to somehow jump it between galaxies. And if whoever did this had possession of your ship, that makes this a targeted attack."

"I know. And it looks like it's from your part of the universe, no less," Charlie said. "Look, I hate to ask you to do this, but you can get there faster than us. Will you keep an eye on the Asbrú until we get there?"

"Of course. And you needn't feel awkward asking me to do this."

"Yeah, well, there's one catch."

"Oh? What could possibly—"

"The ship landed in Wales."

Ara fell silent in his mind, but he could feel the surge of emotions through their bond. She had been trapped in Wales. Thousands of years in a cave, on the verge of insanity by the time she was finally freed. And now he was asking her to return there.

"Look, if there was any other way—"

"No, do not worry about me. I need to revisit the area eventually. To come to terms with what was done to me. While I would have perhaps preferred waiting a bit longer, this is inevitable. I will head there now. When I reach those shores, I will be able to smell the magic. It shouldn't be hard to pinpoint the ship's location."

"Thank you, Ara. This means a lot to me."

"The whole planet is frozen, Charlie. I think it means a lot to everyone."

Charlie and his friends burst through the exit to the surface, rushing through Eddie's door, already open and waiting for them.

"Get us home, Eddie!" Ripley blurted, jumping into her seat.

"Hang on to your bootstraps. We're gonna fly!" the ship replied, blasting into the air.

The distance was too short to get anywhere near Eddie's top speed, but he did manage to accelerate so hard that he broke the sound barrier with a loud boom before rapidly decelerating and dropping down outside of Ripley's sprawling home. The teen was out the door as soon as it opened.

"Get me home, ship," Bawb said through clenched teeth.

"You're next, man. But Rip's my girl. She'll always take priority," Eddie replied, quickly hopping the short distance to the Wampeh's home.

Bawb managed to clear the door before it was even fully open, dashing into his home in a frantic rush. Charlie, Leila, and Rika stepped out and waited for him. They knew what he would find inside, and there was no need to intrude in what had to be a difficult moment for the man.

It would be the same for Ripley. For everyone. Their loved ones, anyone not protected by the Magus stone's protective glow, would be frozen. Even Baloo, wherever that rambunctious fur ball was, would also be motionless.

The one positive was the spell itself. Bawb had recognized it. Part of it, anyway. It was magic from his galaxy, as Charlie had feared. But while massively powerful, and of a particular variety none of them had ever seen, it wasn't a killing spell. It was merely a stasis one. As such, those trapped by it would not age, nor would they wither. They were simply frozen in time. Hunze would simply remain sleeping in her bed, unaware anything had happened.

Charlie doubted that made his friend feel any better.

"I don't get it," Leila said. "The last time we had enemies *anywhere* was hundreds of years ago, and that was before we were thrown backward into your past."

"I know." He turned to Rika. "You have any theories?"

"Hey, I may have worked for the bad guys, but I wasn't one. I hope you know that."

"Of course we do. But you might have insight into this that we lack."

SCOTT BARON

She shrugged. "Sorry, but this is way outside of my wheelhouse."

They stood silently a while, wrapped up in their own thoughts, until Bawb finally stepped out of the house. The look on his face, hidden as it was, made it clear what he had found. Charlie noted he was now also very well armed.

"We need to pick up Ripley," he said, his voice tight with emotion. "Then we must go to the scene of the crime, immediately."

"I agree, but we need to gear up too," Charlie noted.

"Do as you must," Bawb replied, his face once again unreadable.

He boarded the ship and took a seat without another word and didn't speak again until they were well underway to the distant shores of Wales.

CHAPTER SEVEN

Charlie, Rika, and Leila loaded their gear aboard the young AI ship, carefully stowing everything extra securely, just in case Eddie decided to make any more of his sudden maneuvers without warning. He flew well, no doubt, but his youthful exuberance sometimes got the better of him. Then again, they had to remind themselves that despite seeming to be fully grown, the ship had really only been "born" a month or so prior.

Rip had been uncharacteristically quiet since they took off, and all had thought it best to give her a little space to process the sight of her parents frozen in place. Despite her seemingly unshakable take-on-the-world demeanor, even Ripley would be viscerally hit by something like that. They were her parents, after all, and for all her mock whining and eye rolling at her dad's jokes, they were a very close family.

Eddie took the most direct route, bursting through the atmosphere, flying high and fast, like a passenger-carrying ICBM. With the trajectory he was on, they'd be at their destination across the globe in less than a half hour.

Everyone had questions, and he was, technically, a

supercomputer. But the young ship was new to all of this, and thus wisely opted to let the big-brain AIs handle the analysis of what had happened. Routing the comms to the cabin, Cal was able to update the shell-shocked passengers as they flew.

"We have confirmed, this is a global phenomenon," he informed the group. *"There were minimal casualties, thank goodness, but some people were in precarious positions when the event occurred."*

"You can just call it a spell, Cal," Charlie said. "The sooner you come to grips with magic, the better."

"Yes, of course. We have assessed the data, and this magic is indeed a verifiable phenomenon far outside our normal scanning parameters. And the fallout of this spell was, quite unfortunately, not limited to people on the ground."

Rika, being a pilot, was the first to realize the implications. "Oh, shit. How many crashed?"

"As most of the AI ships are involved in the extra-solar survey, the majority of transit is currently being handled by human and Chithiid pilots. When the spell hit, we lost forty-seven craft. Another thirty-five were able to auto-land, thanks to their safety system backups. Naturally, many terrestrial incidents occurred as well."

"But you said this affected animals as well as people, right?" Ripley asked.

"Yes, Ripley. All animal life is frozen. Vegetation, however, seems unaffected."

"So, Baloo––"

"Undoubtedly frozen. Only Ara was able to withstand the event. I posit it was the sheer potency of her inherent magical properties protecting her without requiring conscious effort, much like Leila's unusual pendant did."

"It's called a Magus stone," Leila said, quietly, absentmindedly stroking the green gemstone. "So Baloo is okay, just frozen."

"He'll be fine," Charlie said, putting his arm around her. "It sucks he's not with us, but at least there's one positive of animals being indiscriminately included in this spell."

"Which is?"

"Think about it. If predators weren't frozen in place, all of those people would basically be a giant buffet for the taking."

Leila cracked a tiny hint of a smile, despite her distress, and Charlie's stress ball in his stomach relaxed slightly. He knew she would be okay.

"It is worth noting, all AI, not being flesh minds, were unaffected. However, many basic mechanical systems seem to have fallen victim, though we still do not understand why."

"I can help with that," Bawb said, breaking his icy silence. "If this was a modification of a *verata* spell that incorporated elements of some of the more historically military applications of the spell, then it is highly likely a form of vessel immobilization was woven into it."

"But we're not a magical planet," Charlie said.

"No, but enough basic mechanical parts, such as hinges, or levers, could have been stricken. That alone could cause failure in any number of devices," the Wampeh noted. "It was likely unintentional, judging by what we've observed so far."

"Or it was a crude attempt to disable our defenses by an enemy who doesn't fully understand how tech works."

Bawb was silent a moment as he considered the possibility. "Given that they used your ship as the delivery mechanism, that is a reasonable assumption."

"And let's not forget, we're in our own future now. The *Asbrú* was built hundreds of years before current levels of technology. If it was an attack based on *that* knowledge, or lack thereof, it's only logical that whatever spell they cooked up wouldn't work on newer tech."

"Then this was an attempt against more than just the human population."

"It would seem possible, though how they would know what

to target is a mystery," Bawb said, a distrusting look flashing Rika's way, but gone before she could see it. She was Charlie's friend, and part of the team, but it had not been very long at all since she had been fighting for the enemy, and it would take more than her fellow humans vouching for her before he would trust her completely.

Charlie craned his neck, peering at the monitors as they began their descent. "Eddie, can you zoom in on those fires?"

The displays flicked to a tighter frame. They were looking at the rebuilt city of London, and parts of the city were burning.

"Cal, you said it landed in Wales. What's going on down there?"

"Vic has informed me that several craft crashed into the city proper. Automated fire-suppression systems knocked down most of the blazes, but not all. Unfortunately, the fire-fighting crews in that city were largely human and Chithiid. He is gathering cyborgs to step in to fill those roles as rapidly as he is able, but there was not a terribly robust population of mechanicals in that city. It will take time, but we can rebuild whatever is damaged."

"And the people in those buildings?" Leila asked.

A long silence hung in the air.

"Unfortunately, there will be casualties."

They sat quietly for the remainder of the flight. The situation was worse than they'd originally feared, and they had every reason to expect it would only deteriorate further.

Eddie slowed his descent, leveling into a slow glide as they approached an area of flattened trees and disturbed soil. There, resting in the afternoon sun, was a shape Charlie had thought he would never see again. They made a slow loop, surveying the area from above.

The majority of the team that had been tasked with protecting the ship were still outside, frozen in place near the open door in the hull. The rest were undoubtedly inside, and

Charlie couldn't help but wonder what other booby traps they might have inadvertently sprung.

They would find out soon enough.

"Hello again," Charlie said, taking in the sight of his old ship. "Okay, Eddie. Take us down."

CHAPTER EIGHT

Charlie and Rika looked at one another as they approached the *Asbrú*. After so much time, it was hard to believe, but there it was, looming above them.

"That's definitely her," Rika said. "I'd know our ship anywhere."

"You remember that thing more than you remember me," Charlie said. "I'm flattered."

"Well, I knew her better than you, Charlie. I was second-in-command, after all."

He cracked a little grin and continued to move in for a closer look. A shadow flashed by as his friend flew overhead.

"Ara, do you sense anything?"

"No. Whatever spell caused this, there doesn't appear to be any new activity from the vessel."

"All right. We're going to go in. Let me know the second you sense anything, okay?"

"Of course. And, Charlie, be careful."

"Thanks, Ara. We will."

"Ara doesn't sense anything," he relayed to the others. "Well, no time like the present. Let's go see what's inside."

They walked closer, stepping over the smashed trees that had been flattened when the ship came in for its rough landing. The hull was intact, and looked almost new––except for the crashing part, of course. But there were still some signs of the original damage from the ship's belly-flop onto the hard-pack of the Balamar Wastelands, which had torn away much of the underside.

"You see this, Rika?" Charlie asked.

"Yeah. Rebuilt, but the seams aren't right. It wasn't welded into place. Whatever they used to repair the ship, it's a technology that's foreign to me."

"Magic, actually," Bawb interjected.

"Of course it is," she grumbled. "So, it was a spell to superheat the materials they slapped in place to make them fit and stay put? Like a magical weld, I guess."

"Hardly. I know this spell. It is a rather crude means of patching a hull, but it will do the job in a fix. Additionally, it requires very little continuing power drain to maintain the spell. It doesn't actually attach the patches, you see. Instead, it creates a perfect seal, pulling the replaced sections flush with the hull from the inside. So long as the underlying structure holds up, this will stay in place, even in the event of a crash."

Charlie ran his hand along the new belly of the ship. It *looked* like it was new, but he vividly remembered the ruined ship, as well as the dozen dead crew members, taken when that part had been shorn away. It was such an eerie feeling, knowing this was *his* ship, the result of his long hours and years of engineering work, now resurrected from the grave and turned into a weapon.

"What do you say, Rika? Ready to do this?"

"As ready as you are."

"So not very, then?"

"Shut up and lead the way."

"Okay, then. Let's see what our girl has for us."

The group carefully made their way to the open doorway,

stepping around the frozen men and women in their path. Charlie sensed an ongoing push of magic coming from the ship, likely caused by his bond with Ara.

"You feeling this?"

"Yes. The spell that froze everyone. It is still active. Still sending some sort of continuous signal, though I'm not sure how, exactly. Or to what end, for that matter."

"Well, I guess we'll just have to wing it and see what we find."

Charlie flicked on his flashlight and stepped inside the ship. What he saw was a sharp contrast to the *Asbrú*'s near-pristine exterior.

"Hoooly shit," he gasped.

"Jesus, this place is a wreck," Rika said.

"At the risk of repeating myself, I must once more ask. *This* flew?" Bawb said with a little grin. His familiar calm and amused outlook in the face of death was slowly making a reappearance.

"It didn't always look like this," Charlie said. "They must've just fixed the outside to make it appear as if everything was okay. Trojan horses don't work otherwise."

"Trojan horse? You haven't mentioned this breed before," Leila said.

"Historical reference. I'll explain later," he said, moving farther into the wreck of his ship.

The insides were an utter shambles, much of the debris and ruined equipment not even removed for the scrap pile before the ship was sent on its nefarious mission. Most of the sand from its years in the Balamar Wastelands had been scooped out, but that seemed to be as far as the cleanup had gone.

Charlie had a brief flashback to his short stint as a space pirate. He and Marban had been aboard a ship whose captain had scuttled the craft rather than let it be taken. The craft had plunged toward the planet below, but spells protecting the valuable cargo had slowed and directed the descent, keeping the ship intact upon impact, though just barely.

From the look of things, a similar type of spell had guided the *Asbrú* to Wales. He had to wonder what the significance was, if any. What sort of person had layered that magic into his ship? It was obviously an expensive bit of casting, and whoever had sent it back to Earth had serious resources at their disposal. The sheer expenditure of magic to force a wormhole open would have been staggering.

Leila's Magus stone remained dark against her skin. Whatever magic was still pulsing out from the *Asbrú*, it was of no threat to them. Not at the moment, at least.

They pressed on, moving deeper into the ship, heading toward the ruined command center. Walls had buckled, only magic holding the infrastructure in place. A lot of time and effort had gone into keeping the ship intact, but it was magic-magic doing the work, not "tech-magic" as the residents of that distant galaxy had once called it.

Finally, they reached command. Rika paused in the doorway, immobile, staring at the place her seat used to be. All that remained was a pile of debris. Debris from underneath which Charlie had pulled her to safety. A flicker of the memory tickled the edges of her mind before another sight caught her eye.

Just behind her station, thick bolts jutted from the floor, sheared off when several tons of steel had torn through the captain's chair––and the man seated in it.

"Reynard," she said, quietly.

"What was that?" Charlie asked.

"His name was Reynard," she replied. "I remember him."

Charlie nodded, silently paying his respects to their dead captain, his remains buried in the red sands of a distant planet.

"Come on, Rika. There's nothing for us in here. We need to check out the rest of the ship."

She hesitated a moment, taking in the dark compartment one last time, then turned and stepped out the door to command for the last time.

CHAPTER NINE

Somehow, the *Asbrú* had been turned into a flying weapon. A dispersal device for potent magic the likes of which even the residents of that distant, magical galaxy had never seen. A massive spell––or more precisely, combination of spells–– powered by an incredible amount of magic. Enough to freeze an entire planet.

But the ship was nothing more than a dressed-up wreck.

"I don't get it," Leila said. "There's no one on board."

"We still haven't checked every compartment," Charlie noted. "But from what I've seen so far, I am inclined to agree with you. It doesn't make sense. How in the world did this rusted-out hulk power that kind of spell on its own?"

Rika pulled open a panel, examining the melted circuitry inside. "Could they have hidden something inside the bulkhead, maybe? I mean, there's enough space for it. The ship was designed to have additional equipment installed in the future, which is why there was so much void space in the walls when we launched."

Charlie thought it was fascinating watching her move through the ship. Though she had essentially been lobotomized, the magical, healing waters he'd provided her had restored the physical structure of her brain. It was still wiped, but it was healthy. But now, as she passed from compartment to compartment, an instinctive muscle memory was kicking in.

Charlie didn't say anything, not wanting her to become self-conscious and lose the groove she was in, and after searching through a half dozen compartments, she was moving about the ship with the easy familiarity one would expect of its second-in-command.

The group split into two teams, all of them armed and ready, though both of the AIs in the region, as well as their dragon friend, were certain they were alone. It took some time digging through all of the levels and compartments, but eventually, something began to stand out.

Certain panels seemed to have been re-sealed, the edges of them lacking the years of buildup found elsewhere throughout the ship. Someone had, indeed, been tinkering within the ship's walls.

"Is that what I think it is?" Rika asked as she pulled open a tightly sealed panel.

Charlie shined his flashlight inside, the golden strands gleaming in its glow. "Holy shit. That's Ootaki hair, Rika. A *lot* of it."

"I thought so. But what's it doing running through the walls of the ship?"

Charlie leaned into the narrow space and examined their find more closely. It seemed as though a large, unused conduit had been filled with the power-containing locks.

"This is bad. These conduits run all throughout the ship," he said. "There's no telling how many are hiding this stuff. We need to tell the others. Have them shift their search so we can map out where this hair is hidden."

Charlie passed word over their comms––devices he was thrilled to have access to, rather than using magical skrees to send messages—and over the course of the next several hours, the group managed to roughly map out the location of the hidden power source.

It wasn't hard. It was everywhere.

"Impossible," Bawb said. "This quantity of Ootaki hair simply does not exist. Even at its peak, the Council of Twenty possessed perhaps a fraction of this amount."

"So you're saying it's a lot."

"No, Charlie, I'm saying it cannot be. We have discovered sizable quantities running throughout the entire ship, as if it were an invasive vine living in the infrastructure. But some of it is shorter, some much, much longer. Some highly powered, some minorly so, as if taken from all manner of Ootaki. But it is the sum of it that truly worries me. This much hair? It is impossible."

"And yet, here it is," Leila said, running her finger along the strands.

Her Magus stone began to glow, and a shuddering wave of magic spread through the ship.

"Leila, let go!" Bawb yelled.

She quickly snatched her hand back, the stone's glow fading until the unsettling magic disappeared.

"What was that?" Rika asked.

"*That*," Bawb said, "was a booby trap. Or more likely, a deadman switch. When your Magus stone interfered with the Ootaki hair's ongoing spell, the deadman began to activate."

Leila went pale, despite her olive complexion. "You mean I almost just killed us right now?"

"It is a distinct possibility. Yes," the Wampeh replied. "However, it would seem the gradual pressure your Magus stone applied was perceived as less of a threat than a direct attack. Fascinating, really. Whoever planned this accounted for potential disarming spells. But I wonder..." He pulled a small knife from one of his hidden sheaths and gently probed the hair.

Nothing.

Bawb then pulled a lone strand loose and applied the blade to it.

"You sure that's a good idea?" Ripley asked, peering over his shoulder. "I don't think that's a good idea. Guys? Anyone? That's not a good idea, right?"

Bawb flashed a pointy-toothed grin. "Do not fear, young one. In a vessel this size, with this much Ootaki hair, a single strand should not cause a catastrophic response. It may, however, reveal if there is a non-magical weakness we may exploit."

In one fluid motion he sliced through the hair. Immediately, a flash of magic rumbled through the ship, a distressing buzz lingering long after he retracted the blade.

"This is most disconcerting," he said, re-sheathing the knife.

"That it caused a reaction? Or the *size* of the reaction?" Charlie asked.

"Both. But more the latter than the former. We must consult with the Wise One. I am certain she felt that, and she is far more skilled than I at reading arcane spells. Whatever that was, this ship is a far greater threat than any of us previously believed."

Charlie felt his heart beat a little harder. Bawb was spooked. For the deadliest assassin in thirty systems to be spooked, something very, very bad must be afoot.

"Ara, did you feel that?" he silently asked his Zomoki friend.

"How could I not? I was just probing the layers of spells encompassing that vessel. Someone put a lot of effort into this—whatever this is."

"Yeah, we noticed."

"No, Charlie. When I say a lot, I mean years.*"*

"How is that even possible?"

"I do not know. But this spell is growing stronger. It is a slow process, but I can sense it regaining its potency."

"That would be the Ootaki hair. We found it running all throughout the ship."

"Ah, yes, that would explain it. This planet's sun will recharge the hair's power, as it does mine, given time."

"But what about that other spell? The one that flared up just now? Bawb tried cutting a single hair and we got that reaction. He thinks it's some kind of deadman switch designed to do something if the hair is interfered with."

"I concur."

"But what will it do?"

"I don't know. Fortunately, it is recharging very slowly. The sun's radiation has a much harder time penetrating the hull of that ship. Were it fully exposed, we would have quite a problem on our hands."

"And we don't now?"

"Oh, we most certainly do," she replied with a little chuckle. *"But it could be far worse. And at the moment we have multiple other issues at hand as well."*

Charlie knew she was right. The *Asbrú* was just one part of the problem, and from what she could tell, they had time. And he had learned long ago, it is far better to step back and prepare than rush in half-cocked.

"Come on, you guys," he said to his friends. "Let's get out of here. We need to regroup. We need to talk to the AIs."

He followed the others as they carefully filed from the *Asbrú*, heading back to Eddie's waiting ship, a cloud of doubt hanging thick in the air. But surely the AI minds running the planet would know what to do.

I just hope they have some semblance of a plan.

CHAPTER TEN

When the survey team reached the nascent ship, they discovered that Eddie had gone the extra mile in their absence and whipped up some hot cocoa for the survey team with his rather limited food replicator. He may not have had the capability of producing the more complicated spreads found on larger ships, but at this precise moment, the comfort beverage hit the spot. Especially for those who had never tasted it before.

"This is amazing!" Leila gushed, a good portion of her funk clearing with the first sip of the new treat. "Charlie, your coffee was wonderful, but this? This is so... I don't know how to describe it."

Charlie grinned, pleased to see her spirits rising. Even Bawb seemed slightly more relaxed as he sipped his steaming mug. Ripley and Rika—being native Earthlings—were not nearly so enthusiastic, though the chocolatey treat did hit that nostalgic pleasure center in their brains.

"Eddie, can you patch in Cal and the others?" Charlie asked as the warm cocoa slid into his belly.

"No problem, Chief."

The ship's young friend rolled her eyes.

"Stop calling people chief, Eddie. It's lame," Ripley grumbled.

"You got it, Boss."

"Ugh. You're ridiculous."

"Says you. You're one to talk, you know."

"Guys," Charlie interrupted. "While we all normally enjoy your banter, we really need to focus here."

"Sorry," Ripley replied.

"Yeah, apologies, Your Highness."

Ripley let out a grunt, but held her tongue.

"I heard that," Eddie said. "And, technically, it's correct. Oh, by the way, I have Cal and the others on the line."

"We've been listening for a bit, actually," the super-powerful AI noted.

"Wonderful," Charlie sighed. "So, any new developments on your end?"

"Vic has managed to get the fires out in London, which is positive, of course. We are quite fortunate that cybernetic organisms remained unaffected by this spell. But I've spoken with the other major AIs across the globe, and everyone is still quite befuddled by this magic."

"It makes sense. They only just learned that magic was even a real thing and not some fairy tale, after all."

"Indeed. Unfortunately, the systemic failures of more simplistic systems worldwide have proven to be somewhat of a hindrance. As such, all of our cyborg workforce is tasked with handling the myriad emergencies that have arisen. Damage control is sucking up valuable resources we would much rather deploy toward more directly addressing this new threat."

"Sadly, until we decipher this spell, I don't know there's really much we *can* do," Charlie said. "And on top of that, there are just five of us. We're a ridiculously tiny team."

"I am actually hoping to help with that. Sid, the AI overseeing

Dark Side moon base, has just dispatched a ship with some of his most talented crew. A few dozen men and women with a high degree of technical proficiency should touch down in Los Angeles shortly. So while things are difficult, you will have assistance, at least. Now we simply need to find what they will be able to do to be of help."

Eddie flashed a tracking map on his screens, showing the medium-sized ship's approach trajectory. At their rate of speed, they'd possibly even arrive in LA before Charlie's team made the trip.

"Okay, Eddie. Fire it up and get us back to Los Angeles. We've got all we're going to get from here for now, and I think we could all use a quick shower and a meal before we dig any further into the limited data we have. Maybe catch a little cat nap, even. Everyone agree?"

The others nodded, and Leila looped her arm through his, resting her head on his shoulder. He was glad Bawb was too busy watching the screens to notice. The poor man had to be in hell, but, as was his way, he showed no outward sign of it.

"Cal? Charlie? I do not believe this is normal," the Wampeh said, his eyes not once wavering from the screens.

Charlie looked up and saw what he was referencing. Rika was the pilot among them, but even a layman could see the angle of approach was all wrong.

"Cal, what's going on?" he asked.

"We have lost contact with the ship. Attempts to hail them are being made across all channels, but as of yet, there is no reply."

"Did something hit them? Were they attacked?"

"Nothing of the sort. One minute they were on a normal approach, entering the atmosphere. The next, we lost contact, and they dipped into a steeper descent."

Bawb was transfixed by the line on the screen, rapidly approaching the planet's surface. "Charlie, ask Ara how quickly she can get to that ship," he said, an urgency coloring his voice.

"Why?"

"Because I'm afraid if she doesn't, every soul on board that vessel is going to perish."

Charlie suddenly realized what he was implying.

"Ara, there's a ship streaking toward the surface. It looks like it's going to hit just outside Los Angeles. Can you intercept it? Maybe grab on and guide it down somehow?"

"I'm afraid I would not reach them in time. And, Charlie, I sensed a surge emit from the Asbrú *just now."*

"I figured as much," he replied, turning his attention back to the monitors. "No dice. She said she can't get there fast enough."

"I might be able to," Eddie interjected. "I'd have to do a hard burn out of the atmosphere, and we'd pull some serious Gs on the descent, but maybe––"

"There is simply no time," Cal said. ***"But your offer and efforts are appreciated."***

Powerless, the team watched in horror as the line on the screen tracked the plummeting ship. All the way into the ground. Then the tracker abruptly went dark.

"We've lost them," Cal said.

"What the hell happened?" Ripley blurted, tears welling in her eyes. "Why would they do that?"

Leila gently put her arm around her. "Because the spell is still active, Rip."

"But we're safe."

"Yes. But only because the Magus stone granted us some sort of protection that appears to stay with us. They were not so fortunate."

"She's right," Bawb said. "The ship lost contact as soon as it breached the atmosphere. This spell appears to extend all the way to the edge of space. Any who attempt to reach the surface will most likely fall victim to its power."

"We will need to discuss this in greater detail. The AIs in orbit will run a new assessment. We will reconvene once you are safely back in Los Angeles and have had a chance to eat and rest."

It was a logical step, but Charlie's appetite was suddenly non-existent, and he seriously doubted any of them would now be able to nap.

CHAPTER ELEVEN

"*Uzri ho*," Rika said with a grunt, throwing a low kick in combination with the throwing spell powered by her small konus.

Charlie avoided the kick, but rather than countering the spell, he instead let it take him from his feet, rolling with the force and using its momentum to launch him into a lunging takedown.

Rika flew through the air––her feet suddenly occupying the space where her head had just been––then landed with a slap to the ground, the length of her arm and body spreading the force of the impact. She scrambled to her feet and cast again.

"*Eeflanguley*," she blurted, but Charlie saw it coming, pulling from his internal power and silently casting a dispersing counterspell, followed by one of his favorite diversion spells.

Rika wrinkled her nose in disgust. "A poo-smelling spell? Are you fucking kidding me?"

She was distracted long enough for Charlie to lob a casual foot sweep spell, knocking her to the ground once more. "It distracted you, didn't it?" he replied with a laugh, moving in for a ground attack.

Rika shifted on her back, feet at the ready to block any attempt to reach the mount position. But Charlie expected that, instead using a lifting spell to raise her body from the ground. He dove beneath her before she could react, canceling the spell and dropping her on top of him, her back landing solidly between his legs and grabbing arms.

With a combination of magic and grappling, he had achieved an unconventional, but advantageous, position.

His arms snuck up around her neck, sliding into a rear naked choke. Rika struggled, tucking her chin and very nearly escaping his powerful arms, but Charlie was calm, slow, and methodical. Shortly, Rika reluctantly tapped out.

Charlie released his grip, the two getting to their feet again.

"Not bad," he said. "But you know, I think——"

Rika planted a solid front kick in the middle of his chest, knocking the wind from him, his diaphragm spasming painfully. A flying knee followed, Charlie barely avoiding a full blow, Rika's knee only glancing off his shoulder as he spun away, forcing his lungs to work again. Normally, if you couldn't talk, you couldn't cast. But Charlie wasn't normal in that respect.

She pressed the attack, launching a series of blindingly fast punches. Charlie absorbed some, and blocked others, letting Rika move in closer as she gained the upper hand.

Or so she thought.

Dispanus, he thought, channeling the smallest of power into the spell without verbalizing the word, directing it only into her left leg just as she pivoted into a round kick.

Her limb went numb, the stun spell effectively taking her foot out from under her. Rika went tumbling, her own momentum carrying her to the ground. A moment later, her leg began to regain sensation. Charlie had gone easy on her, she realized, rubbing the pins and needles sensation from her thigh.

This was what they needed. Far more than a snack or a nap, a little bit of good old-fashioned sweat and violence helped calm their nerves. A brief respite from the crazy events of the day they were still trying to understand.

Rika slowly got back to her feet, dusting herself off as she rose. "Okay, I'll admit it, you've gotten a lot better," she grumbled.

"So, you remember some of our old training back in the day?"

"No, not really," she replied. "But I do have a...I don't know. A *gut* feeling that we've done this before."

"We have."

"And that I used to kick your ass on a regular basis."

Charlie laughed. "Yeah, that too. But back then, I hadn't spent years training as a gladiator. I also wasn't an assassin's understudy. Plus, you weren't using magic."

Rika grinned and took a swig from her water bottle. "It seems we've come a long way, Charlie."

"Indeed, it does."

"The thing is, after what the Tslavars did to me. What Malalia did to me. I still feel like, I don't know. Like I don't have a solid sense of who I am. Does that make sense? I mean, I was under the control of another person, and I don't need to remember my past to know that I am fucking *not* okay with that."

"No, that you would not be," Charlie said. "But all of that, it wasn't your fault. Violence was done to you, and you can't blame yourself for any of it."

"But I don't even remember our friendship, Charlie. I mean, I know we were friends. We trained together."

"And you ran me ragged, I might add."

"So you say. But I still only have ghosts of that in my head. I have no *real* memories."

Charlie stepped close, putting his hands on her shoulders and looking deep into her eyes. "It's okay, Rika. You're with friends now. And you know what? Screw the past. We'll make *new* memories, okay?" He stepped back, smiled warmly at her, and held out his hand. "Charlie Gault. Pleased to meet you."

She gripped his hand firmly. "Rika Gaspari. Nice to meet you too, Charlie."

"You know something? I think you and I are going to be good friends."

Rika pulled him in close and gave him a tight hug, her eyes welling up with emotion. She abruptly let go, hastily wiping the tears from her eyes.

"So, firing range next?" she asked with a sniffle.

"Sure. You always were a better shot than me."

"At least there's something I can still beat you at," she said with a chuckle.

"And you can likely outshoot the others too."

"Well, to be fair, our magic friends are kind of out of their element on this world. They're getting the hang of it, mind you, but it's kind of a fish-out-of-water situation for them."

"I know," Charlie agreed. "And far more than our medieval adventure. I mean, that was sort of like visiting a rural world for them. But all of this tech? It's gotta be a mindfuck."

"But we're hundreds and hundreds of years beyond our own time, Charlie, so we're just as much out of our element as they are. Or nearly as much, anyway."

"I suppose," he replied. "But let's go remedy that, shall we? Starting with those pulse rifles. You know I've been dying to try one out."

Rika flashed a warm grin. "I already asked Cal to have a pair ready for us at the range."

"Of course you did. Well, then. Let's go violently poke holes in things from a distance."

CHAPTER TWELVE

Their workout sweat showered off, and their spirits higher, Charlie and Rika joined their friends in Cal's command center.

Leila had opted for a long walk rather than sparring when they got back, but changed her plans when the tranquil stroll failed to set her at ease. The sight of the frozen people may also have spoiled her outing somewhat. So, she opted instead for a run up and down a nearby building's fire stairs, working up a good sweat.

Ripley and Bawb had taken the opportunity to fly to their respective homes. There was nothing they could do for their loved ones, but the visceral need to see them ruled the moment. Charlie felt bad for the young girl, but even more so for his stoic friend. No matter how calm he seemed, Bawb had to be torn up inside. He was just very practiced at hiding it.

They noshed on handfuls of snacks as they sat in the command center. Presciently, Cal knew their hunger would eventually catch up with them, and had arranged for a platter of sandwiches and refreshments to be waiting for the group when they arrived.

"You must eat. It is imperative you keep your energy levels up," he had said.

They knew he was right, and each of them had taken one. Ripley, in particular, hadn't realized how hungry she actually was. The teen downed two of them in short order.

Their blood-sugar stable and their frazzled nerves calmed, at least a bit, the group settled in for their situational review.

"Now that all are present, I have patched in Sid on Dark Side base. Sid, would you care to begin?"

"Thank you, Cal," the distant AI began. "I would like to first thank you all for the work you are doing. I am sure it is not easy, and, unfortunately, the weight of this crisis rests fully on your shoulders. We hope to rectify that, and are working to upgrade a ship with a mid-grade AI to at least provide you more aerial support. But it seems no humans or Chithiid will be able to enter the atmosphere."

"Yeah, we saw that," Charlie said. "And we're really sorry about your people, Sid."

"Thank you. It was hard losing them. They are all valued members of our team, and their talents will be missed. However, we have more pressing issues at the moment. Namely, the underlying purpose of this attack. For this, we must ask the question we currently have no answer for. That being, what do they hope to gain?"

"It's a terror attack," Rika posited. "Something to distract and frighten the population."

"An interesting supposition, however there is no need to frighten or distract a population that is frozen in stasis."

"Shit. Good point," she said. "But what, then? If there are no demands, and no overt acts of aggression, then what purpose does this serve?"

"That is what we are trying to determine," Cal said.

"Charlie?"

"Yes, Sid?"

"Cal and I were discussing one possible line of action. Ara is an immensely powerful being, which has me wondering. Given her abilities, might it be possible for your dragon friend to perhaps unfreeze a single individual at a time?"

"I've already talked with her about that. The problem is, the sheer complexity of this spell makes it a near certainty that anything she tried wouldn't work. A *lot* of effort went into crafting this spell, isn't that right, Bob?"

The pale man nodded in agreement. "Indeed. I too have spoken with the Wise One. Her assessment aligns with mine. There are multiple spells––layer upon layer of them––all interwoven to create this magical amalgam. There is simply no telling how long it might take to devise a working counterspell without understanding of the original in our possession. Or whether we would be able to craft one powerful enough to release the global population. Huge amounts of power went into this spell's creation, and it is still being added to by the hour."

"Ah, yes. That was another aspect we wished to discuss. You say the ship is still emitting this spell, and you cannot directly attack the substance at the root of it."

"Hair," Charlie said. "Ootaki hair, to be exact. It stores magic, allowing the user to draw from it, like a battery pack."

"And can your own magic overpower it? Negate it, somehow?"

"From what we've seen so far, we don't believe so. There's a deadman switch of sorts. If we interfere with the spell, it will trigger whatever the associated booby-trap spell is. Bob, this is more your area of expertise. Would you mind?"

"Of course," the Wampeh replied. "Upon further probing of the power we encountered when we attempted to cut a strand of the Ootaki hair, what we have seen is a multi-layered defensive spell, triggering a full power dump from the magic stored in the hair. I am not entirely certain of the exact spell it powers, but from what Ara and I have observed thus far, our shared belief is it would likely cause the atmosphere of this planet to rupture."

"Which would destroy all life on Earth and render the planet uninhabitable. Hardly a desirable outcome for someone intent on occupying."

"But we don't know that's what they want to do," Charlie said.

"No, we do not. However, if they possess this capability and wanted to destroy Earth's population, they would have deployed it immediately. No, they are waiting for something. The only question remaining is what?"

The group sat quietly, all very aware of the terrible reality of the situation. Finally, it was Rika who broke the silence.

"Well, then. I guess that settles it. We've already lost one team."

"Settles what?" Ripley asked.

"What we have to do next," Charlie interjected.

"You mean figure out whose ass to kick, right?"

"No, Rip. What she means is doing what we have to do to keep any more innocent lives from being lost."

"Again, the ass-kicking thing comes to mind."

"Much as we all want that, we need something more immediate. Cal, you agree, yes?"

"Yes, Charlie. Sadly, I do."

"And, Sid, you're on board as well?"

"Of course."

"Then there it is. As of right now, planet Earth is quarantined."

CHAPTER THIRTEEN

Two days had passed, and nothing had changed. At least, it seemed like nothing had, until an AI from the city of Cape Town checked in with Cal and the rest of the global network. At first, they didn't know what to make of his strange readings, but as they put their collective processing might behind the problem, an unexpected answer became clear.

Someone was out there. And that someone was snatching people.

"Are you sure about this?" Charlie asked when he and Leila came rushing into the command center.

They'd been enjoying a moment of quiet time together, a king and his queen confiding their concerns with one another in the face of a dumbfounding problem. Charlie had found that despite her seemingly rough upbringing as a slave laborer, tending the animals on Visla Maktan's vast estate, Leila possessed the sharp mind of a diplomat. Or perhaps a tactician. Whatever it was, she had a knack for seeing the big picture and poking holes in ill-conceived ideas.

What they had come to agree, in regards to the current problem, was that without the means to counter the spell encompassing the planet, the best they could do was to task teams of cyborgs and any AI machinery up to the task with finding individuals frozen in precarious, life-threatening situations and moving them to safety.

They would still be in a frozen stasis, but at least when they thawed out—*if* they thawed out—they wouldn't find themselves crushed, burned, or run over in their first seconds of resumed consciousness.

But now, something new was afoot. And it changed everything.

"Yes, Charlie. The report was quite conclusive," Cal said.

"And it's happened in more than one city?" Leila asked. "You're certain?"

"We are certain," Cal replied. *"When the first report came in, we parsed the data and performed a comprehensive analysis. Initially, we believed it was a systems error. A glitch. But upon closer review, we realized this was something else. Once the anomaly was identified and they knew what to look for, other AIs around the globe reported in with similar occurrences. There is movement out there. And people are going missing."*

Charlie and Leila squinted at the display screens, trying to make out what the AIs were so flustered about. All they saw was a normal day in a city—if normal meant the sparse population was frozen in place.

"There," Cal plainly stated. *"The woman standing in the bottom left of frame."*

"What woman?" Leila asked.

"I will back up the recording."

The image flowed in reverse, the only sign of motion the subtle drifting of shadows from the clouds above. Other than that, everyone was stock-still. And then it happened. The woman Cal had mentioned tilted slightly, then vanished.

"She disappeared!" Leila exclaimed. "But how is that

possible? That magic doesn't exist. And even if it did, it doesn't exist *here*."

"Precisely why we are so concerned. Naturally, we contacted you as soon as we realized something was afoot."

"Wait a minute. Play that back again," Charlie asked.

The image replayed again, the woman vanishing just as she had before. But Charlie thought he saw something. Something familiar.

"Did you contact Bob?"

"He is on his way," Cal replied. *"Do you believe he may have insight into this phenomenon?"*

Charlie squinted at the looped segment. "Yeah, I think he will."

"A shimmer," the Wampeh said plainly, squinting at the video-magic as they played the scene for him.

"You're sure?"

"Charlie, it is a particular type of concealment I am *very* familiar with. Yes, this is shimmer magic. A very sophisticated variety, I would add. In fact, if not for their taking people from the streets like this, I doubt they would be able to be detected at all."

"But we have no energy readings of any kind from that area. Nor from the other cities in which this has occurred."

"There have been others?" Bawb asked, his curiosity piqued. "How many?"

"Five cities we know of thus far. Cape Town, which is what you see here, then Valparaiso, Chile, Rio, Brazil, Wales, UK, and Honolulu, Hawaii."

"Those are all over the place," Charlie said with a groan. "Seriously. That spans the globe. How the hell are they moving that quickly, and over that kind of distance, without anyone spotting them?"

"I am afraid that particular question is beyond me," Bawb replied. "Have you asked Rika? She was close with our enemy."

"I haven't asked her, Bob. And for the record, again, she's better now," Charlie said.

Bawb groaned, unconvinced. "In any case, if others did in fact arrive along with the *Asbrú*, their use of shimmer magic would explain why their presence was unnoted until now. Of course, that's the point of such stealth castings. If it was easy to track shimmer magic, it would defeat the entire purpose of it."

It was quite a revelation. *Someone* was on the planet, sneaking around and snatching up people, human, Chithiid, and even a few cyborgs, though they were not frozen, the recordings showing their surprise at being taken before they vanished from the video images.

"How can we track them, Bob? You know how this stuff works, and I'm sure you've had to chase people using them."

"That I have, though it was not a pleasurable experience."

"But the point is, you understand how to do it. So maybe if you and Ara have a little pow-wow with Cal and his friends, you'll be able to devise a way to find these bastards. Does a shimmer block you from thermal imaging?"

"What is thermal imaging?"

"Like infrared. It operates on a different premise than the regular visual spectrum, using heat signatures instead of light refraction."

Bawb cocked his head slightly. "That is a rather ingenious methodology. Your world does not cease to surprise me. I will discuss it with Ara and our AI brothers. I have a few ideas that I've put to use in the past that may allow them some degree of tracking and detection. And if it comes down to it, I can use my own shimmer cloak as a test case, if I must. But you understand, it is a very special piece of equipment to me and giving up its secrets should only be a last resort."

"I understand. You never know when you'll need to sneak up and kill someone, after all."

"I'm glad you understand."

"That was sarcasm, dude. But yeah, we'll try the other options first."

"Excellent," the assassin said. "I will speak with the Wise One and relay suggestions back to Cal and his team. But for now, we need to get ahold of Rip and Eddie. I very much want to examine the locations of the abductions firsthand. There may well be something of use to one who knows where––and *how*–– to look."

CHAPTER FOURTEEN

It was the first ever Zomoki/AI confab, and even the mighty Cal found himself in the unusual position of feeling almost giddy with excitement. For a normally staid mind, this was a rather interesting development.

Of course, AIs were designed to evolve and grow—to experience emotions, even—so it was to be expected. And getting to work alongside an actual mythological creature? Well, it was something so unique, anyone, even an AI, couldn't help but be thrilled.

Ara had spoken at length with Bawb before he went to prepare for his reconnaissance, and they managed to come up with several clever methods the non-magical AI network might be able to use to track the use of magic in their cities.

It would be primitive by both cultures' standards, but magic and non-magic users had managed to bridge the gap between their vastly diverse methods of doing things. The "tech-magic" of Earth was a bit confounding for the offworlders to wrap their heads around, but eventually a path was laid out.

It was Ara, rather than Bawb, who provided the first traces of magical power for the AIs to try to get a fix on. She forced a tiny bit of power onto one of the Earth vehicles, doing nothing to it beyond making it an incredibly brief receptacle for magical potential. As it was of the wrong galaxy, the effect would be very short-lived, but it should be enough.

The AIs observed with great interest as Cal recalibrated his many sensor arrays and shifted the spectrum analysis of images on his video feeds to the agreed upon wavelength. If the test in Los Angeles was a success, they could duplicate the process and protect themselves from enemies, wherever across the globe they popped up next.

"Are you ready?" Ara asked, watching the vehicle roll into place with interest.

"I believe I am, Ara. Let us begin."

Once again, Ara pushed a modicum of power into the vehicle, then retreated from the testing area to ensure she would not taint the results with her extremely powerful presence.

"Engaging the revised spectral analyzer," Cal announced.

The vehicle rolled through the testing area, a dozen different cameras monitoring it with every conceivable means of scan at their disposal.

"Do you see anything?" Ara asked. "Besides your normal observations, of course."

"I'm sorry, Ara, but nothing is reading on any of my scans."

"Then we will try again," she said. "But perhaps first you should scan me and make note of my power on your apparatus. The magic I have imparted to that vehicle is a different flavor, but, nevertheless, I fear my very presence might still skew results. The power originates from me just the same, so I think it would be best to take that factor into consideration."

"A very astute observation, Ara. Indeed, it is a possibility that you might throw off our tests. If you would please step into the testing area, we will begin assembling an energy profile for our database so we can keep your signature from affecting our future scans."

The massive dragon flapped her wings, lunging into the air, making the quick hop to the testing area, then settling in between the cameras and scanners. Like Bawb with his specialized shimmer, Ara was also reticent to have her own particulars probed and logged, but a great threat was looming, and the stakes were high. An entire planet's population hung in the balance.

The high-tech machinery hummed, cataloging every possible aspect of the energy gently radiating from her body. Unlike an inanimate object charged with magic, she was a living, breathing being, whose every moment of existence generated more power, which flowed through every cell of her being.

"Thank you, Ara. I believe we have what we need," Cal said. *"You may step out now."*

She did, puffing out a little plume of smoke as she lumbered from the area.

"What did you just do?"

"What do you mean?"

"Something just registered on the readouts. It wasn't much, but the needle definitely moved."

Cal quickly shared his data with Sid and the other AIs monitoring the process. Each ran the calculations themselves, and each reached the same conclusion.

"It seems that you left a residual trace of your signature magic when you did that just now. But we would not have registered it without first having a baseline reading from you directly. I have spoken with the others, and all are in agreement. We believe with a preliminary baseline we should be able to then track the small traces of magical energy in the future."

"So, you need to first observe our quarry before you will be able to track it?" she asked, incredulously. "You do realize, the whole purpose of this exercise is to locate them in the first place."

"Yes, yes, we know. But this is the interesting part. You see, we

already know where those observations took place. We just didn't know how to properly read them."

"Which is a problem, yes?"

"It would be. But many of the cities are in the habit of recording raw data instead of compressing to save space, as had been a practice in the past. With the population so greatly reduced, there has been no need for it."

Tech-magic was not Ara's forte, but, nevertheless, the point was clear. "You can adjust your analysis of prior observations to widen the scope, can't you?"

"Yes. You understand."

"And with this, you think you will be able to approximate the original signature of our quarry?"

"Yes, again. But. There is one issue."

"Isn't there always?"

"Unfortunately, yes. We should be able to detect residual traces of their magical power signature, but we will need to be close if we wish to track it."

"How close?"

"By my calculations, I would think no more than ten miles."

Ara sighed. "Meaning we cannot track from the air. In fact, we cannot track at all, unless we are right on top of them. This is *not* ideal."

"It is not," Cal agreed. *"But for now, it's the best we have."*

"Then we will make it work," Ara replied. "Somehow."

CHAPTER FIFTEEN

The flight to Cape Town could have been exceedingly short, as Eddie had gotten the hang of the ICBM-trajectory reentry angles, but Charlie instructed him to take a lengthier route to better survey the area beneath them as they approached their first stop.

Bawb had also requested a flight change. In his case, though, it was that they alter course several times upon descent.

"You never know who might be watching," he said, looking out at the exterior displays pensively. "It is always best to leave your enemy guessing."

Eddie gladly complied with both requests, making a very lengthy, and very erratic descent. When they finally touched down near the shores of Cape Town, Bawb felt fairly confident that they had likely achieved some modicum of stealth. Regardless, the group was still on edge as they exited the ship.

"I wish we had Baloo," Leila said with a sigh. "He'd smell anyone long before they could get near us, shimmer be damned."

"Yes, he would be most useful in this instance, though spells do exist to mask smell and sound," Bawb noted. "But those are only known to but a select few, and the likelihood of encountering them here is slim to none."

Charlie covered the rear of the procession, while Bawb took point, leading the group toward the area the abduction had taken place. Leila, Rika, and Ripley scanned the area on all sides, weapons held ready, as they walked between the two men.

Eddie had set down a short distance away from the target location, per Bawb's request. As such, they were making their approach via a series of streets with adequate cover should the need arise. But there was not a sound. With all wildlife frozen, along with the few resident humans and Chithiid of the city, the silence was eerie.

"I never really thought about all of those ambient sounds we just ignore," Ripley said. "It's so quiet. Like, I thought it was quiet back home, living where we do, away from the city center. But this? It's nuts."

It was true. With no flights passing overhead, no traffic, and no movement at all, the only sound in the air was the slight breeze gently rustling the leaves of the nearby trees. Other than that, all was still. Frozen.

"It'll let us hear our prey easier, though," Leila said.

"Or let them hear us," Bawb said, hushing the others. Using hand signals, he directed them to follow him as he turned down a smaller street.

They passed several more frozen citizens, each and every one of them stuck in mid-thought or action, like wax museum figures imitating life. But these *were* still alive. Alive but in stasis. Leila shuddered. They'd seen quite a few by now, but every time it still sparked a visceral unease. Looking at Ripley's eyes, she knew she was not alone.

Bawb held up a clenched fist, signaling the team to stop. His hands were faintly glowing, his slaaps fully charged, powerful disabling spells on the tip of his tongue, ready for anything. But nothing came.

He crept forward, carefully stepping around the area they'd seen the woman taken. He then crouched and scrutinized the ground, cocking his head slightly as he read the pavement as a mystic might read tea leaves. The Wampeh sniffed the air, gave the area a final, scrutinizing once-over, then stood up.

"We are alone," he said. "But someone was definitely here. Mind your step in this area," he said, pointing to a large swath. "This is where they came in."

Charlie stared at the ground until his eyes hurt, but all he saw was pavement, some debris, and a bit of dirt blown in by the ocean breeze.

"What are we looking at here, Bob?"

The Wampeh pointed at the blank canvas of ground. "There were seven of them. Tslavar, most likely, given the footwear. And all males, judging by the weight distribution and lengths of their strides."

Ripley squatted down and squinted. "I don't see anything."

"Neither do I," Rika said. "But he's a master assassin. I would trust his assessment over any wilderness scout."

"Thank you, Rika," he said, then began carefully walking the perimeter of the area he had noted. "They arrived from that way, to the west. It seems they were aware this city possessed an intelligence, judging by their approach."

"How can you tell that?" Charlie asked, still seeing nothing but ground.

"Because of the spacing of the steps, and the shift in weight as they walked. Despite being shielded by a shimmer, they were still moving with great caution. It was only a fluke that the briefest of images of the disappearance taking place caught anyone's attention. This was skillful."

"You sound like you admire them," Leila said.

"I appreciate the effort it took to acquire their skills, and the execution of them," he said. "But I would still slay them in an instant, were the opportunity to present itself." He bent, intrigued by something invisible to all but him.

"I don't know how you do that, man. I mean, I get it, you're a trained killer, but this tracking thing––over pavement, no less––it's impressive."

Bawb allowed himself a little smile. "I have told you, Charlie, I am a Wampeh Ghalian. We are not allowed to even touch a weapon for the first years of our training. But in no way does that mean we were idle in that time. There are many things you can learn about your quarry if you but know where to look. For example, come here."

Charlie walked next to him.

"This patch of ground," Bawb said, squatting and pointing. "To the untrained eye it is devoid of information."

"Yep. Seems pretty damn devoid to me," Charlie said.

"But look closer. Do you see this small pebble? The way it has scraped into the surface beneath it?"

"I don't see any––hang on. You mean this one?" Charlie said, poking a tiny piece of rock no bigger than a grain of rice.

"Very good," Bawb said with a pleased grin. "Now, imagine the weight of a man atop it. His footfall as he walks. How the pebble reacts beneath his stride. Do you see the little scratches made to the ground? How pressure was applied, then pivoted slightly?"

Amazingly, Charlie did. And once he knew what to look for, other signs suddenly began to spring out to his newly seeing eyes. "And this one here!" he exclaimed.

"Yes. And what else?"

"And there!"

"Good. You are getting the hang of it. Now, keep your eyes open and follow. Try to see what I see," he said, leading the group as he followed the near-invisible tracks. "The victim was placed on a floating conveyance here. That means Drook power. And I can sense the slightest residue, now that we are standing atop it." He turned to Charlie. "This was a smaller conveyance. A litter to carry the body. You can see the footsteps doubling back the direction they came from following alongside it. Once their load is lightened."

Bawb began to move faster, the trail clear as the kidnappers had clumped together on the way out once they'd retrieved their prize. A sloppy mistake, and one that he hoped to make them pay for. The trail led them to an open park area just outside the city center.

The pale man came to an abrupt stop.

"What is it?" Leila asked. "Are there more tracks?"

"No," he said, scanning the empty ground. "Quite the opposite."

"What do you mean?" Rika asked.

"What I mean is, the tracks end here."

"But that doesn't make sense."

"No, it makes perfect sense," he said. "There was a craft here. One powered by Drook magic and large enough to allow these men and their cargo to easily enter. That would be a sizable vessel."

"So they have a ship?"

"Yes. And this area is still under surveillance. Which means their entire ship is cloaked by a shimmer," he said.

"That's not good, Bob."

"No, it is not. I will work on a counter-shimmer spell, now that I have an idea of the basic variety they are using. It may or may not work, but even a glimpse of them might give us an edge. The power used to sustain it must be quite substantial, but if I can disrupt it for just a moment, the spell I have in mind might work. I need more information first, though."

He turned to Charlie. "We should go see the other locations, though I fear we will find the same results. Someone has a powerful ship. One that we cannot see."

CHAPTER SIXTEEN

The flight back home was the highlight of the day for Eddie's exhausted passengers. They'd made arcing hops through the atmosphere over and over, visiting each and every one of the five cities where abductions had been documented, the disparate points spanning the globe. It was a grind, and one and all longed for the warm comfort of their own bed.

Eddie took Ripley home first, as he always did. Say what you will about his occasionally over-exuberant nature, he was a loyal friend. Apparently, he had been something of a difficult mind to birth. The new system of bringing AIs online, letting them grow more naturally, rather than following a strictly regimented course, was imperfect at best.

The end result, however, was a group of young AIs who, if they'd been fortunate enough to pass the late-stage psych evaluations, would be installed into a ship. Those who developed any one of a variety of deficits or personality flaws would not be so fortunate, dedicated instead to monitoring terrestrial or lunar systems, or even in the worst cases, overseeing waste disposal machinery.

For obvious reasons, flight installation was a goal all of them shared.

Fortunately for Eddie, his precocious young friend happened to be very close to some of the most powerful AIs the planet had ever seen, and when they asked if she might take a look at his "unusual" quirks and talk to him the way only a teenager can, she was happy to lend a hand.

Things had gone better than either anticipated, and what began as a job, wound up becoming a rather unexpected friendship. Ripley was a handful, no doubt, but together, they found a delightful synergy. Pilot and ship. Pals. Working through the training together—and talking a fair amount of trash—Eddie was finally ready for his flight tests.

He was put through his paces, and regardless of Ripley's connections, no leniency or favoritism was imparted. At the end of the demanding test cycle, he passed, and by a good margin to boot. Eddie was officially installed in his ship and tasked with assisting Ripley for his first active year. After that, he would be able to choose if he wanted to stay with her or venture out on his own.

They were in week seven.

"Okay, I'm gonna pass the hell out," Ripley said to her new friends as she disembarked.

"Don't forget to eat something," Leila called after her. "It's going to be another busy day tomorrow. You want me to fix you something?"

"You know there's always a ton of food in my house. Trust me, I'll have plenty to eat."

"Of course. Sorry, I wasn't thinking," Leila said, blushing slightly. Of course she knew there was food in the girl's house. Her father was something of a whiz in the kitchen, and there she had gone, accidentally reminding her of her frozen parents with an offhand comment.

Eddie next made the quick hop to Charlie and Leila's home before setting a course for Downtown and Rika's loft.

"You sure you don't want me to drop you at your place?" Eddie had asked Bawb when he climbed out with Charlie and Leila.

"Yes, I am sure. But thank you for the offer, Eddie. However, this evening, I think a little walk before going home would do me good."

Charlie winced inside. He shared a look with Leila. Their poor friend was going home, and Hunze was still there, frozen in stasis.

"Bawb, are you sure you don't want to take one of the guest rooms? It's no trouble, and we could all have breakfast in the morning," Leila offered,

Charlie got the hint. "Yeah, we'd love to have you stay. And I'll be a sport and even break out the *good* coffee in the morning."

Bawb cracked a pained smile at his friends' efforts. They'd all become exceptionally close over their time together, but Charlie and he had developed a particularly unusual bond. The man with Zomoki blood in his veins—one who would have been a valuable prize for the power-absorbing Wampeh—had become a closer friend than anyone in his adult life.

Their intentions were appreciated, and he felt the love they offered, but on this night, he had plans of his own.

"I thank you for the offer. But I am feeling that a walk along the shores might be a welcome respite from the troubles of our day. I have always found the ocean helps me think. And even on this world, the sound of the waves and smell of salt in the air is familiar."

"Okay, man. Whatever you need to do. But I'm serious, if you need *anything*, don't hesitate to ask."

"Thank you, Charlie. And you, Leila. My king and queen are

most gracious," he said with a wry little smile that told them that, while he was hurting, he would be okay.

"All right. We'll see you at command in the morning. Sleep well," Charlie said.

"And you, my friend."

Bawb was true to his word, and rather than taking the direct route back to his and Hunze's home along the bluffs of Malibu, he instead descended to the shore below. Waves broke against the nearby rocks, the bioluminescence in the water making a slight glow from the agitation. Farther out, the sliver of moonlight reflected across the rippling ocean.

The assassin from another world breathed in deeply, his senses open wide as his lungs absorbed the clean, restorative air. He was in pain, yes. But he was nevertheless able to appreciate the beauty that had somehow inserted itself into his life.

"I wonder if the others would expel me from the order," the assassin mused as he began the walk home, sticking to the damp shore at the water's edge.

Perhaps they would banish him from the Wampeh Ghalian. But given his new life, he couldn't help wonder if that would be such a bad thing.

His stroll lasted a good half hour before he ascended the far end of the bluffs and retraced his way along the dark roadway to the home he and his love had taken as their own. She would be there, he knew. Silent. Still. Frozen in place, exactly where he had left her, lying in bed, softly slumbering.

It would be hard, staying in the same house as her still shape. But it was Malibu, and the property had many rooms, should he want to sleep in one of them. But she was his, as he was hers, and every night he lay at her side. Her protector.

But he had failed. Somehow, he had been unable to keep her safe.

He crossed the perimeter of his property, the first of several alarm spells tickling his senses as he passed. Many layers of magic protected the residence, increasing in power—and deadliness—the closer in you went. Hunze had felt it was overkill, but he hadn't lived this long by being complacent. Besides, she and their friends were explicitly safe from the spells' wrath, a subtle modification added as he cast them.

Bawb placed his hand on the doorknob and was about to open it when something *off* caught his eye. There, on the doorframe, was a tiny fleck of fresh blood.

His fourth layer of spells—those that protected the building itself—were far more violent than the ones guarding the perimeter. And despite a good cleanup job, it seemed someone had tripped the outermost.

He reached out with his konus and tested the spells he had just passed, a horrible truth hitting him as he did. He had been distracted, worried about Hunze. And this was why his kind did not form attachments.

"These are not my spells," he realized.

And in fact they were not. Someone had gone to great lengths to copy his work, but no matter how clever the fake, an artist always knows his own brushstrokes.

Bawb turned the knob, needing to get inside and gather his most powerful weapons to defend his home, and perhaps even his thin armor, lined with a portion of the powerful hair Hunze had gifted him. It was a good plan, but he realized it was already far too late for that. While the innermost rooms' spells would keep Hunze safe with their exceptional violence, the intruders were within reach.

Quickly, he stepped back from the doorway and spun, knives flashing from his hidden sheaths as he dispatched three masked Tslavar mercenaries as their shimmer cloaks sloppily shifted aside to better allow them to strike out.

Despite the added speed they gained, it was poor strategy

against the Geist, and he was simply faster. The dead men quickly fell, and the next two after them––despite keeping themselves properly hidden within their shimmers until the last second––followed their friends to the ground.

Still more attackers emerged, suddenly pummeling him with spells from all directions. He managed to land a hard kick to the ribs of one, toppling them over as at least a few of the ribs in their left side cracked. Another took Bawb's hard elbow to the weak point in the neck, snapping it as the assassin had been trained to do without a second thought.

Bawb fought with the ferocity of a man cornered and knowing he could not possibly win. As such, he would be sure to take as many down with him as he could. But the onslaught was too great, and a series of stun spells landed with great force.

They want me alive, was the last thing he noted before slipping into darkness.

Even unconscious, the deadly assassin inspired fear. And with good reason. Those tasked with capturing him knew full well what a Wampeh Ghalian could do. Bawb's inert body was rapidly stripped of both weapons and clothing, his captors ensuring he was not wearing any hidden device, or even a layer of Ootaki hair woven into an undershirt.

Trussed like so much wild game, he was hastily loaded onto a floating conveyance and hauled away, the bodies of the many he had slain carried along with them into the depths of the night.

CHAPTER SEVENTEEN

"A stealth tech ship? This complicates things significantly," Cal said. *"And while we have adapted scans to better track the masking technologies of our worlds, this magic is an entirely novel manner of power use and device shielding."*

"Just think of it as plain old magic and it'll be easier," Charlie said, sipping a cup of coffee as he reclined on one of the command center's comfortable couches, Leila curled up next to him, likewise nursing a steaming cup of caffeinated joy. "I had a hard time wrapping my head around it as well at first. But once you simply accept it as honest-to-God magic, it's a lot easier."

"Kind of how we were with the workings of your tech," Leila added. "We all thought of it as tech-magic for the longest time. But once we arrived here, in the place, and time, where it powers *everything*, it became clear that we just had to accept it as how things work here."

"You have all adapted quite well. It is an admirable flexibility you and your friends have demonstrated. I'm sure it wasn't an easy transition," Cal said.

"After months living here in this world without magic, it did somewhat ease our transition."

"But that doesn't exactly count, Leila. I mean, we were in medieval times, after all."

"Regardless, you've learned the workings of this time and civilization quickly. It shows an impressive flexibility and quickness of mind."

"Who has a quick mind?" Rika said, walking into the room, making a beeline for the coffee dispenser. "Not Charlie. You *must* be talking about Leila."

"Hey!" Charlie objected.

The snarky pilot flashed an amused look at Leila. "Us girls gotta stick together, right?"

It was slow going for Leila, accepting this woman from Charlie's past as part of their circle. She had tried to kill them, after all, and having been so recently under the thrall of Malalia Maktan's magic, there was still a slight hesitancy to trust her.

Then there was the fact that despite Charlie being with her fully and completely, a history still existed between him and this other woman. Leila knew it was just friendship, but a little nagging awkwardness nevertheless reared its head from time to time. Fortunately, Charlie put any concerns to rest the moment they arose by simply being himself. Her man. Her king.

"Hey, gang," Ripley grumbled, trudging into the room. "Why, again, are we meeting this early?"

"It's ten a.m., Rip," Charlie said.

"Yeah, like I said. Why so early?"

"Teenagers," Rika said with a laugh. "Though, to be fair, I was quite a night owl too, until I became a pilot, that is. Then those late nights became a thing of the past, for the most part."

"It's my body clock," the groggy teen replied. "I can't help it if my natural sleep cycle doesn't align with all of you weirdos."

Rika filled a second cup of coffee and brought it over to the sleepy girl. "Here, it looks like you need this."

"Thanks, Rika."

"No problem."

"So, we gonna get this shindig rolling?" Ripley asked, sipping the steaming beverage.

"Soon, Ripley. We are waiting on one more arrival."

"Hey, weren't you and Eddie going to give Bawb a lift?" Charlie asked.

"He didn't show."

"Did you go by his house?"

"Hey, the guy was kind of out of sorts, in case ya didn't notice. I figured if he wants some alone time with his frozen lady, I totally get it. Give the dude some space."

Charlie hated to admit it, but she was right. Bawb had put on a strong face and done an admirable job, but his distress at Hunze's condition had to be constantly weighing on him. Hell, Charlie had only just recently gotten together with Leila, and he knew how bad he would feel if he were in those shoes.

"Yeah, you're right," he admitted. "Let's get started without him. We'll just fill him in when he gets here."

"As you wish," Cal said. *"So, to begin with, I have some bad news. There have been more abductions observed. This time on this continent. Seattle and San Francisco, just last night."*

"Again? And in our part of the world? How did we not see them coming? Aren't you guys on the lookout for things after we got all that intel yesterday?"

"We are refining our scanning. Ara was very helpful in devising methods to track these cloaked parties. She has an impressive intellect, being able to understand our technology so quickly despite being a space dragon."

Charlie laughed. "Still kinda weird saying that, isn't it?"

"A bit, perhaps," Cal conceded. *"In any case, we had extrapolated possible disturbance patterns and devised an experimental algorithm to track minuscule incidents that might combine to suggest the presence of one of these invisible vessels or its men."*

"And?"

"And we actually did encounter something in San Francisco. The AI there was recently installed—the original was destroyed in the war. She is a more modern design, and quite powerful, though I must admit, calling herself Fran was lacking creativity, in my opinion. In any case, Fran also possesses a new array of automated defenses, which she used to target what appeared to be nothing."

"But there *was* something, wasn't there?" Rika asked.

"Yes. The Chithiid that had been snatched was not recovered, but she used a targeting algorithm to follow likely movements of cloaked foot troops. Instead of randomly firing, as some of the older systems did, she fired individual rounds. Not only did that keep collateral damage almost non-existent, but it also resulted in a response from the hidden attackers. Observe," he said, flashing on a pair of the display monitors.

Images of the city on the bay flashed on screen. With the spell in place, it was eerily silent, not even the pigeons moving, but rather, laying where they fell. Then a few shots rang out. Triangulating in, walking the rounds closer to *something*.

A flurry of debris launched into the air, flung at the cannon, followed by a wave of power. Normally, that would have ended things, but this was not an AI who would easily give in. Instead, Fran brought multiple other defense cannons to bear––some from across the city––lobbing rounds in all manner of trajectories, pummeling her invisible quarry.

That certainly elicited a reaction, and the sheer power and speed of the counterattack took Charlie aback.

"Shit. I recognize that spell," he said. "This is bad."

"How bad?" Leila asked.

"Either someone has a *very* powerful slaap to cast those spells, or we have an emmik on Earth. Maybe even a visla."

"So, this is a substantial adversary?" Cal asked.

"Oh, yes," Charlie replied. "This does not bode well."

The possibility of natural power users of that level being on the planet was a complication none of them had expected. Sure, they had encountered, and defeated, Malalia on Earth's soil, but that was thousands of years in the past, and she had been blasted back to her own galaxy, and in that same time, no less. Malalia would have long become dust by now.

But some other powerful entity appeared to be interested in their world. And from what they'd already seen, a larger play than just snatching random people was in motion. But without more information, they had no idea what that might be. Charlie knew one thing, though. Whatever it was, it was undoubtedly not something good.

CHAPTER EIGHTEEN

"Come on, stop pussyfooting around and hit me!"

Leila weighed the invitation and finally snapped out a jab, catching Rika on the chin.

"That's more like it," she said, obviously pleased as she shook off the punch. "Sparring isn't any good if you go half-assed. Now, let's go again."

Rika had offered to spend some time working with her olive-skinned teammate to improve her hand-to-hand skills, as well as basic magic. It was a bit odd, the human helping the woman who grew up using a konus her whole life, but with the tactics implanted into Rika's mind, she possessed a decided advantage when it came to martial matters.

Charlie and Bawb had been working with Leila for some time as well, but after watching one of their training sessions, Rika suggested a woman might be able to help her in ways they could not. It wasn't that the boys weren't skilled. They fought incredibly well, but they fought like men, relying on techniques designed for their physiques and strengths.

A woman, on the other hand, was better suited for speed and

leverage than brute strength, and there were specific moves that would suit Leila's already lithe and athletic build just fine.

The two had been at it for a good ten minutes, starting with light sparring to get the blood flowing and the muscles loose, while Cal and the other AIs were crunching numbers and sorting the mountains of data at their digital fingertips, working on a better methodology to perhaps track the mysterious kidnappers.

In the meantime, that left the tiny handful of unfrozen people on the entire planet with nothing to do but wait. And if waiting was on the menu, why not hone some skills while blowing off a little steam?

"Try to square your hips and throw a series of punches from your midline rather than looping them wide," Rika instructed.

"Won't that be weaker?"

"If you get your hips solid as your base of power, then no, not really. It's all about leverage and transfer of power. Physical, that is, not magical," Rika noted. "But we'll get to that stuff too, in a little bit. But for now, try throwing four punches like this," she said, demonstrating a quick Wing Chun flurry.

Leila stepped over to the three-sectioned punching bag and aimed for the middle one, churning her fists over one another as she had been instructed.

"Nice! You're a natural."

"I wouldn't go that far."

"Well, you've got a knack for it," Rika said. "Some people, it's like they have two left feet. Take Charlie, for instance."

"But he's a great gladiator. I've seen him fight, as have you, obviously."

"Well, yeah. He's great *now*. But when we were crewmates, it was like pulling teeth getting him to train at all."

"So you remember training with him?" Leila asked, her interest piqued.

Rika furrowed her brow. "Not exactly. I mean, I know we did those things, and I have vague flashes every once in a while. But specific memories are like ghost images flitting at the periphery of my memory. But now that we're training like this, that particular bit felt a little, I don't know, *fresher*, if that makes sense."

Leila supposed it did. When she walked the hills above their home, there were occasional smells that would take her right back to Visla Maktan's estate and her former life there, tending the animals. Memory was a tricky thing, like that.

"What do you say? Another few rounds before we call it a day?"

"Sure. Why not?"

Rika smiled. "Good answer." She then launched an attack, forcing Leila to react, not think.

Leila quickly threw her hands as she'd been shown, pivoting at the waist and using her hips for power as she used Rika's momentum and power to pull her out of position, while situating herself to her side for a clear shot.

Rika winced at the blow, spinning away and throwing a low kick, nearly sweeping Leila off her feet. But Leila was wearing a konus. It was a little thing, barely charged, but it was enough for her to fling a diversionary spell at her opponent, following it with a physical and magical counterattack that took Rika right off her feet.

The stronger woman bounced back to her feet and pressed her attack, forcing Leila out of her comfort zone. But that was Rika's plan. To make her stretch her abilities and exceed her own expectations.

The spell Leila used wasn't one they'd been training with. It was one Charlie had shown her, but that she'd never been able to make work no matter how hard she tried. Charlie had explained that the more difficult a spell, the more crucial it was that she not focus on the words as much as the intent and feeling of the energy behind it. And that was what suddenly flowed through her as her lips barely uttered the words.

"*Dispanus rahm!*" she barked, the konus on her wrist flashing to life at her words.

Rika found herself abruptly upended and stunned, the combination spell leaving her dazed on the ground.

"Oh my God! I'm so sorry!" Leila said, bending over the downed woman with concern etched into her face.

Rika, however, was laughing. At least as much as a stunned woman could, given the magic still immobilizing her.

"Now *that's* more like it," she said, shaking off the spell and slowly sitting up.

"Are you okay?"

"Yeah, I've had worse," Rika replied. "She didn't make me a killer in a day, after all." A dark shadow flashed across her face as the memory of what had been done to her paid an unexpected visit.

"I'm so sorry. I didn't mean to dredge any of that up."

"Leila, it's not your fault. What happened, happened, and I've got to live with that. And part of that process is learning to talk about it. To accept it. I don't have to like it, but I can't pretend it didn't happen, you know?"

"Yes, I suppose I do."

"Good. So we're cool. This wasn't anything on you. It's just she messed with my head, and every so often, well..."

"I understand."

"Thanks, Leila," she said, taking her offered hand and getting to her feet. "And besides, it wasn't all bad."

"You've got to be kidding."

"No, I mean it. I mean, the torture and mindfuck weren't cool, but I came out the other side intact, miraculously, and I've got the residual benefit of having retained pretty much all of that skill set she embedded in here," she said, tapping her head. "So while some memories are bad, others are useful. It's a trade-off, is all," she said, mopping her forehead and neck before peeling off her soaked sweatshirt. Leila caught a brief glimpse of a nasty bruise wrapping around her left rib cage before she slipped into a clean top.

"Are you okay?"

"Yeah, I'm fine. Just a little sore is all. You?"

"I feel great."

It was true. They'd worked up a good sweat, and the exercise felt fantastic. Leila's energy levels were topped off from the excitement of sparring. Rika, on the other hand, was moving a little slower.

"Electrolytes?" Rika asked, offering her sparring partner a pouch.

"Are these the salty/sweet things?"

"Yeah. Glucose to help it absorb into your system faster—we call it an isotonic solution—and electrolytes to keep your muscles and nerves all happy after you sweat all of them out."

"Then yes. Thank you," Leila said, taking the beverage and sipping the odd concoction.

Rika studied her quietly for a moment. "Leila, I'm sorry to ask, and I hope it's not inappropriate, but with everything such a jumble in my head, I was wondering. Did Charlie ever say anything about me?"

Leila stopped drinking. "Uh, he did say that he lost his friend not long after he arrived in my galaxy."

"Right. But nothing else?"

"You mean...?"

"So we weren't...?"

"Oh. Uh, he said you were just friends. *Good* friends, but that was all," Leila replied.

"Oh, thank God," Rika said, relaxing a little. "It's just he treats me so well despite what happened at the castle, and I know we were friends once upon a time, but I still can't remember details. If there ever had been something, I didn't want to accidentally say anything that might make him uncomfortable, ya know? I may not remember that life, but that doesn't mean I might not go blundering like a fool and put my foot in it, if you know what I mean."

"I think he would have said something, Rika, so you're fine."

"Whew. Thank God. That would be awkward," she said with a bright laugh. "And besides, you two are disgustingly perfect together."

"Aww, thank you."

"I mean it. I just hope one day I'll find someone who looks at me the way he looks at you."

Leila pulled her into a tight hug before she could object.

"Hey, what's that for?"

"For being my friend," Leila said. And this time, she meant it. "Now come on. We should go clean up before we meet the others."

"Good call. And Bawb should be there by now. I have a few theories I want to run by him."

"He'll be there. I know he's dealing with some tough things with Hunze frozen, but even with that, he wouldn't miss two briefings in a row."

CHAPTER NINETEEN

Ara and Charlie sat quietly perched atop the tallest building in the city, looking out across the clear blue skies, taking in the unobstructed view that spanned from the distant mountains to the east, all the way to the crystal waters to the west. To any passing below, it would almost appear as if a giant gargoyle had been installed on high to guard over the city. And they wouldn't be entirely wrong.

Since her arrival, the mighty Zomoki had been something of a comforting sight to the sparse population of the reconstructed city. While the war was long past, having a powerful--and quite legendary--new champion, was nevertheless reassuring. And Ara, for her part, had taken to the role.

Of course, flying low, learning every inch of her friends' new home had also been something she felt a pressing need to do, having been surprised and trapped in an unfamiliar cavern until not so long ago. That had been across the planet, but the memory was still fresh, and Ara was keen to ensure no such surprises would sneak up on her again.

Fortunately, the humans' solar system possessed a wonderfully powerful sun, and every moment spent under its revitalizing rays healed her in both body and spirit. And now, just as she was finally feeling like herself again, there was some new danger threatening her and her friends.

As for Charlie, his own internal powers were growing rapidly, his blood link to the dragon as strong as ever, some of her magic ability flowing through his veins now as well as her own.

And there was another anomaly. Something about being here, in this place, linked to this man, had somehow increased the speed at which she was absorbing the sun's power. She had confided this in Cal, the two sharing their theories as to why this might be happening, and he had some interesting hypotheses.

For having just had the existence of magical space dragons proven to him––their being mythological creatures only now disproven with the hard fact of her very tangible presence––the AI was surprisingly flexible in his ability to work his mind around magic-based problems. Most pressing at the moment, however, was finding their invisible enemy.

"They were able to devise a way to observe traces of my power," she said to Charlie, pensively staring out over the city. "It is imperfect at best, and very limited in range, but the fact remains, if they are able to observe the origin of the power, they can then trace its signature, to an extent."

"Interesting," Charlie said, staring out across the hills to the north. "All we need now is to find whoever is doing this, which leaves us pretty much where we already were."

"I know. But at least it's a start," Ara replied.

They sat together quietly, mulling over their options. The problems they faced were many, and solutions were painfully few.

Charlie took a deep breath, filling his lungs with the fresh, coastal air. "You know, last time I was in LA, that would have smelled like exhaust fumes."

"What are exhaust fumes? I'm afraid this is an aspect of this new world I am yet unfamiliar with."

"Ah, yeah. Well, those would have actually been from way back in *my* time. We still used a type of engine that was powered by combustion. It made the air a bit smoggy. Sorry, smog is, I mean *was* the residual smoke and fumes from those engines. But with the war, and Earth losing so much of its population for so many years, it seems the planet has managed to undo all of the damage mankind had inflicted."

"Nature finds a way," the dragon noted.

"That it does. But we certainly didn't make it easy."

"So you have said. Non-magical explosions driving a conveyance? I am impressed with your world, Charlie, but I must admit, that does not sound like a terribly efficient means of transit. Or safe, for that matter."

He laughed. "No, when I say combustion, I don't mean big booms, but small fires taking place within a closed environment, used to create combustive pressure. And you're right, it wasn't the most efficient of things. But, hell, before my day they even used a version of it to launch ships into space."

"Into space?"

"Yeah. They were basically giant, flying bombs with tiny craft stuck on the tips. And every once in a while, they would blow up before even making it out of the atmosphere."

"And people would willingly fly in these craft? Yours are a daring, and foolish, people, Charlie."

"I certainly won't contradict that," he said with a chuckle. "But we got past that tech. Eventually, we devised clean, efficient drive systems. And no matter how ridiculous some of our population's old practices may seem, they're still my people. Which brings us back to our problem at hand. One of them, anyway. How do we unfreeze them?"

"On that, I am afraid we are still unsure. Even on individual subjects, it has so far been impossible to break the spell—it is an incredibly complex one, and it will take time to devise something that might work, at least on a small scale. But this is global, and the Ootaki hair powering the spell is growing stronger every moment it is in the presence of your world's sun."

Charlie paused, a light bulb flashing on in his mind. "Holy shit."

"What?"

"Hunze's gift."

"What of it?"

"She gave half of her hair to Bob. And the *way* she gave it."

Ara cocked her head slightly. "That's a good point. It is fully charged. Supercharged, even, thanks to this world's sun."

"Exactly. And her hair has been here for a lot longer than the stuff in the *Asbrú*, so it should be exponentially more powerful, despite being a smaller amount. I mean, it was already far more powerful than any other source of magic on the planet, besides you, of course."

"And if we could devise a manner to incorporate its power into the counterspell—"

"Now we're on the same page," Charlie said with a grin. "This just might work."

"But the Geist is the lone being capable of wielding that hair. It was given out of love, and as such, is bound to him and him alone."

"Yeah, but he's a very talented user. Working together, I'm pretty confident we could find a way he could add all of that power to a focused spell. But first things first. We need to unfreeze one person to know it will work. And if you can truly craft a counterspell, then Hunze would be my first choice."

"Mine as well, but only if I have the highest degree of confidence she will not be harmed should the spell fail. I will discuss this with him when he arrives."

"He's still not here?"

"I have not seen him arrive."

"It's not like him to sulk around his house. But knowing him, he's probably planning some violent revenge. I mean, they didn't *hurt* Hunze, technically, but they might as well have. And you know how protective he is of her."

"Oh, yes. Indeed."

"Yeah. You do not want *that* assassin angry with you," Charlie said with a little grin. "I'd hate to be on the receiving end of that retaliation. Someone is going to be having a very bad, and very short, comeuppance. Possibly in several pieces."

CHAPTER TWENTY

It was quiet. Not soothing, peaceful quiet, but disconcerting quiet.

Several humans, a few four-armed Chithiid, and even a lone, flesh-covered cyborg lay strapped to form-fitting tables made of some strange, self-illuminating material that seemed to be almost like stone, but malleable. And on those devices, they lay. Captives in a smooth, windowless chamber.

All were firmly restrained across their legs and torsos, and were further bound at each wrist. Their bodies were positioned at an incline, unseeing eyes staring blankly at the ceiling. The cyborg among them, however, was actively looking around, his head restrained but his eyes free to roam. And roam they did.

Tall, green-skinned men came and went, periodically collecting one of the frozen captives and taking them from the room. When they returned the hapless person some time later, they had been unfrozen from the spell, but remained in a dazed state. They also had a thin blindfold over their eyes. Had he been from another galaxy, the hapless mechanical man would have recognized his green-skinned captors as Tslavar mercenaries.

And he would have been afraid.

The process was repeated every several hours, a different captive taken away, then returned a while later. The reason behind it, however, remained a mystery.

The cyborg watched the comings and goings with great curiosity––at least, as much as he could see with his head strapped firmly in place––taking note of the limited things he could observe. It seemed the strange, green men were releasing the others from whatever kind of ailment had befallen them. But why they all remained restrained, he was unsure.

The situation did not make sense. At least, not to the tin man covered in flesh.

To the greatest assassin in thirty systems, however, it made perfect sense.

Bawb had been stripped to his undergarments, his captors making sure he had no weapons hidden anywhere on his body, hidden from view. He was secretly glad he had not been wearing the armored vest he had fabricated and lined with some of the powerful hair Hunze had gifted him. It would have been useless to anyone else, the hair being bonded to him for life, but he'd have hated to lose it.

Of course, had he been wearing it in the first place, he very likely would not have found himself in his current predicament to begin with.

He had been separated from the others in the compartment by a partition, rendering him unable to observe the goings-on with the other prisoners. Unable to see, that is. But to his sharp ears, a lot of information was there for the taking.

It seemed there were at least a few others held in the chamber, judging by the number of breathing mouths he could hear, though that number would increase each time the Tslavars––he could tell by their voices––would remove something, bringing it back with a breathing occupant some time later. It was a vexing mystery, but he remained unconcerned.

He had time. If they wanted him dead, that aim would have already been achieved long before now.

The Tslavars weren't giving up any additional information as they went about their work. But without the translation spell Bawb had provided himself and his friends, the other captives wouldn't have known what was being said anyway, were they aware.

"Oh, you're aliens," the cyborg said when the green men stepped into his field of view. "I haven't seen your species before. What are you called?"

"This one isn't affected," one of the mercenaries said, ignoring the cyborg.

"That's strange. We should tell Sindall. He'll know what to do."

"I'm sorry, I can't understand you," the metal man said. "What language are you speaking? I thought we'd assimilated all of the allied races' languages into our database."

"This must be the hybrid being Sindall brought aboard to experiment on. One of the ones with a strange metal beneath its skin," the nearest Tslavar said. "I heard Purak talking about them yesterday. Apparently, the spell does not affect them. Something about them renders them immune."

"Then why is he here?"

"Well, the capture and transit spell still immobilizes them the same as others, so perhaps he was accidentally rounded up with the others. Whatever the reason, Sindall will soon learn all there is to know about this breed."

"I have no doubt. Such an unusual magic at work in this system."

"I agree. But it's not our job to figure all of that out. Now, come. We must transport this one for study."

Bawb could hear the men activate the conveyance spell to lift the table.

Ah, so there are others held in this place, he realized. *But they are still in the grip of the spell. Frozen and unbreathing. No wonder I hear so few. This is a start. Now I need more information.*

Bawb, bound as he was, found himself limited as to the methods of intelligence-gathering at his disposal. One, however, was still available to him. Provided, of course, the green men were loose with their tongues. But first, he would need to get them to engage in discourse. *Then* he would ply them for information.

"You should know, you will be unable to enchant that man," he called out past the partition.

The footsteps stopped.

"That's right, it's true. You cannot enchant his kind, if that's what you are trying to accomplish. Their minds are made of code, not meat."

If that does not pique their interest, I don't know what will.

The silence told him that despite their likely orders to not speak to the segregated prisoner, the men were second-guessing that command. The footsteps growing louder confirmed that suspicion. Bawb contained his grin and waited.

"How do you understand us?" the green man said, stepping around the partition. "No translation spells have been provided, and any on your person would have been negated when you were brought aboard."

"Ah, about that," Bawb said. "I have a little secret."

"Which is?"

"That my own spell is quite a good deal more robust than your counterspell. I assume it's located at the entrance to this place, yes?"

The man did not answer, but his partner joined him, both looking at the pale man with a heady mix of confusion and distrust.

SCOTT BARON

"And is this how you were not frozen with the rest?" one said.

"A good question. But first, tell me. Why are you even here?"

"I can't answer that."

"Can't, or won't?"

"You killed several of my friends."

"Their fault, I assure you. And if you were attacked by shimmer-cloaked men outside your own residence, you likely would have reacted the same."

He could see the slight glimmer in the man's eye as he mulled over that statement. Despite his killing their friends, the point was a valid one that any man of action would be remiss to deny. It still didn't make them forgive him, of course. But, suddenly, their captive seemed just a little bit more like one of them. As he had intended.

"Please, won't you at least tell me what you want from me? I'm not much use to you here. I'm not even from this world. Or this system, for that matter."

The Tslavar mercenaries didn't know what to make of the odd man. He was the one strapped down, yet they were the ones strangely ill at ease.

"You're a Wampeh. Someone from our realm, so far from home. What is it you are doing here?"

"I might ask you the same," Bawb replied. "And what interest are these people to you? It seems beneath mighty Tslavar warriors to snatch helpless civilians from the streets."

This was what he wanted. A discourse. Normalized communication with the men, gradually lowering their guard. Soon, they would slip. Soon, he would have the information he sought. Or at least some of it.

The sound of footsteps approached, and judging by the pace, their owner was in something of a hurry.

"What are you doing conversing with that prisoner?" a man barked.

"Captain Sindall, we're sorry, sir. But this one possesses a translation spell. We just thought we'd, uh, help question him. Maybe get some answers."

A loud slap rang out as the captain's hand met the man's face. "Imbecile. You have no idea what you're dealing with. You weren't getting answers from him. He was getting them from you."

Oh well.

"Now do your jobs and get this one to the examination chamber."

Chamber, not room? So we're not in a building, then. We're on their ship, Bawb realized. In his haste, the captain himself had slipped, providing a nugget of valuable information. *A Tslavar ship. Interesting.*

"Where are we going?" the cyborg asked. "Won't you talk to me?"

"Do not fear, friend," Bawb called out. "Their magic will not work on you. Be brave."

"Wait, they're not here to help me? What's going on? They aren't helping the others?"

Bawb knew it had to be confusing for the cyborg. One moment he was minding his own business, the next he was in a strange place surrounded by an alien race he'd never even seen before. And he couldn't understand a word his captors were saying. As it was, only Bawb's spell allowed them to communicate.

"No, they are not here to help you. But you will get through this. Stay calm and keep your wits about you and you will be okay," he said, comforting the cybernetic man, but not believing his own words.

Time would tell if he was correct. The time when the confused cyborg was either brought back to the chamber intact, or if he was never heard from again.

The three men's footsteps faded as they moved deeper into the ship, leaving the bound Wampeh alone. Alone to ruminate and plan.

CHAPTER TWENTY-ONE

Two days had passed, and Bawb's disappearance had quickly gone from, "Where the hell is Bob?" to something far more concerning. He hadn't been absent terribly long, but when he failed to show up for the second strategy session, Charlie and Leila had taken it upon themselves to do a wellness check of their friend, figuring he needed a little nudge to get out of his funk.

They even brought a container of chicken soup––something Charlie swore could make anyone feel better––but when they reached his home, the magic around it was crackling with residual energy from the recent disturbance.

"Ara, I need you at Bob's place, ASAP," Charlie called to his Zomoki friend.

"I am not far. I will be there momentarily," she replied, and two minutes later, the familiar shadow of his dragon friend flashed across the ground.

Ara landed with a crunch, the urgency of Charlie's call making her eschew her usual restraint in touching down.

"What is it?" she asked, golden eyes flashing as she took in the surroundings, assessing the disturbance to Bawb's magical defenses.

"You see what I see?" Charlie asked.

"I do. Something happened here. And recently, it would appear." She leaned in close, sniffing the ground outside the front door. "Death. Blood. Several fatalities, it seems. Tslavar, from the smell of it. And they took the bodies with them."

Charlie knew that race all too well, having been taken captive and forced into slavery by them several years ago. "At least we know who we're dealing with," he said. "But this is not good."

"No, it is not," the dragon agreed.

Leila stepped to the doorway and bent low, studying the traces using her natural skills as an animalist from the Maktan estate, as well as the new tricks she'd observed Bawb teaching to Charlie.

"They didn't kill him," she said, stepping back and tracking the faint hints of combat on the ground. "Charlie, does this look like dragging boot prints to you?"

He stepped close and scanned the ground. "Yeah, you're right. I think they captured him. And look, the tracks drag off then vanish."

"A floating conveyance again," Leila noted. "Just like in the other abductions."

"Only this one didn't go as smoothly as planned," Charlie added.

Ara focused her intense gaze on the front door. "Someone triggered one of our Wampeh friend's more violent spells, it appears. Look there, on the doorframe. Blood, and older than the other traces. Someone was dispatched attempting to enter his domicile. From what I can see here, it would appear Bawb returned home to an ambush."

"And made a pretty good showing of it," Charlie added. "But

this is Bob we're talking about. How is it that any of them survived, let alone took him captive?"

"If they were using the same shimmer spells as before, he might not have noticed them until the last second," Ara replied. "Leila, will you please check inside and make sure Hunze is unharmed? The interior spells appear untouched, but I am too large to check on her myself."

"Of course, Ara. I'll be right back," Leila said, hurrying into the house. As a close friend of Bawb's she was granted passage free from harm, and if any of the Tslavar trespassers had attempted further ingress, there would be ready signs of it as she moved through the house. Likely in the form of their body parts from the spells' wrathful carnage.

Charlie looked at his Zomoki friend with concern in his eyes. "This isn't good. We've got to get Bob back, Ara."

"I know, Charlie. He is our friend, and we will do all we can. But there is another consideration as well."

"Which is?"

"Without him, the Ootaki hair stored inside is useless. Hunze's gift will only serve one person, and that man has been taken."

She was right, of course, and any hopes they had harbored that Bawb's cache of powerful hair might help them counter the spell holding Hunze and the rest of the world in stasis were now put on hold until they could somehow locate and free their friend.

"Whoever did this had some serious power backing them," Charlie said. "And shimmers aren't easy to come by, not to mention requiring a fair bit of training to be any good at using one." Charlie slowly made another loop of the scene of the abduction, noting the tiny details Bawb had clued him in to finding. "I'm counting what seem to be a dozen or so footprints. Well, traces of them, anyway. What does your nose say?"

"Yes, that is a fair approximation."

"So, a squad of Tslavar mercs on a snatch-and-run mission, only Bawb got the upper hand. At least for a moment. That there's no Wampeh blood is a testament to their professionalism. These weren't just any kidnappers."

"No, they were not," Ara agreed. "It would seem a disciplined team carried out the deed."

"And if not for Bob's booby traps catching them off-guard, they'd likely have taken him unaware."

"It would seem that way. Also, it is worth noting they were able to deactivate his more benign repelling spells at the perimeter of the property. That alone is a sign of their skill. But to then replace them with counterfeits of their own? That shows a level of planning and sophistication far beyond your ordinary mercenary."

The front door swung open with barely a sound. Leila's steps were light and silent, her years working the grounds of Visla Maktan's estate, keeping his animals maintained and looked after, had made it second nature.

"Hunze's fine," she said as she exited the house. "Looks like no one dared go inside."

"They caught on quickly after their buddy got splattered at the doorway," Charlie noted.

"Indeed," Ara agreed. "Whatever happened here is long-done, and Hunze remains well protected by the spells Bawb has in place." Ara glanced around the area doing one last survey, then leaned down low. "I am afraid there is nothing more we can do here. Climb onto my back. We must go speak with Cal and the others at once. We need to devise a new plan."

CHAPTER TWENTY-TWO

After a quick flight to Downtown, Ara had jumped right in with the greater minds of the global AI network to devise a means of sussing out the whereabouts of the cloaked ship she believed now housed their friend.

As Ara was far too large to fit inside the loop tube station where Cal had set up shop, a nearby rooftop landing pad high above had been converted into a jury-rigged situation analysis center, with a series of screens now sharing data with the massive dragon.

The AI network had been vigilant as only never-sleeping computers could be, scanning every byte of data from their scanners continuously for a hint as to the whereabouts of the alien threat. None were to be found, save for the few moments when a frozen body blipped off their radar.

Whatever type of shimmer spell they were using, Ara conceded it was beyond her substantial ability to unmask. And without a baseline gauge of the ship's signature when it was uncloaked, there was simply no way to effectively trace it. At least, not yet.

The AIs ran simulations, gauging the speed at which the

craft would have had to travel in order to carry out its abductions at the disparate locations around the globe. People had been snatched from nearly all continents, and in fairly rapid succession.

Ara pointed out that if she could make the trip in that short a time frame, a well-powered ship could undoubtedly do so as well, though how they managed it without even leaving a re-entry signature as they leapt through the atmosphere was beyond her.

"I would think that a disruption in the clouds at that speed would be one way to track a rapidly moving object, even if it was shimmer cloaked," Ara said.

"Yes. Akin to a contrail from a craft as water vapor parts around it at high speed," Cal agreed. *"And yet, there have been no such signatures. We are all unfamiliar with the intricacies of this magic—beyond what you have told us, of course. Is it possible for a shimmer spell to create some sort of field around the craft, preventing even the air from shifting as it passes?"*

Ara had to admit, it was a novel concept she had not considered. It had never been done, that she knew of, but that didn't mean it was not possible.

"I suppose it is within the realm of feasibility, though I've never seen such magic," she conceded. "But I wonder if such a spell would be able to fully negate the heat generated as they re-entered the atmosphere."

"If they are making orbital hops, that is."

"Well, naturally. There must be something we are missing. Some means of tracking them. No shimmer is perfect; we simply have to discover this one's flaw."

Down below, in the comfort of the command center, the four remaining members of the team were poring over the data, a vast array of monitors displaying every bit of information they'd gathered thus far.

Ripley had claimed one of the couches as her own, a small bag tucked beside it, along with a blanket and pillow. The news of Bawb's abduction had been a gut-punch for her. Here he was, the most deadly member of their little group by far, snatched from his own house without a trace. And his house was not so far from her own.

"Screw that," she had said when she arrived at command in a rush. "I'm not sticking around out there with those Sleever things busting into our houses."

"They're *Tslavars*, Rip. And I think they went after Bob for a reason," Charlie said.

"Great, so they took the most badass fighter first. Leaving us all more vulnerable. Don't you see?"

"I do. However, Bob also possesses the single most powerful source of magic on the planet, besides Ara. It looks like they were trying to get *that*. And when they couldn't get past his spells, they settled for the next best thing. Probably in hopes of having him give them access to it."

It was the first time Charlie had voiced his concern out loud, and it felt, somehow, like that made it more real. Until that point, it was just one of many hypotheticals floating around in his head. But he knew it had to be something to do with Hunze's hair. It made sense, tactically. Negate the most powerful threats first, then complete whatever the hell it was they were doing.

Ara wouldn't be lured into a trap again, and her sheer size and power made even a sneak attack highly unlikely to succeed. But Bawb, despite his considerable skills, was still just a man. And a man could be taken, if the stars aligned, along with a carefully laid plan.

"Would you feel better taking our guest room?" Leila asked. "Charlie and I will be there to protect you."

"No way. You're, like, only a mile from my place. Nope. I'm not going anywhere near there."

"You can stay with me if you like, Rip," Rika offered as she scrolled through images of the abduction sites. "I've got a massive place all to myself. I can get one of the other rooms made up for you."

Ripley seemed to be considering the offer a moment. Rika did live high up in a residential tower, and it would be much, much harder for anyone to sneak up on them through all of those doors and elevators. But even so, it could be done.

"Thanks, Rika, but I'm just gonna stay down here with Cal. It's the safest place in the city."

"As you wish," Rika said. "But the offer stands, should you change your mind."

The four of them turned their attentions away from their teen friend's housing status and back to the much larger problem at hand. Namely, how the seemingly random abductions could possibly be connected. And how they managed to snatch people from all over the globe without being spotted once.

Between the network of cube-satellites observing from on high, and all of the myriad scanning being done by city-sized AIs across the planet, it was a statistical impossibility that they wouldn't have at least *something* by now. But they didn't, and it was driving them all batty. Even the AIs seemed unsettled by their inability to apply logic and math to come to a solution.

"Put up the list again," Charlie said. "On the main screen, please. And then next to it, let's slap those cities onto the map and put that there too. And include time stamps on each of the abduction pinpoints."

Rika quickly compiled the data and arranged it as he requested, swiping the gray-scale image from the smaller tablet up onto the main display screen. It was information they'd been staring at for hours, and still were no closer to an answer.

Charlie walked to the screen and stared. "Cardiff, Rio, Cape Town, Valparaiso, Honolulu, Seattle, San Francisco, and now Los Angeles."

"There may have been another one," Ripley said. "Uncle Cal mentioned a fisherman in Sydney may have been taken."

"How did we miss that?"

"There was a storm there shortly after, and the AI was focused on saving all of the frozen people who were in harm's way," Ripley replied. "I guess this just slipped through the cracks until he was able to go back and review the data again. That's when he saw the guy didn't fall off the dock, but just seemed to vanish."

"But why a fisherman? And why on a dock? It seems there would be easier places to take someone," Rika noted.

Charlie crossed the room and got himself a cup of coffee from the food dispenser. "Anyone else want a cup?"

"Yeah, that would be great," Leila said. "Rika? Rip?"

"Me too, please," Ripley said.

"Ditto," said Rika.

Charlie procured the caffeinated pick-me-up for his friends and set back to work, deeply inhaling the steam wafting from his cup. It made him think of Ara and her ability to *smell* magic. It was incredibly disconcerting that the invaders had devised a spell that actually kept her from even picking up a whiff of them over so many days.

"It's crazy, you know," he said.

"What is?" Leila asked.

"That even Ara can't pick up their scent. I mean, she's got this incredibly powerful nose, and she can smell not just people, but even magic. And even so, she still can't find even a tiny trace of them. It's like someone just took a big old mop and wiped down the world, taking every trace of these bastards with them."

Ripley's eyes went wide. "Holy shit!"

"What is it, Rip?"

"Wiping the world! Don't you get it?"

"English, Rip. What are you talking about?" Rika asked.

"I can't believe we didn't see this. It's so obvious."

"Again, not making sense. What are you talking about?"

"Look. Here," she said, walking to the main display. "Look at the cities. Look where they are."

"Yes, Ripley, we've seen them a million times," Charlie groaned.

"No. *Look*. Use your eyes."

The others did use their eyes, but only to give her confused looks.

"Ugh, hang on," she groaned, punching in a quick series of commands on the screen.

The map shifted from gray-scale to a full-color topographical image, including the heights of the tallest peaks, as well as the ocean's deepest depths. And then it hit him. What Ripley had meant.

"Hooooly shit," Charlie gasped.

"I know, right?" she said, beaming proudly.

"Damn. Now that was impressive, Rip."

"Thanks."

Rika and Leila stared a moment longer before it dawned on them as well.

"Those are all coastal cities," Rika said.

"Yep."

"And the oceanic trenches..."

"Yeah," Charlie said, his pulse spiking at the first real progress they'd made. "That's why the satellites and city scanners can't see them. Why Ara can't smell a trace of them." He walked to the screen and took in the image with an entirely new perspective. "Those bastards aren't flying. They're traveling underwater."

CHAPTER TWENTY-THREE

"This is bad," Ara said.

"How bad?"

"Very bad, Charlie," the dragon replied. "*Extremely* bad."

She and the AIs had been churning through tracking options when Ripley had rushed onto the rooftop landing deck in a blur of excitement, her new friends in tow as she blurted out what they'd learned about the alien invaders. That they were avoiding detection by traveling *under* the sea. And Ara was *not* amused.

"Hang on," Ripley interjected. "I thought this was a *good* thing. I mean, we finally know how they're getting around now, right? And how they're picking cities. We just need to have the guys along the coast step it up, right?"

"As I've already informed our coastal AIs," Cal informed her.

Ara looked at her unknowing new companion with sympathetic eyes. "I'm still afraid this is not good news, Ripley. While, yes, we can now narrow down potential areas of incursion, the fact remains that the quantity, strength, and most especially the *variety* of magic needed to power and maintain a craft of any size beneath a body of water as large and deep as your oceans is extremely expensive."

"Which means whoever is doing this is well funded," Charlie noted. "And also well versed in asymmetrical tactics. No one expects them to travel beneath the sea."

"Yes, obviously. But this also means they are an exceptionally well-connected adversary. The magic they would have to be using is incredibly rare. Only a few are able to cast such spells. And of those, a mere handful in all the known systems could sustain a vessel in the manner they are for such long durations."

Ara had used the word *sustain*, and it had not gone unnoticed.

"Are you saying there's a natural-born power user on this submerged ship?" Leila asked. "An emmik, or even a visla traveling with them?"

"That's exactly what I'm saying," Ara replied. "We have gained valuable information today, but also learned just how dangerous our adversary truly is."

The group stood quietly as her words sank in.

"This is bad," Charlie finally muttered.

"Yes, Charlie. As I had said."

"And even knowing this now, you still can't, I don't know, like, switch your scanners for water or something? Refine your nose?"

Ara laughed. "Oh, if only it were so simple. But no, my senses are what they are, and any magic would be muted by a large body of water, even more so by one so deep as this. If I was able to track them down, my magic is more than adequate to protect me in the void of space, but it would not serve me in the crushing depths of the ocean. But even if it could, I would still be unable to breathe fire upon them while they travel in that manner. So you see, I am at quite a disadvantage so long as they are submerged."

Charlie's brow furrowed as he ran through their options.

None were good, and some were just plain bad. But there had to be something they could do to gain an advantage. Or at least put themselves on somewhat equal footing.

"Cal? I was just thinking. Do you guys have any submarines?" he asked.

"We've not had use for them in hundreds of years—the war caused the global fleets to eventually sink. There have been a few research craft made serviceable again by local salvage operations, but none that would be of use to you."

"Okay. I figured it was worth asking."

"And a good idea, in theory, but it would be a needle-in-a-haystack type of situation were you to attempt to track this craft. If Ara is correct, from what I've learned of magical propulsion systems, there would be no engine sounds for sonar to home in on. And cloaked by this shimmer spell, there would almost certainly be no signature from other forms of scanning either."

"Yeah, well, I was just thinking if we could lob a few torpedoes at them, if we managed to get close enough, the concussion might make them slip. All we need is for that shimmer to be dropped and we'll be able to track them, even if they do manage to make a run for it."

"Excuse me," a female voice interrupted.

"Everyone, this is Nat, the AI currently running the San Diego region down south of us," Cal informed them. *"What is it, Nat? We were just discussing potential tracking options."*

"Yes, I heard," she replied. *"And I do believe there may be a sub of the type your friends are looking for tucked away in the underwater research facility in San Francisco Bay."*

"Really? Why didn't I know about this?"

"There was no reason for you to, Cal. As you know, the city was leveled during the war, and no one was concerned with old military facilities when the rebuilding began," she replied. *"But that's not what I wanted to tell you."*

"Has something happened?"

"I received your message about waterfront incursions, and happened to notice what appears to be a stealth mission currently taking place near my shoreline."

"That's perfect!" Charlie blurted. "Ripley, how long will it take Eddie to get us down there?"

"I don't know. Maybe ten minutes. It's not like we have to go far, and there's no need to breach atmosphere for it. I'll pull him up on comms and get you a better answer."

"Thanks, Rip. Come on, we need to gear up and prep for a fight. Cal, Nat, do you guys have any cyborgs nearby who could join in?"

"I know at least a handful nearby who are willing to help," Nat said. *"I will contact them and ask them to prepare and stand by."*

"And there are a few close at hand here as well who will be very willing to accompany you down south," Cal added.

"Great. All we need to do is get to––"

"Oh, dear," Nat blurted.

"That's not good. What happened?"

"I was playing possum, allowing the anomaly to progress deeper into the city while I tracked it."

"A good tactic."

"I agree. However, it seems they came upon one of the unaffected cyborgs within my borders and have engaged him. Things seem to be spinning a bit out of control."

Charlie felt the opportunity about to slip through his fingers, and he had no idea when they'd have another chance.

"Can you slow them down?"

"I've already had my smaller auto-cannons lay down a suppressing fire barrage to keep them from retracing their steps, but I dare not break out the truly big guns with so many frozen civilians in the line of fire. And as these are invisible adversaries I simply cannot tell if I'm actually holding them back or am merely firing into noth––Oh."

"Oh?"

"I appear to have hit one," Nat said. *"These Tslavars, they bleed green, do they not?"*

"Yeah."

"Then, yes. I definitely hit one."

"Ara, I can't wait for Eddie. Can you get me down there while he loads the others?"

"You know I can," she said, stooping down low so he could climb aboard her back.

All he had in the way of firepower was the carbine he'd been carrying since Bawb's capture and the konus around his wrist. For this fight, he would need more.

"Leila, have Eddie swing by the house. Grab my go-bag and some more ammo. I'll meet you guys in San Diego."

"What are you going to do? I can come with," Rika said.

"I need you to get your guns and hustle down with the others. Me and Ara are going to do what we can to keep these fuckers from getting back out to sea."

"I've dispatched the few cyborgs I've been able to arm to meet you at the waterfront, Charlie. I'll be tracking you while you fly in. Do you have a combat comms set?"

Cal popped open a compartment on one of the console tables he'd had brought to the roof. A row of wireless earbuds rested inside in small, clear cases.

"He does now," Cal said. *"And I've re-tasked the few AI ships in the air to provide extra eyes. They do not possess weapons, but it may give you an edge nevertheless."*

"Thanks, Cal," he said as he slid the device into his ear. "Okay, Nat. I've got comms and am on my way. Talk me in when we get close, I'll relay to Ara."

"As you wish, Charlie. Fly safe, and I will see you in San Diego shortly," she said before focusing her attentions on the fight on her streets.

"Be careful, Charlie," Leila said as Ara straightened up and prepared to launch herself into the sky.

"You know it," he replied. "Love you."

"Love you too," she said as the mighty dragon leapt into the air. Leila turned to the others, a fierce determination in her eyes. "You heard him. Let's get moving. There's a fight going on, and we don't want to miss it."

CHAPTER TWENTY-FOUR

The small puffs of smoke and faint sound of projectiles breaking the sound barrier as they were fired from their weapons greeted the massive dragon and the man on her back a good mile before they could see the fighting clearly. Buildings blocked their view, and it was only once they were directly above that their angle of view was such to allow them a glimpse.

What they saw was a dozen or so cyborgs firing at what appeared to be nothing.

"*Shimmer cloaks,*" Charlie said. "*Any idea how we can help?*"

Ara flew another pass, banking to better see the entire field of battle as she did. "*I think I can. But it will take a moment to prepare.*"

One of the cyborgs abruptly flew through the air, a *kika rahm* variant being cast at him, taking him right off his feet.

"*Yeah, they're here, all right,*" Charlie noted. "*Okay. Drop me on their flank and I'll provide some cover for those guys until the others get here.*"

Ara flew away, clear of the combatants' line of sight, then dropped low, just skimming the tops of buildings before dropping to the street in an intersection several blocks from the fighting.

"They will not have seen us land," she said. *"I will work on a means to disable their shimmers."*

"You sure you can do it?"

"Not one hundred percent. But I have a clear scent of the magic now, so I am confident I can at least inconvenience them, if not outright negate their magic."

"That's my girl," Charlie said with a grin, unslinging his carbine. *"I'll see you in a bit,"* he added, then took off at a fast jog toward the sound of fighting.

Ara leapt back into the air, sharply altering her direction so she was at the opposite side of the battle before flying high enough for the camouflaged troops to see her. Charlie, on the other hand, was moving in low and fast. Whoever he came across, they were going to be in for a nasty surprise.

The smell of burning cordite was thick in the air as the cyborgs fired the projectile weapons in the general direction of their adversaries. It was essentially firing blind, but once in a while, it seemed the air would ripple from their efforts.

One of the cyborgs briefly froze in place, hit full-force by one of the invaders' spells. She went rigid a moment as her flesh covering hardened and cracked. Charlie recognized the spell and knew full well that no breathing creature could survive a direct hit.

But this was no breathing creature.

The cyborg recovered quickly, her flesh breaking off in dusty chunks at the joints as she re-entered the fight, firing a volley at the seemingly empty space where her attack had come from. Soon enough, the rest of the flesh exo-body covering her endoskeleton would fall away. But she could just get another one grown. If she survived the battle, that is.

One thing the alien invaders hadn't taken into consideration as they launched volley after volley of magical attacks was something utterly foreign to their brains. These flesh-and-blood men and women they were fighting were not actually alive. Not in the traditional sense, anyway. Nor were they only flesh and blood.

Powered by tech, not meat, the killing spells were ineffective against beings whose core form was composed of metal and science. It was something they would eventually adapt to, if given time. Switching their plan of attack to physically brutal spells rather than physiologically deadly ones. But for the moment, at least, the city's defenders had a slight edge.

The auto cannons were being extremely selective in their firing. Despite the sparse population of the city, the body snatchers had come seeking fresh prey, and in this spot, there were simply too many civilians to allow for free-fire.

"Ara, you seeing this?"

"Yes. It seems the concentration of fighting is contained to the intersection ahead of you."

"Okay, that should make the next bit a little easier," he replied. "I'm going to hit up Nat on the comms and have her tell those little ships she has circling high above to come in a bit closer and fan out to look for their ship. They're pretty far into the city, and I don't think they'd want to trek all the way back to the water's edge if they didn't have to."

"You think they flew their craft into the city?" Ara asked. "That would be tactically foolish."

"Yeah, but these guys are cocky. They think they're untraceable, and that makes them sloppy."

A familiar shape flashed overhead, banking sharply and looping back before dropping down on the opposite side of the area of engagement from Charlie.

"Looks like Eddie's here with the others," he noted. "We'll keep these guys busy. But what I need you to do—besides working on some way to mess with their shimmers—is to join those ships and look along the shore areas for signs of water."

Charlie's idea suddenly clicked into place for his dragon friend. *"Very clever,"* she said with an appreciative tone. *"The shimmer makes the craft invisible to the eye, but the water running off of it would still flow onto the ground."*

"Yep. And so long as they haven't been out of the water too long, that means there will still be some sort of trail showing where they went. We don't know the size of the ship, but I'd think it would have to travel in the less-dense areas. Maybe look for highways or parks."

"I shall," Ara replied as she changed course toward the nearby coastline.

"Hey, you guys hear me?" Charlie transmitted over his comms.

"Loud and clear," Rika replied. "We're set up on the enemy's three o'clock."

"I saw you come in. But that means they probably did too, so keep it tight. They're using killing spells," Charlie informed them. "Ara got a good whiff of their shimmers and is working on a disrupting spell. But until she does, just follow the targeting from Nat's auto cannons. She seems to have a pretty good idea where these bastards are pinned down."

"Copy that," Leila said over the comms. "Did I do that right?"

Despite being in battle, Charlie chuckled. "Yeah, babe. That was right."

"I'm getting the hang of these ear-skree devices," she said. He knew the satisfied tone in her voice. Leila was undoubtedly grinning.

Eddie dropped low, his cannon firing off a series of rapid bursts at likely areas of cover for the enemy before he veered off. Good thing he did, because a blast of deadly debris was flung into the air he had just occupied.

"You see that?" Charlie asked, rhetorically. *"That* is why we have to be careful, Eddie."

"Yeah, but I thought I saw one of them," the AI said, a slight hint of concern in his voice.

"Well, just hang back out of their reach until we can properly target them."

Ara's familiar shape flew past, swooping low over the battle.

"Why can *she* do it?" Eddie whined.

Another blast of debris was flung skyward, but the powerful Zomoki's magic easily batted it away.

"That's why, Eddie. This is a fight she's far better equipped for than any of us," Charlie replied.

And it was true, though he and his friends were also wearing slaaps and konuses should the need—or opportunity—to use them arise.

"That was what I needed," Ara sent to Charlie. *"Their foolish use of that particular spell has given me the last piece I believe I require."*

"You have the spell ready?"

"It's imperfect, but I think it will serve our purposes well enough," she replied. *"Stand by a moment while I give this a try. Oh, and be ready to attack."*

"Ara's going to try something. Target the hot zone. This is about to get interesting," he called out over their comms.

The deep red Zomoki focused her magic as she dove down toward the fighting, then cast a rumbling spell, the mix of power blowing out power in the surrounding buildings as the wave of magic hit the ground.

It also damaged the enemy's shimmers, rendering them partially visible.

"Shit," Rika blurted.

The others shared her sentiment. This wasn't just a handful of attackers. There were well over a dozen of them. Only a few had been actively engaging, hoping to lure their opposition farther forward, where the other members of their cloaked force sat quietly waiting to strike. It was a classic maneuver.

This was no amateur operation, Charlie realized. This was high-level military strategy at play. And it might have worked, but for one thing.

"We've got eyes-on," he called out. "Light 'em up!"

CHAPTER TWENTY-FIVE

"Charlie, the other ships believe they've found a patch of wet ground," Eddie relayed to the man on the ground.

"Copy that. I'll tell Ara," he replied. "Stand by."

"Hey, the ships think they found that wet spot you've been looking for."

"Yes, I see where they're focusing their search. Damn, they're going in too close. Tell them to fly by and pretend they do not see it. Quickly!"

Charlie relayed her instructions without hesitation or question. He knew better by now. *"You mind telling me why you're giving them a free pass?"*

"You'll see," she replied. *"But for now, you have more pressing matters."*

She was right. The fighting raged across the battlefield, the formerly cloaked invaders now visible—more or less—providing tangible targets for AI and human forces alike. The Tslavar mercenaries had prepared for much, but the loss of their camouflage was not something they'd expected.

They moved to a fallback position quickly enough, but not before giving up all of their tactical positioning advantage. No longer were the Earthlings walking into a crossfire. Rather, they were driving the Tslavars back on their heels.

"Why aren't these things taking them down?" Leila shouted over the gunfire.

She fired off another volley, the shots traveling true––she had been a very quick study at the range, and her accuracy was exceptional for someone from a world where firearms didn't even exist. Yet, somehow, the Tslavar fighters remained upright, the shots deflecting into the ground and neighboring buildings.

It was the same for the other forces, Charlie saw. Their fire was simply not effective. Only the larger projectiles from Nat's city cannons were causing damage, and even those were largely stopped, though the sheer kinetic force of the much larger rounds was still enough to drive the Tslavar mercenaries back.

"Well, that's new," Charlie grumbled as he fired off a quick spell from his konus, slinging his ineffective carbine over his shoulder.

"These aren't working, Charlie!" Rika yelled through the echoing concussions of the auto-cannons. "What the fuck? Their magic shouldn't be able to stop these. It's not designed to adapt so quickly."

"Well, they've seen this before," Leila noted. "We used guns a few times against them. The Balamar Wastelands, for one. So they've had time to plan and prepare for it."

"That was almost a thousand years ago, Leila," Charlie said over her comms. "What kind of people pass down a grudge for that many generations? It's nuts."

Even across the battleground, he could see Rika's wry grin. "I'm half Italian. Trust me, people can definitely hold a grudge a lot longer than that."

Another flurry of magical attacks took a pair of the advancing cyborgs off their feet, slamming them violently into the building behind them. Any flesh being would have been broken irreparably. The metal men, however, would be fine if they survived the battle long enough to have their bent parts swapped out.

The Tslavars were making a move, and his friends were pinned down, the mercenaries rapidly closing the distance between them.

Shit. "You've got company!" he called over comms.

"Yes, Charlie, we can see that!" was Rika's terse reply. "But our goddamn guns aren't doing much, here."

Charlie realized he had to act immediately or they'd be overrun. He quickly focused his attention on his slaap, channeling his internal power as well, building both to peak readiness.

Well, here goes nothing.

He leapt from cover and charged across the intersection toward his friends. The Tslavars shifted their attention to him, as he expected, but he was ready. Each of their spells was met with not only a counterspell, but one with a redirection twist. An unusual addition of his own making that threw their own magic back in their faces. More than a few of the mercenaries fell victim to their own spells in that manner.

Charlie cleared the street, ducking for cover beside his friends.

"*Now* you break out the magic?" Rika complained.

"I've only got so many things I can do before they expect it," he replied. "They seem to be entirely focused on Earth weapons, at the moment, though I have a feeling that just changed."

Indeed, their attackers had shifted tactics, deploying defensive spells in addition to their increasing barrage of attacks.

"This isn't looking good, Charlie," Rika said.

"I know, I know." He poked his head out, quickly surveying the approaching men's formation. "Okay, I have an idea. Did you guys bring your pointy things?"

Leila and Rika both flashed their swords and knives.

SCOTT BARON

"Excellent."

"What are you thinking, Charlie?" Leila asked. "There's no way we can fight magic with knives from here."

A little smile curled his lips. "Nope, you're right. That means it's time to ditch those carbines and get ready to move fast."

"Are we running away?" Rika asked. "Doesn't seem your style."

"You're goddamn right it's not my style," he replied with a chuckle. "We have to go on the offensive. Do something they won't expect. Something I learned from my pirating days."

"Which is?"

"We get so close that they can't use their magic without the risk of hitting their own men. Listen, I've watched you two train, and I know you're more than ready for it. I'll cast a series of diversion and counterspells until we're upon them. Then we let loose. It looks like they're relying on slaaps, and only a few have anything more than a basic blade on them from what I could see. If we do this right, we'll have them on their heels."

The women looked at one another, determination in their eyes.

"Okay, let's do this," Leila said. "You ready?"

"Oh yeah," Rika said. "Stay close, right?"

"Right."

Charlie felt a surge of pride. The two most important women in his life were impressively badass, and now they would be fighting on the same side.

"All right. On three," Charlie said, beginning his countdown. When he reached one, the spells were already flying fast and wide, a barrage of magic hurled like a massive burst of scattershot.

Several Tslavars were taken off their feet, their defensive spells not prepared for the unusual assault. All of them were forced to divert their energies to broad-ranging defensive spells as they attempted to cope with the odd strategy. It was all the time Charlie and his friends would get. And it was all they would need.

They sprinted across the area, Nat's auto cannons blasting out a stream of projectiles, further knocking the mercenaries back, focusing on the cannons until, finally, the three of them were in close. Too close for the invaders to use magic. And with only their hands and short blades, they suddenly found themselves at a most unexpected disadvantage.

Rika and Leila whirled into action, a pair of dervishes unleashing their flashing steel. The Tslavars wore armor, but a light variety designed more for maneuverability and protection from minor impacts than Valkyrie-like attackers.

Charlie felt a surge of energy flow through him. The initial adrenaline surge was long gone. Now he was in the middle of it. And he was in his element. For the former gladiator, it was a surprisingly welcome sensation.

He truly let loose for the first time since they had escaped the clutches of King Horgund's men a few thousand years in the past. But now, on what felt far more like his own home turf than an ancient castle, Charlie was a sight to see. And despite the violence they were unleashing themselves, the two women fighting at his side couldn't help but note his skill with appreciative glances before refocusing on the opponents in front of them.

Leila dropped low, punching a mercenary in the groin. The man didn't have time to react, though, as Rika spun, her sword catching the seam above his shoulder guards, nearly taking his head clean off.

Blood sprayed, the ground becoming slick with gore as the three worked their way through the greater numbers of mercenaries. The cyborgs watched, unsure what to do. They'd been hastily armed with firearms, but these were not military-grade units, and they had absolutely no experience in hand-to-hand combat. Nat and Cal, wisely, instructed them to stay clear, lest they become an unintentional hindrance rather than a help.

Several more invaders fell to the flashing blades, the trio throwing the attackers into confusion, when a new volley of magic blasted toward them, forcing Charlie and his friends back as he frantically cast defensive spells, barely stopping the barrage.

"What the hell?" Rika blurted, looking for any sign of the new attackers.

"Ara, what's going on? We've got new attackers here."

"Yes, Charlie. They appear to have sent more men to reinforce their ranks when it appeared you might defeat them. As I had hoped."

"Hoped? What the hell do you mean, hoped? We're in the shit, Ara. What are you up to?"

"We found their ship, Charlie. We found it, but pretended it remained unnoted. And now they have sent men to your position."

He realized what she had done, and it was brilliant. "You know where they are. Even with their shimmer cloaks, they came from point A to point B."

"Now you get it," her amused voice chuckled in his head.

Charlie started laughing along with her.

"What's so funny? We're getting our asses handed to us!" Rika growled.

"You know something, don't you?" Leila added.

Charlie smiled wide. "Just wait. You're going to love this."

A massive shadow crossed overhead as Ara lined up for a low pass. Dropping in as low as she could, Ara then lay down a massive stream of her magical fire, incinerating the dozens of invisible men as she torched the entire path, all the way back to their ship.

Its doors had been closed when she reached it, so whatever troops remained in the staging area managed to escape her wrath. The ship, however, took the full force of her magical flames, the shimmer dropping in an instant.

The captain of the craft knew his men were lost, or as good as lost. They were hired mercenaries anyway, and knew what they were in for, so as fast as he was able, he spun his ship and flew straight for the coast, diving deep beneath the waves.

Ara, however, was unconcerned. They might be able to get their shimmer back up and functional eventually, but the entire craft had been doused in fiery magic. *Her* magic. And she knew that smell like her own shadow. There was nowhere they could hide from her now, no matter how deep they may dive. Not for long. Once they came near the surface, she'd be able to track it anywhere.

CHAPTER TWENTY-SIX

The carnage the dragon had wrought was a destruction of the enemy force that was frightening in its totality. The men who had fallen to Ara's flaming barrage had been invisible to the eye when she ignited them, and they remained that way even in death, no more than little piles of ash where men had once been.

The few remaining combatants still engaging Charlie and the others had quickly shifted their course of action and attempted to flee, but their route of escape disappeared as the flaming ship lifted off and dove into the ocean in a cloud of steam.

Charlie had briefly considered attempting to capture them for interrogation, but these were hardened fighters. They'd never talk, but he still wondered if they might be of some strategic use. Before he could think on it further, Ara landed atop them, immolating some, while snatching up and devouring the remaining few in a single bite.

He and his friends were ready for the spectacle. The domestic cyborgs pressed into combat service, however, were not.

"It...it..." a wide-eyed cyborg stuttered––which was saying something, as his mind was a state-of-the-art computer, and his eyes were mere flesh-and-blood enhancements covering his true sight apparatus.

"Yeah, it's kind of a trip, right?" Charlie said with a low chuckle.

"She-she ate them."

"Yup. That she did," Rika said, giving Leila an amused elbow.

"I think he may need a little bit of time to process this," Leila added, hiding her amusement as best she could.

Eddie touched down nearby, and Ripley bounded out of his door the second it opened.

"Did you see that? It was awesome! The way she was all, 'whoosh'! Spitting fire and just messing up all of their shit! That was so cool!"

"Thank you, Ripley. I'm glad to have provided you a touch of entertainment," Ara said.

Ripley spun around. "How did you land so quietly? I didn't even hear you."

"Ah, that," the dragon said with a grin. "With age comes certain talents one picks up over the years. And I have found the spells that prevent my wings from throwing wind or making noise to be most useful when hunting some of my more skittish prey. I didn't mean to sneak up on you, though. I was merely still rather caught up in the moment and cast without consciously thinking about it."

She turned to Charlie as he surveyed the carnage.

"So, did you enjoy that?" he asked.

"Quite," the Zomoki replied with a contented sigh.

"You know, it might have been nice to question one of them."

"And you know as well as I that they would not have talked. I merely saved you the problem of providing a guard for captives."

"Very considerate of you, Ara," he said. "That was a pretty

clever trick, by the way. Though I'm not exactly thrilled with being bait."

"Oh, I was watching you three fight. Given the skill each of you displayed, you were in no real danger. At least, not until the reinforcements arrived."

"And about that. You say you found their ship?"

"Yes. It was a little ways over there, back toward the water."

"Just follow the trail of incinerated mercenaries, eh?"

"That's one way, yes. But the ship, though thoroughly doused in my flames, nevertheless managed to make it back to the ocean. It was a rather impressive maneuver in its speed and efficiency, if I'm being honest about it. Whoever their captain is, he or she is very skilled."

Charlie pulled a small nutrient bar from his pocket, curbing the grumble in his belly. They'd left for San Diego in a hurry, and now that the action was done, he realized just how hungry he was. Fortunately, one of the little conveniences of being back in a time where certain creature comforts were readily available meant he needn't rely on hard bread and tough jerky.

"So, it got away," Rika said. "Kind of defeats the whole purpose of all of this, doesn't it?"

"Not really," Charlie said as he chewed. "You wanna fill them in, Ara?"

"Gladly. You see, Rika, we've been unable to track the invaders' ship, as we had no baseline signature by which to hone our efforts. That is now no longer the issue."

"But it's underwater again," Leila noted. "I thought that even if you had its scent, you were unable to track it when it was submerged."

"Normally that would be the case. However, this ship has just been thoroughly covered by my flames. *My* magic. And in so doing, its shimmer spell was damaged, possibly beyond repair. At least for the time being. They were forced to expend a lot of power defending themselves. So much that I suspect all of their resources have been focused on maintaining the magic protecting them from the depths of the ocean."

"Right. So it's out of range," Leila said.

"Ah, but you forget. The ship was covered by my magic, and a mere ocean will not simply wash that away."

Rika realized what that meant. It wasn't perfect, but it was a start. "So you can actually track it? Even underwater?"

"Yes, depending how deep it goes."

"Awesome!"

"Hang on," Leila interjected. "But Ara can't travel underwater." She turned to her Zomoki friend. "You already said you didn't have the magic for it."

Ara grinned, her lengthy teeth glistening in the invigorating sunlight. "No, I do not," she agreed. "But if you follow the burn field, I believe Cal and Nat have a little surprise you will be quite fond of."

CHAPTER TWENTY-SEVEN

The team stood at the coastline, staring out at the choppy waters of the Pacific.

Cal had tasked a team in the Northern California bay area with tracking down what was believed to be the lone surviving naval research facility that had survived the Great War intact. It had been spared the wide-scale destruction on the surface, as this particular facility was accessible only via a handful of surface accessways. Beyond that, the only way in or out was through a series of locks, deep beneath the bay's waters.

Once the hostilities had finally ended, the area had been deemed too much of a loss to reconstruct. With the sparseness of the global population, it made no sense to attempt to re-settle the region. Land that had once held great value in the bustling hub of the tech industry was now left to fallow, a rusting remnant of a time long past.

"What do you have for us, Cal?" Charlie asked over his comms. "Ara says you and Nat have something we might like. It wouldn't have to do with that sub you were looking for, would it?"

"Interestingly enough, the research facility in the San Francisco

Bay was located by the team of cyborgs I sent to investigate. The old records were accurate, it seems, and though the surface accessways were long ago destroyed, the underwater lock system was found to be intact."

"Holy shit. You found us the sub up there? That's awesome. How long until you can have it moved down to our location?"

"Well, that's the interesting part. You see, my men were able to gain access via the launch tunnel's peripheral lock system, but what they found was not what was expected."

"Meaning?"

"Meaning the facility was empty."

Charlie and the others were crestfallen. This was their one hope to properly pursue the alien craft beneath the waves, and they'd come up empty-handed. Leila put her arm around him, her familiar warmth putting him at ease.

"It's okay, Charlie. We'll find another way," she said.

"I was not finished," Cal said.

"What's that supposed to mean?" Rika asked.

"Yeah, what aren't you telling us, Uncle Cal?" Ripley added.

"I feel that Nat might be better able to answer that question. Would you mind?"

"Not at all," Nat said. "As Cal noted, the research facility up north had been discovered to be empty. But there was reference to another facility. A top-secret Naval testing lab where vessels would be put through their final paces before being cleared for launch."

"Okay, but I thought that was the top-secret facility," Charlie said.

"It was a level of top-secret," she replied. "But this other facility, it was something of a secret even among those with clearance. And, apparently, it was located at another Naval base. The largest on the West Coast, in fact."

Charlie could see where this was heading. Before the war, the largest Navy base had been right there in San Diego. It had housed a sizable chunk of the Pacific Fleet, as well as been home to Naval special operations, DEVGRU. All of the best toys the Navy had to offer passed through Coronado at one time or another.

"Are you telling me there's another facility here?" Charlie asked. "One that's still intact?"

He could almost hear the smile in the AI's voice. *"Yes, there is, Charlie. And you'll never guess what we found inside, hidden for centuries."*

Apparently, Nat had a knack for theatrics, because at that moment a small, sleek attack sub breached dramatically, coming to rest atop the churning water.

"It was in dry dock, actually," Nat said. *"I had our most skilled cyborgs give it a quick once-over before launching. Fortunately, it was originally crewed by mechanicals. Only the command positions were slotted to humans."*

"Meaning?"

"Meaning some of the original cybernetic crew survived the war and were still functional. And a few actually remained in San Diego for the duration of the war, surviving, hidden from the world. Well, they were glad to reintegrate once the war ended, and they still live here. So I took the liberty of requesting they join you aboard your new ship. They were thrilled at the chance for action, by the way. It's still going to be running with a skeleton crew, but it was designed to operate with one, anyway."

The hatch opened, and a strong-jawed woman with ebony skin stepped out onto the craft's exterior. A cyborg, no doubt. Military. And one who had chosen a fitness model's face and physique for her meat suit aspect. She called down to her crew, and an inflatable boat quickly filled with air and launched, carrying her to the shore.

She jumped into the surf as the boat wedged up onto the sand, ignoring the water as she walked to meet the waiting group.

"Captain Theodora Watkins," she said, striding toward them.

"You must be Charlie Gault. A real pleasure to meet you," she said, shaking his hand with a firm grip that had nothing to do with her being a cyborg. "And you'd be Rika Gaspari. Quite a pilot, from what I hear." She turned to the olive-skinned woman, sizing her up. "And Queen Leila. Pleased to make your acquaintance."

"Nobody calls me that anymore."

"Just because you're not in your kingdom doesn't make you any less a queen, Highness," Captain Watkins replied.

Leila blushed slightly at the unexpected attention.

"Hey, what about me?"

"I'm sorry. Of course. You're the one who has been working with Eddie, the ship parked just over there, right? Ripley, if I'm not mistaken."

"Just call me Rip."

"Okay, Rip. You can call me Ted."

"Ted?"

"Short for Theodora."

"Oh. Cool," Ripley said with a grin.

"I hate to break this up," Charlie interjected.

"Yes, of course. Time is of the essence," Captain Watkins said. "The sub is ready to go when you are."

"I'm coming with," Leila said. "Don't try to talk me out of it."

"Wouldn't dream of it," Charlie replied. "Rika, how about you and Rip get with Cal to set up a welcoming party? Captain Watkins and I are going to see if we can maybe drive the Tslavar ship up onto the shore somewhere along the coastline between here and LA. Once it's out of the water, we'll need forces to hold and storm the ship. Bawb is almost definitely on board, and we're damn sure going to get him back."

"On it," Rika said, turning on her heel. "Come on, kid, let's get moving."

"Good luck, guys," Ripley said as she took off after Rika.

Charlie and Leila waded out to the inflatable boat and climbed in.

"Ready?" Captain Watkins asked.

"Good to go."

"Okay, then." She nodded to the crewman at the helm. Moments later they were flying through the chop back to the submarine.

"Ara, you still have a fix on them, right?"

"Yes. They've not gone far. It seems their ship may have sustained more damage than I originally believed. I think they are trying to effect repairs just offshore. They believe themselves safe at that depth."

Charlie grinned. *"Well, they're about to be in for a nasty surprise."*

CHAPTER TWENTY-EIGHT

The sub was the height of human technology––that is, until war destroyed nearly the entire planet. With no need for this sort of machine in the current day and age of peace and reconstruction, it was a deadly device out of time. And it was exactly what Charlie needed.

"Ping them with the sonar," he said as Captain Watkins positioned the craft on the offshore side of the hiding Tslavar ship, drawing in close. "They'll hear it. Even if they're running on totally different systems, at this range the sound will echo through their hull."

"We could just as easily torpedo them," she noted. "But I know you need them in one piece. Which makes this whole maneuver a hell of a lot more difficult."

"I know, I know. But once we push them ashore, the rest should be relatively easy." At least, he hoped it would be.

As anticipated, Ara had no difficulty pinpointing the hiding vessel. Relaying the information to Charlie with their silent connection, they had managed to sneak right up on it in the murky waters.

"This seems almost too easy," Leila said as she watched the gritty image on the sub's monitors.

Despite the advanced array, it was still nearly pitch-black so far down from the surface. Of course, the sub was also sporting a wide assortment of other, non-visual, scanning equipment, allowing them to see their prey. And it was those readouts Captain Watkins was studying with great intensity.

"Ping on my command," she said.

"Aye, aye, Captain."

"Aaaand, ping."

A solitary tone blasted through the water, illuminating the Tslavar ship on the sub's screens with the reflected sonic waves. The reaction was immediate.

"It's on the move!" the crewman at the helm called out. "It's accelerating around us and aiming for deep water."

"Head it off," Watkins commanded.

"Can't, Captain. We're at three-quarters full already, but it's way too fast. I don't understand how they're moving so quickly."

"Shit. We need to drive it the other way," Charlie blurted.

"I know. Full speed," Watkins called out. "Gun it."

"Aye, aye, Captain."

The sub lurched as it accelerated even faster, but the fleeing craft was nevertheless widening the gap.

"No! We can't let it get away," Charlie groaned, realizing what was happening. "It's using magical propulsion. Something more efficient underwater than we are."

"Magic?" Captain Watkins said, incredulously. "You just said magic."

"I take it you weren't fully briefed, then?"

"I was told to get underway and meet you ASAP. Nothing about any magic. So, is that some code word classified tech? I didn't think we still used those, after the war, I mean."

Charlie chuckled despite the dire situation. "Nope. Real magic, I'm afraid. Like storybook stuff."

"Wands and wizards? Are you for real?"

"Real as it gets. And interestingly enough, our friend, who we think is captive on that ship, actually *does* have a wand. A bunch of other cool toys too. I just wish we had a few of them right about now."

"You're pulling my leg."

Charlie silently cast an *ogeufne* spell, igniting a tiny fire above the deck, then quickly extinguishing it.

"Holy shit."

"You said it."

"Uh, Charlie?" Leila said, putting her hand on his shoulder. "I took this when we were at Bawb's house. I didn't know if it would be needed, but his gear was just sitting there, and I thought it might come in handy."

In her hands was the Wampeh's drookonus. The slender rod contained the stored power of dozens of Drooks, more than enough to power a ship for weeks. Charlie kissed her, a gleeful look in his eye.

"Babe, you're the best." He took the rod into his hand and turned to the captain. "Okay, I'm going to try something. What I need you to do is try to steer as best you can and stay on that ship. Can you do that?"

"Should be able to. But it's much faster than we are."

"Not for long." He shifted his attention back to the device in his hand, dredging up the spells he had learned long ago during his first weeks of captivity. He'd used them on Earth tech once before. There was no reason they shouldn't work again.

The Drookonus began to glow slightly as he incanted the spells in his mind, guiding their power into the very metal of the submarine.

"Captain?" the pilot said. "We're accelerating."

"Keep after them," she replied, hiding her surprise as best she could.

"Aye, Captain."

The Tslavar ship took note of the craft now steadily gaining on them and took another sharp turn, heading straight for the drop into the deepest parts of the sea floor. The agile sub matched course, staying on their tail.

"Charlie, what's happening down there? They are moving fast, and away from the coastline."

"I know, Ara. I'm using Bawb's Drookonus to help this thing keep up, but they're so damn fast."

"Obviously. It's a specialized series of spells that part the water just ahead of their ship."

"Huh. Like a push spell, but focused."

"You could say that. But I'm losing their scent, Charlie. I never realized the depth your oceans reach. And it's hard to communicate with you. I'm barely able to reach you."

"We're going deeper."

"I know. And I'm just barely above the waves as it is."

Time was running out if they hoped to succeed, and Charlie knew it.

"They've got some sort of water-parting spell that's letting them pull ahead," he informed the captain. "I don't know that we can catch them, even with the Drookonus helping."

Captain Watkins glanced at her executive officer. "XO, do you think the splitter could be made functional?"

The burly man looked pensive. "I suppose so, but there's risk in firing it up. That part of this bucket was never fully tested, you know."

"I do. But we've run out of options." Captain Watkins glanced at her crew and passengers, then made a choice. "Okay. Do it."

"Aye, aye, Captain," her XO said, jumping to action, unlocking a series of red covers protecting blinking switches. He activated several arrays and turned to the captain. "Armed and ready."

"Then let's do this. Engage."

He turned a knob, then pressed a large, red button. The ship hummed and vibrated, the pitch increasing to the point of discomfort. Then it was gone. Or *almost* gone. The sound, it seemed, had become focused at the front of the craft, where it remained with a faint hum. Captain Watkins smiled broadly.

"Now let's show these bastards tech the likes of which they've never seen."

CHAPTER TWENTY-NINE

"Uh, what just happened?" Charlie managed to blurt as the submarine he was helping power with his drookonus suddenly launched into high gear.

Captain Watkins kept her eyes on the control display showing their speed, course, and proximity to their quarry. They were not only increasing their speed, they were gaining on them, albeit slowly.

"The Moses system. It's something we never got to properly test out," she replied. "It looked promising, but then the war hit, and everything kind of got back-burnered after that. But the tech is still good, and the ship is solid."

"So what is it?"

"An audio-vibratory physiomolecular transit device."

"You mean——"

"Yes, Charlie. A device which is capable of breaking down the bonds of water, projecting forward and creating a force-gap between the ship's hull and the waters. Essentially, it parts the sea for us."

It was impressive, Charlie had to admit. And if they were chasing any other type of craft, he had little doubt they would have already overtaken them. But this was no ordinary pursuit, and the ship so quickly fleeing them was not going to give up so easily.

Had Charlie learned the specific spells for underwater transit, maybe, just maybe, he could have given them the little extra boost they needed to close the gap. But it seemed that even with the Moses device firing at full power, they were only slightly more than matching pace.

The magic these guys are using is incredibly specialized. And powerful, he realized. *They must've spent a pretty penny acquiring someone capable of wielding it.*

The ship shuddered as a loud bang rang out through the hull.

"What was that?" Leila asked, a look of concern flashing across her face. Charlie instinctively put his arm around her as they both looked at the monitor the captain was so intently staring at.

"Whale," she informed them.

"What's a whale?" Leila asked.

"A huge sea animal. Really big, and really peaceful. Kind of like cows, but if the cow was about thirty times bigger and lived underwater."

"I think I would have liked to see this whale thing," Leila said. "Poor creature."

"Sorry, it can't be avoided," Watkins said. "At this speed, maneuverability has to be sacrificed. It's a trade-off. Hence the shape and reinforcement of the sub's prow."

"Well, I guess at least it died instantly," Charlie said. "And it was floating in stasis, so it didn't feel a thing anyway."

"At this speed, it wouldn't have felt much in any case," the captain said. "But I'll tell you what. If this crazy plan works, I'll gladly take you both on a whale watching expedition when this is all through."

"I think I'd like that," Leila said.

"Then it's a deal. But for now, we've got to get that ship turned around and heading back toward shore. Charlie, you seem to know something of their tech. Do they have countermeasures aboard?"

"You mean like sonic chaff? I don't think so. They'd never have had need for it. Their stuff will be geared toward repelling magical attacks."

"Magic," Watkins grumbled. "Freaking magic. Y'all are just tossing this stuff around like it was normal or something."

"Uh, you did see the giant, red dragon, right?"

"Of course. But at least we got a heads-up about *that* beforehand."

"Her," Leila corrected.

"Sorry. Her. But the magic bit. Well, you'd think they would have found that relevant to mention."

Charlie understood where she was coming from, though to be honest, she was handling the whole thing far better than he had when he first encountered magic. "So, to answer your question. No chaff," he reiterated.

Watkins turned to the crewman to her left. "Cooper, load a Mark-Twelve. Set detonation to forty meters proximity."

"Aye, aye, Captain."

"What are you planning on doing?" Charlie asked. "That sounds a lot like you're going to fire a torpedo."

"That's exactly what we're going to do."

"No, we can't do that. Our friend is on that ship. That's why we have to drive it to shore."

"And that's exactly what we're doing."

"But you said you're launching a torpedo——and how can you even do that at these speeds?"

"To your first point, I'm launching a torpedo on a trajectory to *pass* the ship before it detonates, which should cause them to alter course back toward shore. And to your second point, the torpedoes aboard this sub possess the same technology as the ship itself. And with their decreased mass, they go a lot faster."

Charlie realized what she was going to do. Fake a miss and draw out a reaction. It was a classic maneuver. "Okay, then. Let's do it."

"Ara, we should be forcing them to change course. Can you still sense them?"

"Yes, but only just. You're very deep, Charlie, and moving from shore at a high rate of speed."

"I know. But if this works, that'll change in just a minute."

"Ready, Captain," Cooper called out.

"Fire," she replied without hesitation.

A dull gong sound rang out through the hull as the torpedo burst from the bow, piercing the sonic bubble surrounding the front of the sub. "Fish is running straight and hot," Cooper reported. "Detonation in ten."

The assembled crew stared at the screen as the blip closed in on its target. "Five seconds."

They held their collective breaths––at least the pair who were actually breathing––as the blip passed the target then went dark. "Detonation confirmed," Cooper called out.

The alien ship veered, just as they had hoped.

"It looks like it's working," Charlie said. "We're still a long way from shore, but at these speeds, we should be back there by the time––" He paused, a look of confusion flashing on his face. "Uh, Captain. Is it supposed to look like that?" he said, pointing to the blip suddenly closing in on them on the screen.

"That is not normal," Watkins said, a hint of alarm in her voice.

Charlie watched in shock as he realized the Tslavar ship was now on a direct course, heading right for them.

"What the hell are they doing?"

CHAPTER THIRTY

"A goddamn Crazy Ivan?" Captain Watkins shouted to the walls. "Seriously?"

"What's a Crazy Ivan?" Leila asked.

"It's what that crazy sonofabitch is pulling on us. It's insane. We'll all die at this speed."

"Can we torpedo them?" Charlie asked.

"We can sure as hell try. Cooper, launch tubes five through seven."

"Aye, aye, Captain."

Seconds later, the now-familiar sound of the torpedoes leaving the bubble surrounding the sub rang out.

"Fishes away, all three running straight and hot."

The three flashing lights on the display were quickly closing the gap between the two vessels, which made sense as they were on a collision course. Then, all of a sudden, they froze in place.

"What the hell happened? Cooper, did we lose them?"

"No, Captain. They seem to have just stopped."

"Stopped? All three?"

Charlie watched as the Tslavar ship's blip flashed past the frozen lights of the torpedoes, closing fast.

"Oh no. This is a mechanical ship. Abort the pursuit! Get us out of here!"

"What's happening, Charlie? What are they doing?"

"No time, captain. We have to get clear before they can—"

A blast of magic rocked the ship, the metal straining as the drive systems groaned to a halt. The lights stayed on, powered by batteries, but the turbines and generators were suddenly quite silent. As were the air scrubbers.

"Ara, they hit us with a version of that damn spell. The sub is frozen."

"I will relay the information to Cal and the others. Can you surface?"

"I don't know. Gotta do a quick sitrep. I'll let you know in a minute."

"What was that, Charlie?" Watkins asked as she quickly surveyed the systems readouts still functioning.

"A spell. Same one that froze the whole damn planet. Well, a smaller version of it."

"But how did it stop the sub? It should have been unaffected."

"No, I think it was deep in storage when the first spell was released, so it wasn't hit. But now it's out in the open, and got hit at close range, no less. AIs and the most advanced systems aren't susceptible, but anything mechanical tends to be affected."

"This sub is state of the art."

"*Was* state of the art. But that was hundreds and hundreds of years ago. By today's standards it's old tech, even if it was mothballed and remained in pristine condition all that time."

"Well, shit," the captain groaned. "So we've lost power and all our systems are offline. Just fucking great."

Charlie couldn't help but be amused at her ire. It made sense, of course. The whole situation sucked, but it could be worse, he figured.

"It's all right. Once we float up to the surface, they'll tow us back to shore. But the Tslavars are gonna be long gone by then."

Watkins slowly shook her head. "No, Charlie. It's not that easy."

He did not like the look on her face.

"What don't I know, Captain?"

"Long and short of it? We have no power."

"Obviously. But that isn't the end of the wor––"

"And we're sinking."

That got his attention.

"Fuck."

"You said it."

He quickly ran through the scenario in his head, then realized he didn't possess enough knowledge about the parameters to even make a wild guess.

"How deep was it where we last had readings?" he asked.

"Just over nine thousand feet."

Fuck.

"Okay, can this bucket take that kind of pressure?"

"It should be able to. It's rated to seven thousand, but they're always very conservative when they come up with those numbers."

"Okay, okay."

"You keep saying that, Charlie. But it's not okay."

"I know. Just give me a minute."

"Ara, you there?"

"Yes, Charlie. You're getting hard to hear. What's happening?"

"In a nutshell, we've lost power, we're sinking, and if the pressure doesn't crush us to death, we'll suffocate soon enough without the air scrubbers. At least the crew is cyborgs, so they aren't sucking up all the air. But still, on a small sub like this, we won't have too long."

"No, that is not acceptable."

"Sorry, but believe me, it's not by choice."

"Can you escape? Is there a hatch, or a—"

"No go, Ara. We're already too deep. And besides, the hatches can't pressurize without power. And thanks to that damn spell, the manual overrides are almost certainly frozen solid. Do you think you can get to us before we get too deep?"

"You already are," she replied. *"I'm so sorry, Charlie, but my magic simply won't hold out that far down. And you're quickly approaching a depth where you'll even be out of range for us to communicate."*

Charlie stood quietly a moment, listening to the ship creak and groan as it sank deeper and deeper, the pressure increasing with every atmosphere they passed.

"Well, I guess it's time to say it, then. You've been a great friend, Ara. The best I've ever had, really. When we first met, never in a million years did I think we'd wind up on such an adventure. And while I'm sorry you got dragged into all of this, I'm grateful for our time together."

Silence was his reply.

"Ara?"

"What is it, Charlie?" Leila asked, noting the look on his face.

"Nothing," he replied, wrapping her in his arms.

A short while later a dull thud echoed throughout the hull as the sub touched down on the ocean floor. Charlie and Leila curled up together on the deck, wrapped in a blanket and nestled in each other's arms, trying to keep their breathing as shallow as they possibly could. Charlie's magic was useless. His engineering skills, likewise. And there was nothing he could fight that would make the situation any better.

Stuck in a little sub on the bottom of the ocean, all they could do was wait.

CHAPTER THIRTY-ONE

Captain Sindall reclined in his seat and allowed himself a little smile. Their pursuers had been disabled, and the expenditure of magic against a lone vessel and at such close range was minimal, all things considered.

It had been quite a surprise, the humans possessing so powerful a craft, and one able to pursue them at great speed beneath the waters, no less. He had no idea they had such a potent form of this tech-magic that allowed them to travel beneath the waves as he did.

And the weapons they launched at him. Another surprise, though they were easily observable as they approached, unlike a magical attack. Nevertheless, the explosion had been far greater than anticipated, and his vessel had been rocked by it.

A formidable enemy in any other circumstance. But in this mission, he possessed a tool he was somewhat unfamiliar with having at his disposal—powerful magic beyond anything in his usual arsenal.

It was almost a shame letting the unusual craft sink to the bottom of the sea, but after the Zomoki's attack had caught them off-guard, the Tslavar captain was not about to waste a single drop of precious magic that he didn't have to. The residents of this planet were resilient, and surprisingly powerful. More concerning, some did not appear to be affected by their globe-spanning spell.

This was a problem. It *should* have frozen everything, leaving him free to collect his specimens for experimentation and study. Yet it was clear that was not the case. Adjustments had to be made.

But Captain Sindall was used to plans not going exactly as anticipated. Any with his years of combat and service under their belt would be the same. Plans had a way of going sideways, and only those who learned to adapt would live to fight another day.

"How is the shimmer coming?" he asked his second-in-command, a lean, wiry man missing the index finger on his left hand from a particularly brutal campaign he had been engaged in, battling bravely at the captain's side.

"The Zomoki was powerful, Captain."

"Yes, I saw that," he noted with a wry grin. "She did manage to get the better of us. A clever beast, capable of higher thought. An older one, no doubt."

"Indeed, sir. And the amount of damage she wrought with her flames leads me to believe she is even older than any we've encountered previously. That she completely eliminated our forces on the ground so entirely required immense power. And our shimmer spell was not only destroyed, but her residual magic is making it exceedingly difficult to cast another."

"What?" the captain blurted. "That was a top priority. It should have been nearly complete by now."

"I know, sir. But as I said, she was far more powerful than we first assessed."

Captain Sindall stroked his angular chin in thought. "Very well. Have the casters keep at it."

"I will, sir."

"But even with this setback, things are progressing. And how is our Wampeh guest faring?"

"Stubborn. Strong. Difficult."

"Yes, I expect he would be," the captain said. "We were told he was a dangerous target, but the way he reacts to threat of death or violence makes me wonder."

"Sir?"

"It would seem we very well may have a Wampeh Ghalian in our midst."

His second-in-command shifted slightly at the words. Even the fiercest of warriors would be a fool to not be wary of the deadliest guild of assassins in the known systems.

"Are you sure, sir?"

"Sure? No, I am not. But I have learned to trust my instincts. And on this, they are telling me this man is more than just an ordinary Wampeh." He rose from his seat, opened a pouch on his hip, and slid the thick konus held within onto his wrist. "Let's go pay a visit to our guest."

Bawb lay strapped to his table, restraints holding his legs, torso, and wrists firmly. He had no outward bruising or wounds, but that was in no way indicative of the treatment he had received at the hands of his captors.

Being who he was—and possessing the strength not only of body, but also of mind—the Tslavars had quickly learned that threats of physical violence did not faze the man one bit.

Captain Sindall figured if his theory about his captive's true nature was correct, that would make perfect sense. Pain would do nothing against his ilk. But perhaps with magical torture rather than physical, he might eventually manage to break the man.

That one of the deadly sect was even present on Earth in the first place meant that the planet was far better connected than he had been led to believe. And the state of the planet, as well as the unexpected variables they had been encountering, all pointed to a far more complex world. One that would potentially be a much greater challenge to subjugate.

"Hello," Captain Sindall said as he stepped around the partition separating this one captive from the catatonic others. "I see you are resting comfortably."

Bawb turned his head and smiled. He had been thoroughly worked-over, yet his face was as serene as if he'd just woken from a peaceful nap.

"Nice to see you again, Captain," he replied. "It seems you've had something of an interesting day today."

"Oh?" Sindall replied. "Why would you say that?"

"Because the usual men who visit me throughout the day are not here. And because your ship seemed to have abruptly pushed itself to a rapid pace––so much so that the Drooks powering it couldn't entirely dampen the effects."

"Ah, that. Just playing with the locals," the captain said.

"Perhaps," Bawb replied. "But that does not explain the smell of Zomoki flames that still linger in your ship. Someone didn't quite get the doors closed in time, perhaps?"

Captain Sindall had to admit, the Wampeh was good. Observant. He would have to be very careful in choosing his words, lest his interrogation be flipped on its head.

"It was an interesting encounter, of course. But then, when is a run-in with a Zomoki not?" Sindall said lightly. "Though it is rather interesting, I must admit. I believed this planet did not have a native Zomoki population. Nor Wampeh, for that matter. So, you see, it has been a very enlightening week."

"Yes," Bawb said, still sporting that damned, infuriating smirk. "I suppose that would be a bit disconcerting for an invading force. Discovering your spell did not have quite the effect you intended. And that the defenders of the planet were still quite capable."

"But are they?" Sindall countered. "Are they, really? I mean, it was clearly a mighty civilization once, and we deployed that spell in hopes of minimalizing bloodshed as they were brought under the yoke. But something happened here, and despite the unusual defenses that somehow escaped our spell, it is clear as day that something terrible has taken place. The once-mighty civilization appears to have vanished, struck down by an even more powerful adversary. All that remains now are survivors. What I wish to know, is how and why."

Bawb laughed. The poor Tslavar was so out of his element it was funny. "I know what happened here. And I know why you are going to fail in your efforts. But you'll not hear the story from me."

The captain stared at him a long moment. He was wearing his konus, and casting the torture spells would be as easy as breathing for him. But the way the Wampeh was calmly staring at him almost seemed a dare.

No. He would let the underlings handle the dirty work for now.

"It's been nice chatting with you, Wampeh. I do look forward to our next conversation."

With that, Sindall left the room. Soon enough, his men would begin the torture once again. And once more, Bawb would easily endure.

It was one of the benefits of being the rare strain of Wampeh that he was, able to absorb the powers of natural magic users by drinking their blood. It had been some time since he had drained the powerful Emmik Yanna Sok, but some of her power still lingered in his veins, and with it, he was able to negate most of the effects of the Tslavar torture.

Of course, they didn't know that, which made their lack of progress even more frustrating.

"What was that all about, Bawb?" the imprisoned cyborg on the other side of the partition asked.

His name was Tim, Bawb had learned, and he had been a maintenance worker prior to his abduction. While some of the metal men with flesh skins were foppish and soft, designed for service and manners, Tim was a bit of a character, his initial programming making him more relatable to the humans working in his field. But they had all died in the war, leaving him no choice but to tone down his gruff language for more polite company.

But now, as a prisoner, his old ways were beginning to show once more, and Bawb couldn't help but like the spunky cyborg.

"I'm sorry you could not understand, Tim. If I had my tools, I would gladly equip you with a translation spell. But as it stands, I shall play the role of translator, for the time being."

"So, all those rumors I've been hearing about magic users arriving on Earth? It's a real thing, not just talk?"

"Indeed."

"Huh, so that's why I could understand them for a bit when they took me into the other room for questioning. A translation spell, you say?"

"Indeed."

"Funny. I don't think they realize how good a cyborg's hearing is. And even though they walked out of human earshot, man do those guys talk. Especially the one you were just talking to."

"That was the captain who visited me. And he wishes to learn what happened to the planet. About the war. And why your people are not affected by their spell. It would seem they still have a hard time understanding how your kind works."

Tim let out a chuckle. "Yeah, they tried the whole, "cut-into-him-and-make-him-talk" thing, but I just muted the pain receptor alarms in my systems. That seemed to annoy them to no end."

Bawb laughed. "You know, Tim. For a man built with no heart, you seem to possess one all the same."

"Thanks. I just wonder when they'll realize they can't magic a machine. Still, it sounded like some crazy big plans they had for Earth."

Tim relayed what he had overheard, and the scheme at work was indeed audacious. But if they were able to put the right pieces into motion, Bawb feared they may very well gain a solid hold over the planet, setting the stage for a full occupation.

"We need to get this information to Cal and the other AIs," he said, testing his restraints once again. They were firmly attached, as always. "This could be critical for them to know. We need to escape."

"I'm with you on that," Tim replied. "But how?"

Bawb gazed at his surroundings once more with his calculating eyes.

"I'm working on it."

CHAPTER THIRTY-TWO

Ara sat perched above Downtown Los Angeles, her mind racing as she tried to devise some way to reach her friends on the bottom of the ocean. From her vantage point, the blue of the waves could be clearly seen, but while they'd been a soothing sight on other days, on this one they merely served to remind her of Charlie and Leila's plight.

Far below, inside Cal's command center, Rika paced back and forth, barely containing her agitation, while Ripley sat on a couch, her leg bouncing incessantly. Both were on edge, and with good reason.

After the victory in San Diego they had hurried back to Los Angeles to plan the next course of action and coordinate a warm welcome for the Tslavar invaders when Charlie and the submarine drove them ashore.

Then it all went to shit.

All of their planning immediately shifted from a capture operation aimed at a craft emerging from the sea, to a rescue one for the sub now trapped beneath it. Both were difficult prospects, but the urgency of the current situation had sent everyone into overdrive, including the network of genius AIs.

Unfortunately, no one had been able to come up with a solution as of yet.

"What about modifying Eddie, or one of the other ships?" Rika asked, pivoting on her heel one hundred eighty degrees and setting off across the room in the opposite direction.

"They are not designed for that type of pressure. The vacuum of space is far different than the ocean," Cal noted.

"Please, stop pacing," Ripley said. "You're making me nervous."

"You should be nervous. We *all* should be nervous. They're stuck, Rip."

"I know. But I can't think with your pacing. I'm trying to come up with a way to save them."

"We all are. And I think better when I'm moving."

"Ugh! You're so difficult," Ripley groaned.

"Please, ladies. We have to focus our attention on the situation," Cal interrupted, hoping to put a stop to their back and forth. *"Now, from what I have been told by Ara, because of the extreme depth at which the sub has come to rest, no magic will hold out against that pressure long enough to reach them. It is simply too deep."*

"Yeah, we know that," Rika said. "But what if we were to break out the stockpile of konuses and use them to power some kind of super spell?"

"Again, I have discussed this with Ara, and she says a spell simply will not last. It is not that it couldn't be cast. But rather, it is that the spell would not withstand the forces working against it long enough to make the dive to over nine thousand feet."

"So not even if we triple up the konuses?"

"I am afraid not."

"Even if Ara taught us the protective spells, it wouldn't last, is what you're saying? So what if we take a lesser sub, one that can't dive quite that deep, and only cast the spells when we get close?

That would drastically cut down the amount of time the spell would be required to hold out."

"I will ask her," Cal said. *"Please stand by a moment."*

He opened the comms line to the improvised communications nest on the roof of the nearby building, where he'd set up an array of displays to share data with the dragon, and relayed the question.

"An interesting idea," Ara said. "And one I wish could work. But the maximum depth of those craft is simply not sufficient, from what you've told me. To avoid being crushed by the pressure, they would have to stop several thousand feet above the trapped sub, if I am not mistaken. And that far away, the spell would still dissipate long before they reached them," she said. "Five minutes, I would estimate. That's all they would have."

"Your spells work how, exactly?"

"The ones that would be of use would create an air pocket, as well as providing protection from the pressure of the waters," she replied. "I'm sure you know, the problem that most creatures have with those kinds of conditions is the way their bodies react to those forces. If, say, they were to exit a pressurized craft into an unpressurized setting, well, there are a number of unpleasant ways they could die."

"And if they didn't, by some miracle, the return to the surface could surely give them the bends, or an air embolism."

"I do not know these terms, but I assume they relate to the shift in bubbles within the fluid areas of a body," Ara said.

"Very astute."

"I've been around, and have seen a great many unpleasant things," she replied. "In any case, the simple answer to your question is no, it simply won't work. With more time, I could teach them the spells, certainly, but even then, they would not last long enough to carry out a rescue."

"Thank you, Ara. I will relay to the others."

Cal shifted his focus back to his command center.

"Ara says that at that depth and pressure, you would have perhaps five minutes, tops," Cal relayed. *"But given the range of our smaller subs, you would be too far out to reach them in time."*

Ripley punched a cushion on the couch. "No, I don't accept this. There's gotta be a way."

"I'm sorry, Ripley. I truly am. But it is looking as if we do not have an option, here."

"But their sub was able to make the dive," Rika noted. "Surely there are others."

"That was a highly specialized war sub, designed to survive extreme combat conditions and depths. The only other submarines anywhere near that one's capabilities are still simply research craft. Subs that have not been launched in hundreds of years and would need an overhaul before use, I might add."

"So we figure something out. Modify one of them or something."

"Yeah," Ripley agreed. "Like, what about building some kind of diving bell and dropping it down the last way to them once a sub hits its max depth? So long as it's pressurized, it should be able to survive the drop."

Rika gave her a curious look.

"My folks liked to make me watch educational shows when I was a kid," Ripley explained.

"That is a very creative idea, Ripley. However, the problem still remains that there is simply not enough time to attempt your plan, even if it could be made to work. The clock is running, and without power, the sub's air scrubbers undoubtedly remain offline. Even with the cyborgs on the crew not using much air, they'll still run out by morning. I'm sorry, but there's simply nothing more we can do."

CHAPTER THIRTY-THREE

Without power beyond the battery reserves, the temperature aboard the stranded submarine had dropped steadily in the frigid depths as it rested on the sea floor. The cyborgs were unaffected by it, simply turning off their sensory input for temperature.

Charlie and Leila, however, sat on the sub's deck, wrapped in blankets and huddled against each other as they leaned against a slightly less chilly interior wall. Under other circumstances, it might even have been a little romantic. In their current dilemma, that was most certainly not the case.

They'd spent the first hour on the bottom of the ocean working through options. Potential escape plans, mechanisms that might be jury-rigged to allow them to at least surface. One and all had resulted in a dead end. Emphasis on the 'dead' part.

What was really bothering Charlie––even as he faced a watery demise––was that as they sat there, thinking and conserving breath, he had actually come up with what he thought might be a working means to detect the enemy craft from afar, allowing them to launch a sneak retaliation before they even knew what hit them.

"Bioluminescence," he said.

"I'm sorry, what?" Captain Watkins replied.

"You know, the stuff in sea water that glows a little when you swish your hands around in it in the dark."

"Right, I get that bit. But how does that help us?" the captain asked.

"Stuck here, it doesn't. But for tracking the Tslavars? Big-time oversight on their part. Their shimmer––if they get it working again––makes them invisible to the eye, but if we adjusted scans for tiny traces of organic light in a linear pattern, the fluorescence they cause when they churn up the water, *that* might be enough to track them. To determine their next target, and even prepare a defense against them."

Suddenly it made sense to the captain.

"So you mean to use aerial surveillance to pick up bioluminescence as their ship moves. With all of the whales, sharks, and other creatures frozen in place, it would be the only signature out there," she said appreciatively. "Hot damn, that's actually a clever idea, Charlie."

"Thanks. Now, if only we could get word to the surface, they might be able to actually put it into practice. But comms are down, and at this depth, even my link with Ara isn't working."

"Your what with who, now?"

"Ara. The dragon. We have a sort of connection. A bond. It lets us communicate across pretty great distances."

"But not underwater?"

"Not this deep, no."

"Seems like a kind of flawed system," she said, laughing grimly.

"Yeah, but we never tried it out this way. Surprise," he grumbled.

After that, he resigned to settle into as comfortable a spot as he and Leila could curl up in, the couple talking quietly, conserving air, while saying things they might not have another opportunity to voice if things didn't take a turn for the better.

They'd only been together a short while—romantically, that is—their time living together as king and queen notwithstanding, as they only consummated that situation at the end of their reign. But they'd been through a lot. More than most couples have to deal with in a lifetime, and they'd handled it with great aplomb in just a matter of months.

And now that things were finally going well, and they'd made it back to a version of Charlie's world that had running water and didn't include ample amounts of mud sticking to your clothes no matter where you went, *this* had to happen.

"You know, even if it all ends like this, I'm glad you were my queen," he said, arms firmly wrapped around her warm body. "I mean, obviously, I'd rather we don't die at the bottom of the sea. But you know what I mean."

Leila turned her head and kissed him gently, then rested her head back on his shoulder. "Things certainly didn't turn out the way I thought they would, that's for sure."

"Tell me about it."

"I figured I'd live out my days working Visla Maktan's estate, looking after his animals and never leaving the planet. And now look at me. On another planet, in another system—that's in another galaxy! Oh, I wouldn't have believed it if someone told me this would be a possibility."

"I know. Kind of like how I wound up in a magic world instead of a tech one. But here we are. Two fish out of water."

"But surrounded by it."

"Touché."

She nestled in closer, breathing in his smell she knew so well. "We turned out pretty good, though, didn't we? After all we've been through, you and I, we're good, you know? Like, real good."

"I know, babe," he said, softly.

"And I don't want this to end. So don't give up just yet. I need you to use that brilliant brain of yours and think of something. You've done it before, so I'm challenging you now. Do it again, Charlie. Figure out a way to get us out of this mess. Promise me you'll try."

"I swear I will," he replied. "Or die trying."

He sincerely hoped the latter would not be the case.

CHAPTER THIRTY-FOUR

"New Jersey?" Rika said. "Seriously? Last we saw them, they were off the coast of California. How in the hell did they get to Jersey?"

"I don't know," Cal replied. *"But if their cloaking tech—I mean, magic, has been repaired, it is entirely possible they took to the air and cut across the continent. Conversely, we don't know exactly how fast they are able to travel underwater. Magic is far different than technology, and any estimates I would normally make based on water pressure and hydrostatic resistance are moot points where it is concerned."*

Ripley was too busy staring at the display showing the location of the sunken submarine to partake in this particular discussion, though she did catch snippets of it peripherally as she focused on the image in front of her.

Something was nagging at her, tickling the back of her brain. Something just on the tip of her tongue. Or, mind, more appropriately.

"What has Ara said?" Rika asked. "Has she smelled any of her magic surfacing from the ocean?"

"She has not mentioned anything to me, but I will confirm with her."

Ara had been listening in. Cal had left his comm link open at her request so she could better follow the goings-on inside the command center while she simultaneously scanned the horizon for signs of their enemy. As of yet, she hadn't sensed a thing, visually, olofactorally, or otherwise.

"You may inform Rika that I've not smelled anything, but given the length of time they've been submerged, as well as depth they descended to, if the Tslavar craft moved far enough away from these shores before surfacing, it could make detecting them––even with my magic coloring their ship–– significantly more difficult."

"Thank you, Ara," Cal said. *"Rika, Ara has informed me she has not sensed anything."*

"Well, that's just fucking great. So somehow these bastards made it clear across to the Eastern seaboard, then went and snatched a half dozen people right out from under Atlantic City's AI's proverbial nose."

"Which would imply their camouflage is functional once more."

"No shit. And they're still at it. Whatever *it* is. I just don't get it. How the hell did they move so fast?"

Suddenly, Ripley started bouncing up and down excitedly. "Holy shit! The loop tube!"

"What are you talking about, Rip? There's no way the Tslavars are using the loop tube."

"No, not the Tslavars. Shit, hang on," she said, flipping through display options. "Hey, Uncle Cal, can you put up the map of the loop tube network on the big display?"

"Of course," he said, the requested image flashing onto the screen. *"But I am with Rika on this. I fail to see how the loop tube has anything to do with the current predicament."*

"You guys need to think outside the box."

"I'll remind you, as an AI, I am, essentially, a box."

"Ha-ha, very funny. That joke was already old when I was six. But listen. You guys see the links in the network that cross the Pacific? They run all over the place, from LA and Frisco and a bunch of places in between. And then they cross over to Hawaii, and Japan, and a whole ton of other locations."

"Right. It's the loop tube system. That's what they do."

"Gah, you're being dense!" Ripley grumbled. "Uncle Cal, would you please overlay the loop tube map with the oceanic one showing the sub's location? But do it on the same scale, okay?"

"Oh, my," Cal exclaimed.

"What?" Rika asked. "I don't see—oh, shit. Rip, that's brilliant."

"I know, right?" Ripley beamed.

The map overlay took the two disparate images, and lo and behold, an unexpected meeting of the two just so happened to exist, and right where they needed it most. The little dot marking the location of the downed submarine was close to a leg of the loop tube network where it crossed the seabed.

"It's still several miles down," Rika said. "And we don't know exactly how close the sub is to the tube, precisely. But if it's close enough, I don't know. Maybe we could make something work. Cal, could you run a quick calculation on depth and distance, then share it with Ara?"

"I have already done so," he replied. *"And she has agreed, despite the depth, the sub appears to be close enough to the loop tube that the spell* should *be able to hold out long enough to effect a rescue."*

"Awesome!"

"Not so fast, Rip. This is all theoretical. And if we're going to do this, we'll need to achieve pinpoint accuracy when we stop the loop tube car. At the speeds they travel, it'd be easy to overshoot by miles."

"I believe the other AIs linked into the system and I should be

able to stop the car within four hundred meters of its desired location. I wish we could achieve greater accuracy, but the system was never designed for this type of operation."

"Hell, that's far better than I was expecting," Rika said. "But I'm going to need backup on this one. If the spell starts to fail and I can't catch it fast enough, we're all going to have a very bad, very wet time of it."

"What do you suggest?"

Rika turned to her young friend. "You ever want to learn magic, Rip?"

"Oh my God! Really?"

"We have spare konuses, and I don't think there would be any harm teaching you, especially given the circumstances. You agree, Cal?"

"I do, but what would her parents say?"

"They're frozen solid––sorry, Rip."

"It's okay."

"So, given that little detail, I don't think it'll be a concern at this point."

Cal was nothing if not practical, and after a millisecond's thought, he came to the same conclusion. *"Well, then. I think it would be wise if you gather your equipment and have Eddie fly you to meet Ara at the shoreline. She has informed me that you are both going to receive a crash course in some rather archaic magic involving water and force shields."*

Ripley was floating on air as they raced for her ship. "I'm gonna learn magic!" she squealed with glee.

And despite the gravity of the situation, Rika couldn't help but enjoy her young friend's enthusiasm. And if she and Ara were able to bring the girl up to speed, the two of them just might stand a chance.

CHAPTER THIRTY-FIVE

The beachfront training of the teen had started off a bit sketchier than Rika had expected, and Ara had seemed far more brusque with her than she and Ripley had normally known her to be.

Given the intensive nature of her training, and the pressure they all faced, however, it was understandable. Charlie and Leila would die if they failed.

"No, no, not like that!" Ara grumbled as Ripley once again butchered the most basic of the spells the mighty Zomoki was trying to teach her. "You're *shouting* the words––the *wrong* words, I might add––which does not play into the power and efficacy of a spell. Forcefully yelling does not make it work any better. It must come from *within*."

"I'm trying," Ripley replied, throwing her hand up in frustration, then attempting the spell once more, but to no avail.

"And what is this hand waving?" Ara asked.

"I'm casting. Like in the old movies. I mean, I've got this koonus thingy on my wrist."

The dragon sighed. "No, you're still not listening. None of that matters. The spell comes from inside you, Ripley. From your intent. The words are nothing if you do not first tap into that internal direction. And it's called a konus, by the way, not koonus."

"Tomato, tomahto. And hang on a minute. Charlie does it without even saying the words. I've seen it," she countered.

"Yes, but Charlie is unique. He shares my blood, and that makes him capable of a bit more than the rest of you. But take Bawb for example. You've seen him cast, and I'm sure you can't hear his spells every time. He's been practicing continuously, and has made great progress in that. Nowadays, he barely makes a sound. And one day he may even succeed in casting as Charlie does. But for now he must still draw from that internal wellspring by tapping into the words. Just as you will learn to do. Now, try again."

Ripley turned toward the waves and once more spoke the words that *should* have created a parting of the water, the waves held back by the power pulled from the konus.

But nothing happened. Again.

"Like this," Rika said, enunciating the spell more clearly and quietly than her young friend.

The water pushed back, as if the waves were suddenly breaking against an invisible rock, forcing them to part and go around it. This was the least of the spells Ara was teaching them, but they had to start somewhere.

"Well done, Rika. Did you see what she did there, Ripley? How she was not forcing the magic, but rather, letting it flow through her without strain? Try again, but in the way she did."

Ripley started to raise her hand, then lowered it, self-conscious of her overly dramatic casting method. She was the first person on the whole planet the newcomers had agreed to teach magic to, and she was *not* going to mess it up.

She messed it up, the spell firing wild, splashing into the water before careening into the sand and dissipating.

"Ugh! This sucks! And why is Rika so good at it? She only just learned the spell too," Ripley griped.

Rika lightly punched her on the shoulder. "Hey, it's because I've been doing this longer than you," she noted. "And I also had some pretty nasty business done to my head, you know. All sorts of magic got crammed in there against my will. Along with a bunch of other things I'd rather not think about," she said, a slight shadow flashing across her face at the memory.

"Yeah, I know," Ripley said. "I'm sorry. I didn't mean to be a bitch, Rika."

"It's okay, Rip. I know you didn't," Rika said. "I just wish there was some way we could help you take in all of this new information. I understand how frustrating this must be."

Ripley nodded, her jaw twitching as she struggled to keep her frustration in check. Then her mood abruptly shifted, as it so often seemed to do.

"Oh my God," she blurted. "I've got an idea. But we need to talk to the big brains. Eddie, fire up the engines. We're going to see Uncle Cal," she said into her comm unit. She then turned to her dragon instructor.

"Couldn't we just talk to him over the comms?" Rika asked.

"Sure, but if I'm right, we'll need to see him in person." She turned to Ara. "Meet us back Downtown. I think there's something that might make this work. If Uncle Cal agrees to it, that is. And I've got a good feeling he will, given the circumstances."

After a short flight to Downtown, they set down beside Ara on the rooftop landing pad a few short minutes later.

"Absolutely not. You know your mother's wishes on this," Cal said. *"Not to mention, something of this nature has never been attempted. The risks are unacceptable."*

"But Uncle Cal—"

"Your mother was very clear about this, Ripley. And so was your aunt. And if anyone has relevant experience with neuro-stims, it would be her."

"I'm sorry," Rika said, "I'm confused. A neuro what, now?"

"It's called a neuro-stim," Ripley informed her. "It was a type of tech they used to drip feed training and mission information into spaceship crews while they were in flight. That way the people could learn new, mission-specific skills while they slept in cryo."

"That's wild. We'd hypothesized about cryo stasis back in my time, but never did we envision *that* kind of tech."

"It was invented several hundred years after the Asbrú *disappeared, Rika. And it was a very useful system, for our purposes, and it is available for all to obtain linguistic fluency with alien races."*

"Nice. But I have to say, our translation spells are a bit more useful."

"True, but we work with what we have. In any case, beyond that one use, the neuro-stim is reserved for those who need it for specific purposes, not just willy-nilly downloading into a malleable brain. And while the safeties have been greatly improved, we restrict neuro-stim use to adults over the age of twenty-one, and only after a thorough evaluation beforehand."

"But this is important! Can't we waive the age thingy just this once? It's for a good cause."

Rika and Ara shared a look.

"I don't mean to step on any toes here," Rika said. "But if what you've just described is really an option, I think, given the circumstances, that it's worth making an exception."

Ara shifted on her haunches, taking in the implications of this tech-magic. "Cal, if I am understanding this process correctly, are you saying that the proper use of spells, from the pronunciation to the actual casting itself could be imprinted in a person's mind instantly?"

"Oh, no. Nothing like that," Cal said.

"Ah, I see."

"It would take several hours to do safely. And even then, it would be for a tiny fraction of information. The system is designed to be a slow feed of knowledge. To force it any faster is to risk great neurologic damage."

"Not always, though," Ripley said.

"Yes, I know, Ripley. But she was a special case, and she could very well have lobotomized herself in the process."

"Who?" Rika asked.

"My aunt Daisy," Ripley replied. "She's a total badass, and she's got, like, all of this awesome stuff in her head. And it was all put there with a neuro-stim."

"And it nearly killed her," Cal said, effectively neutering Ripley's enthusiasm.

Ara was intrigued by this device. This use of science to accomplish what only a few rather arcane bits of magic could achieve—and usually while causing a fair amount of damage to the recipient. But this? If it could be modified to deliver just the most necessary of spells, then Charlie and Leila might stand a chance.

"Rika? How do you feel about the use of this neuro-stim device? You've had your mind tampered with enough already. Would you be willing to subject yourself to this new form of mental alteration?" Ara asked.

"Hell yes," she replied without hesitation. "If this saves Charlie, then I say let's do it, consequences be damned. I owe him that much. A lot more than that, to be honest. So let's stop yapping and start neuro-stimming." She looked at the others, her adrenaline flowing high from voicing the somewhat frightening decision. "Uh, what exactly do I have to do now?" she asked.

Cal remained silent a moment as he conferred with several of the other AIs who were very familiar not only with the precocious teen, but more importantly, with her mother as well. She was not one to be trifled with, and tampering with her child's brain was a line they would not normally even consider crossing.

But these were not normal times, and despite her mother's wishes that Ripley learn everything the old-fashioned way until she was an adult, the situation was one that they all agreed she would definitely see the importance of. And knowing her, that meant she would, reluctantly, perhaps, let her daughter load magic into her mind.

"Very well," Cal finally said. *"But this is not a well-defined insertion of data. We will have to retrieve the relevant information directly from the source, then parse it into injectable packets, which will then be drip-fed as rapidly as we can safely do so. All aspects will be closely monitored by the top AI minds on the planet."*

"Aww, I feel so special," Ripley said.

"If anything happens to you, there will be hell to pay," Cal replied. *"Your mother would turn me into scrap."*

"You know she wouldn't."

"But not for lack of trying," he replied.

Ripley and Rika shared a nervous smile. It was a little terrifying, knowing they were about to have a computer tap into their minds. For Ripley, it was her first time actually using the device she already knew so much about but had been forbidden from trying.

"Mom's gonna shit when she finds out," she chuckled with glee. "And I'm gonna learn magic!"

As for Rika, she faced a different flavor of fear. She was a brave woman, and not even death scared her—at least, not much—but harm had been done to her in a very similar manner, and she'd been robbed of not only her memories and her old self, but also her free will. At least for a time.

Fortunately, the healing waters Charlie had steadily provided her from their dwindling reserve, along with the efforts of the cutting-edge medical machinery in this time, had finally put her right.

The enormous dragon watched the two women with interest, smelling the emotions and fears wafting off of them. It was good they were scared. This was not something to go into lightly.

"What do you need of me?" Ara finally asked.

"I have already tasked the fabricators with combining and modifying a set of neuro-stim headbands to fit you, Ara. Now, while we have worked together for a while, which has afforded us some knowledge of your physiology, the workings of your brain remain beyond us."

"I suppose they would."

"As such, we will need to ask you specific questions as we attempt to download the correct information. It will be a bit hit-and-miss at first, but once we dial it in, I believe we should be able to process the data. Then it is just a matter of whether it will stick in its new recipients."

"I have the utmost confidence in you," Ara said. "Now, let us begin. Time is of the essence."

And so, just like that, it was decided. Ripley and Rika both were going to get a very small and very specific upgrade to their magical skill set. Just a pair of spells for this one task, plus a tiny refinement of casting style to help the neophyte teen better grasp the actual act of casting.

Of course, there were plenty of other spells the Zomoki thought might be of use to them in the course of their rescue attempt, but by Cal's calculations, there was simply not enough time to even begin to perform the collection and subsequent transfer before the subs ran out of air.

With the clock ticking, they set to work as fast as they were able. The results surely wouldn't be perfect by any stretch, but this would have to be enough.

CHAPTER THIRTY-SIX

A small contingent of cyborgs had volunteered to help in the undersea rescue operation and were all crammed into the single loop tube car with the two magically enhanced women as it sped toward its destination deep beneath the sea.

The mechanical men and women would have seemed a logical addition to any rescue effort, but, with the exception of some very specialized military units that were not on the planet at the moment, the cybernetic population found themselves rather susceptible to extremes of pressure. Especially when saltwater was involved. And thus, at that depth, the mission was as dangerous for them as the two humans.

"How much longer do you think?" Rika asked, fidgeting with the thick konuses now gracing each wrist.

"Cal and the others had to really dial down the speed on this thing so we wouldn't overshoot the target. I'd say maybe another three or four minutes," Ripley replied, likewise toying with the powerful magic devices now sported on her forearms.

It was an odd sensation, she found. *Knowing* something so innately that had been utterly foreign to her just hours prior.

"So, this is what it's like," she had said upon removing the neuro-stim headband, her mind loaded with proper casting technique and a few particular spells. "So freakin' cool."

Even Rika had to admit that this process, while still invasive in its own way, was far less disconcerting than what had been done to her in the past. Of course, that had been done against her will, and the voluntary nature of this particular bit of mental fiddling sat better with her, for obvious reasons.

Ara had been both thrilled as well as somewhat horrified at the success of the process. It meant a rescue had a real chance of success, which was the entire point, but she could also see the potential for abuse of the merging of technology and magic.

"Cal, this has been a fascinating process, but I feel we need a particularly high level of security for this neuro-stim information I have fed into your storage facilities."

"We're one step ahead of you, Ara," he informed her. *"As soon as we agreed to attempt this, the other AIs and I devised a quintuple fail-safe storage protocol specifically for any magical information loaded into the systems both globally, as well as on any ship that comes within transmission range of Earth and its moon. It's an automatic process that, once activated, will only allow access to this data with a minimum of three top-tier AIs confirming the release. Additionally, there are several false files to serve as a further deterrent. Download one of those, and you'll find yourself not only unable to use magic, but also using any magical device in such a way that we will be able to track its misuse."*

Ara felt herself relax. Cal was a good person, even if his mind was made of circuitry rather than flesh, and she trusted him. And so, with the magical upload secure and safe, her two pupils headed out to save their friends.

Miles beneath the surface of the ocean, the loop tube dropped deeper and deeper as Cal and the others made minor adjustments as the car sped toward its destination. The problem was the entire system had been designed for hypersonic transit, a vacuum in the tube allowing frictionless travel at ultra-high speeds.

Now, with passengers not only needing air once they stepped out of the car, but also requiring the vehicle to stop where no stop was intended, the AIs found themselves forced to do something rather uncomfortable for machines who lived in a world of mathematical precision.

They had to guess.

Arriving within a few hundred meters of the target was a given––they were supercomputers, after all––but given the nature of the mission the two women and their assisting team were about to carry out, every additional step outside the safety of the loop tube was one more chance for catastrophe.

They were cutting it awfully close, so far as the AIs had been able to tell. Given the size of the sub and the length of time it had been without power, they estimated they'd be running very low on oxygen by now. Charlie and Leila would likely be delirious from the tainted air and unable to flee the doomed sub once the hull was breached.

That's where the cyborgs came in.

A small team ready to assist in any way possible, but also knowing that they may simply need to get out of the way if that was what was required. As for the cybernetic crew of the craft, they would undoubtedly be able to self-rescue once the hull was opened with the portable plasma cutter Rika had tucked into her pack.

It was a marvel of technology to the woman from the past. Where her ship had possessed a similar tool, it had been many times larger, and required enormous tanks of compressed gasses in order to function. This cutter, however, was light, portable, and for simpler types of cuts, was able to separate the required gasses out of the atmosphere around it.

The sub's hull would cut like butter. Even a military-grade

ship could not withstand the fierce heat of the plasma. But cutting into the advanced naval vessel was the easy part. The hard part was going to be getting there.

The plan was for Rika to cast the first spell, creating a sort of force field against the wall of the tube and beyond. Ara had explained to them that the spell she was providing them was not constrained by the metal in their way, and an air pocket would form outside of the loop tube as well as within. If all went according to plan, when they cut their way out, they would be safely able to step out onto the sea floor.

From there, the two would leapfrog spells, creating an overlapping passageway of air. A magical tunnel leading to the sunken submarine. The sheer quantity of magic required was staggering, and no one person would have been able to maintain the spell.

But with the two of them, as soon as one spell failed, the other would pick up the slack while a new overlap was cast. And quickly. Ara estimated they would have less than one minute before each casting would succumb to the pressures of the deep.

It would be a run to the sub. They only hoped the seabed was firm and not boot-sucking sand. For the heavier cyborgs, that could prove a deadly obstacle if their feet began sinking in, bogging them down.

But that was intel they simply did not have, so they would just have to go as-is and let the cards fall where they may. As the loop tube car began to slow its descent, Ripley and Rika shared a nervous smile.

This was it. Go time.

CHAPTER THIRTY-SEVEN

A subtle wave of fear, adrenaline, and magic washed over Ripley as she crawled out of the emergency exit panel of the loop tube car and stepped onto the empty track. As far as the eye could see, the tunnel stretched out into the distance in either direction.

Where she stood was just a tiny speck on the map of a network spanning the entire globe. And that speck had been reached with near pinpoint accuracy by the greatest AI minds on the planet.

"You should be within twenty meters of the target location," Cal informed them, his voice strangely echoey over the tunnel's emergency intercom system. *"The automatic breach-sealing locks are currently on override. So long as you prevent water from entering the tunnel, the hole you create will not trigger them."*

"And if water *does* get in?" Rika asked, shouldering the small backpack with the plasma cutter in it.

"Then we will not be able to bypass the hardwired safeties, and the tunnel will seal."

"Which would suck," Ripley noted. "So let's avoid that, 'kay?"

"You got it, Rip. Teamwork makes the dream work, right?

Every forty seconds we replenish the bubble covering the breach. The overlapping time should be enough to prevent any leakage."

"Right. Just like we practiced."

Rika turned her attention to the cyborgs exiting the car. "Okay, Cal. Everyone's clear. Pull the car back to the cut-off point."

It was part of the safety plan. Just in case the safeties triggered prematurely––but with no water in the tunnel––the AIs would be able to release them via the onboard relay on the car. But it had to be outside the sealed section, and sending a new car would simply take too long in an emergency situation.

"Moving the car," Cal confirmed, the transit vehicle backing up fifty meters to the exact line of the massive hydraulic seal built into the walls of the tunnel.

"Okay, let's do this. You ready?" Rika asked, rolling her shoulders more out of habit than actual tension in her neck.

"Yup," Ripley replied.

"And you guys?"

"We are," the nearest cyborg replied. "But are you sure you don't want one of us to carry the cutter? We don't fatigue like you do. No offense."

"None taken. And thanks for the offer, but if I get winded running a couple hundred meters with this much adrenaline in my system, then I really need to rethink my cardio regimen. And besides, you guys weigh a lot more than we do. Just in case you get stuck on the way out, it'd take too much time to circle around to swap packs."

"Understood," the artificial man replied. "We will keep pace just behind you and stay ready to assist in the breach and rescue once we reach the submarine's hull."

Rika gave him a little nod, then turned her attention to her human counterpart as she pulled the cutter from her pack. "You ready, Rip?"

"Already casting," the teen replied, the heavy konuses on her wrists faintly glowing as she created the first force bubble protecting their segment of the tube.

"Copy that. Protect your eyes," Rika said, dropping her goggles in place as she fired up the plasma cutter.

The device hummed in her hands as she adjusted the cutting edge, immediately setting the flame to the metal wall, wasting no time. Ripley could hold that portion of the spell for a minute or so. And the cut needed to be completed before they had to swap out.

Rika worked fast, her practice on shore paying off as she sliced a person-size hole in just under thirty seconds, leaving plenty of time for her to cast her own spell. Rika then shouldered the magical load, while Ripley re-packed the rapidly cooling cutter into its heat-proof box and slid it into its backpack.

"Got it. Let's go!"

The cybernetic component of the team wasted no time, the first kicking out the panel and jumping out onto the seabed, pulling the piece of metal aside while the others scrambled to join him. They then slid the section back into the tube where it would be standing by, ready to weld back into place when they returned.

"Amazing," one of the other cybernetic men said in awe as he took in the sight.

All around them a perfectly clear force field held the crushing waters back. It was like standing inside a crystal ball. Only, one where the world outside could kill them in a flash if the shell gave way.

The two magic-wielders tapped into the new spells embedded in their minds as naturally as if they'd known them their whole lives. Ara's gift was working perfectly.

They cast together, rapidly overlapping their spells as they ran forward, charging in the direction of the dark shape looming in the inky waters, barely visible, despite the massive, million lumen lights their cybernetic team were aiming ahead of them, the beams startling the denizens of the ultra-deep.

"I see it," Ripley said, her sharp eyes making out their target.

"Toward the front," Rika called out as she refreshed the bubble protecting their loop tube escape route.

"Got it," Ripley replied, shifting course slightly as she cast the next section of the spell.

The cyborgs were in luck. The seabed happened to be atop a section of hard stone, providing a firm base for the layers of sand and sediment. At that depth the pressure had compressed it all into a surprisingly walkable surface.

Of course, at that depth it could also crush their entire team in a heartbeat.

The spell, however, was working perfectly. Ara had thought to put to clever use what was essentially a reversal of a variety of the boarding spell Charlie had used back in his pirating days. The spell would create a passable tunnel when connecting ships in the vacuum of space, fighting the powerful forces trying to suck the air out of it.

Now, on the bottom of the sea, the inverted spell was pushing outward rather than pulling inward, fighting the ocean's full weight. It was inspired in its design, but there was little room for error. So far, however, the neophyte spell casters were doing an admirable job.

The submarine's mass was growing closer, and they were making good time, casting in rapid succession. And in just another minute or two, they'd finally have an answer to their most pressing question.

Were their friends were still alive?

CHAPTER THIRTY-EIGHT

Charlie and Leila drifted in and out of consciousness as they lay on the floor of the sub wrapped in blankets and each other's arms. They'd been submerged a long, long time without the benefit of the craft's CO_2 scrubbers to replenish their breathable air.

The resulting hypoxia had left them lethargic, their brains not fully functioning, as they were starved for oxygen. They were breathing, but the dank, stale air contained only a small percentage of the vital gas needed for life. With such a low partial pressure, unconsciousness, seizure, and death were all but inevitable in short order.

They had stayed calm, whispering the important things they needed to say to each other well before the air had begun to thin. After that, there was little to do but hold onto one another and wait. Charlie just hoped it would be painless.

The hallucinations had kicked in several hours prior as their minds began entering a waking dream state. Charlie had thought he saw actual pink elephants for a moment. Something he would have probably found amusing in any other circumstance. And Leila had been talking to Baloo, hallucinating her fur baby's comforting presence.

But Baloo was frozen, trapped in stasis mid-hunt somewhere in the hills near their home. And there were definitely no pink elephants on board. For one, they didn't exist. And if they did, there was simply no way one could have ever fit into the tight confines of the submarine.

Knock, knock, knock-knock-knock.

"Shave and a Haircut" rang out on the hull.

Charlie was roused by the familiar—yet unexpected–sound. "Did you hear that?" he asked, sitting up, propped on his elbow.

"Hear what?" Leila slurred.

"Uh, never mind. Just the pressure on the hull," he said, slumping back to the deck.

Knock, knock, knock-knock-knock.

I could have sworn I just heard it again, Charlie mused in the barely alert corner of his mind.

The cyborgs, though covered in living flesh, had no such need for oxygen to function, and Captain Watkins's boot-falls rang out as she came racing forward into the compartment. Wrench in hand, she banged out a quick reply.

Knock, knock.

"Wait, you heard that?" Charlie said, forcing his eyes open.

"You bet your lily-white ass I did," Watkins said. "There's someone out there."

Defying his oxygen-starved body's wishes, Charlie forced himself up onto his elbows again, just in time to see sparks begin to flash through the hull.

"Protect your eyes," Watkins said, pushing him over, facing away from the blinding light.

"But we'll drown," he managed to say. Or, at least, he thought he said it. He couldn't be entirely sure, his tongue felt so thick and unwieldy in his mouth.

"I don't think so." Captain Watkins turned and shouted out

down the sub's corridor. "Crew, take up arms! All hands to me! We've got company!"

Racing feet rang out on the metal deck as the rest of the crew hurried to their captain, taking up positions to repel boarders as best they could. Someone was breaching their hull, despite their depth. And no one in Earth's navies had that sort of capability.

The sparks quickly transcribed a large oval, the hot slag dropping off and rapidly cooling on the deck where it fell. Captain Watkins recognized the effect.

"Plasma cutter," she said with curiosity. "That's Earth tech."

The piece of the multi-layered hull pulled free from the sub, clanging to the wet sand outside. Miraculously, water did not come flooding in. Fresh air, however, did.

Charlie and Leila both sucked in great lungfuls of the briny air, their eyes coming back to focus as their bodies processed out the first bits of the massive carbon dioxide buildup in their tissues.

"Hey, guys!" Ripley said, poking her head in through the hole in the bulkhead. "Damn, it is *ripe* in here," she chuckled, the knot in her gut relaxing as she saw Charlie and Leila moving and still very much alive. "So, we *really* should go, if you're able."

Charlie lurched to his feet, then promptly collapsed.

"Carry them," Captain Watkins ordered.

Her cybernetic crew lifted the two struggling people and carried them to the opening.

"Hand them to us," the cyborgs waiting outside called out.

Charlie and Leila were quickly passed through the opening into their waiting hands. Rika gave him a quick, tight hug then stepped back. The cyborgs were far better able to carry his weight, and besides, she needed to cast the next spell.

"Holy shit," Charlie managed to say, marveling at the wall of magic keeping the waters at bay. "*You* did this?"

"We both did," she replied, nodding to Ripley.

"Wait, since when does she know magic?" he asked, thoroughly confused. "Am I still hallucinating?"

"Long story, and no time for it right now. Can you walk?"

"I don't think so," he said. "But I'll try."

The cyborgs lowered his feet to the sand, and for just a moment he felt the marvel of standing on the bottom of the sea. Then he passed out. Leila, likewise, slipped into unconsciousness.

"What's happening to them?" Ripley asked, alarmed.

"Focus, Rip. You've got to cast next."

"I know. But what's going on? Are they okay?"

Captain Watkins climbed through the hole in her ship with the rest of her crew, jumping down to the sand beside them. "They were hypoxic," she informed them. "They'll be okay. This is just an effect from the sudden spike in oxygen after breathing high concentrations of carbon dioxide for so long. The increase in the partial pressure of O_2 can do that."

"Got it," Rika said. "You heard her. We carry them, guys."

The cyborgs hefted the man and his queen over their shoulders, the entire team taking off at a quick run down the shimmering, magical tunnel. Small rivulets of water were beginning to trickle in. Not much, but a little. But it was enough to cause great alarm in the two casters.

"They're failing," Ripley said after casting the next overlap and reinforcing the bubble over the tube with an extra layer for good measure. They couldn't afford any water getting in there. Not until they were well clear.

"We're pushing the envelope," Rika replied, glancing at her chrono. "Double-time it everyone! We've gotta *move!*"

The cyborgs reacted immediately, increasing their pace, running as fast as the two casters could form their protective tunnel ahead of them. The loop tube was visible, a giant worm of steel stretching out across the ocean floor.

"Almost there," Rika said, the effort of maintaining the spell taking its toll.

A trio of cyborgs hurried through the opening in the tube, quickly taking the unconscious burden from their counterparts still outside on the seabed. They then took off running, racing the fifty meters to the waiting loop tube car.

Rika and Ripley had given up on their carefully timed overlap schedule, both of them growing weaker by the minute. Instead, they cast back-to-back, using the last dregs of the magic in their konuses to maintain the bubble over the section of loop tube.

"There's not going to be enough time to weld the piece back into place," Rika called out. "We need to make a run for it."

"But the water will catch us," Ripley said, fear thick in her voice.

"No it won't," Rika replied, grim determination in her eyes. "We're going to make it. Now run!"

The two took off as fast as their exhausted legs would carry them, each casting with the last of their might, barely maintaining the bubble. Rika had dumped the plasma cutter the moment they entered the tube, but nevertheless felt as if she were running through tar. Ripley was just as exhausted, if not more.

And then she tripped, going down hard on the cold metal floor.

Rika felt the massive shift in the spell holding back the water, the loss of a caster placing all of the weight firmly on her shoulders. She cried out, digging deep and casting as hard as she could, the world going red, then browning out around her.

She had to hold on to the spell. It was all that mattered, no matter what happened. And then, as she felt her mind stretched to the limit, her body suddenly became light, as if it were floating. Flying. Moving without her input or control.

Rika was vaguely aware of the sound of rushing water as her

magic hold finally gave way, followed by the sound of the emergency seals slamming shut, closing off the breached section of loop tube from the rest of the network.

Miraculously, she was not drowning.

With great effort, she opened her eyes. A warm face was looking down on her. The sub's captain, she realized. A groan caught her attention. Rika turned her head to the side and saw Ripley sprawled out beside her in the cramped interior of the loop tube car. The cyborgs had saved them.

She turned her gaze back to the woman studying her as she lay on the floor.

"You did good," she said, smiling down on the exhausted woman. "Now rest."

Rika didn't need to be told twice. She finally let go, her eyes slipping shut as she drifted off into welcome unconsciousness.

CHAPTER THIRTY-NINE

Bawb had been moved from his partitioned area into the general holding space for Captain Sindall's captives, and it was not a pleasant sight. All but Tim, the cyborg their magic would not work on, were blankly staring at the ceiling, human and Chithiid alike.

One by one, they'd been taken away and experimented upon, and one by one they had come back released from stasis, but mentally altered in some way.

Bawb assumed this was a ploy to get him to cooperate with the Tslavar captain's efforts to gain intel on the planet they were hoping to subjugate. What he failed to take into consideration was that while the captive Wampeh indeed cared about *some* of the denizens of this planet, none of them were here.

As an assassin with a particularly bloody past, while he would rather not see the innocents aboard the ship slain needlessly, he also did not truly care, and would gladly allow their sacrifice rather than give in to Captain Sindall's pressure. But as of yet, none had been killed, though that could change at any moment.

Further insulating him from worry was the fact that all but

one of the people he actually *did* care about––the one who was undoubtedly still protected by the brutal spell-traps he had left in place––were unaffected by the Tslavar stasis spell. And judging by the smell of Zomoki flames he had noticed earlier, they were coming for him.

"You really think your friends are going to find us?" Tim asked.

Bawb turned to look at the cyborg. Now that they were not separated by the partition, he could look him in the eye as they spoke. "You are a mechanical man, Tim. Can you not smell the scent of fire still lingering in the air?"

"I just assumed it was smoke from the fighting."

"Oh, that it is," Bawb said with a grin. "And that smoke came from a friend of mine. What your kind would call a dragon."

Tim's expression shifted to one of surprise, but not the shock he might have shown just a day earlier. Magic was a thing, he had discovered first-hand, and apparently, so were dragons.

"So, this dragon friend of yours. She's the one who attacked the ship?"

"Yes."

"And is that why they seem so shorthanded now?"

Bawb smiled brightly. "Oh, yes. That other scent in the air? That is burnt Tslavar flesh."

"That's disgusting, Bawb."

"They are our enemies, Tim. They have taken us hostage, harmed innocents, and attacked my friends. A quick death by incineration is far more generous than the fate they would receive by my hands."

Tim cast a funny look at his pale compatriot. "You're a kind of violent guy, Bawb."

"You do not know the half of it," he said, once again pulling at his restraints, hoping for an inch of slack for him to leverage to his advantage. At the moment, however, no such luck was to be found.

"You really think you can escape?" Tim asked.

"I've freed myself from more difficult imprisonment than this," Bawb said. "Though I do try to make it a point to not become captured in the first place. At least, not without it being intentional."

"Why would you intentionally be captured?"

"It can be...*useful*," he said with a knowing grin.

"Freedom isn't so bad, either," Tim replied, shifting in his restraints, trying, as Bawb had, to release himself.

But just like the Wampeh, he was bound fast. The effort did, however, cause a fresh trickle of blood to run from his back, dripping to the floor beside him.

"You are injured," Bawb said. "When did this occur?"

"Oh, I almost forgot," Tim replied. "I turned off my peripheral sensor units when they started cutting into me."

"They were attempting to break you with torture? But surely they quickly discovered your true nature beneath that flesh exterior."

"You'd have thought, but they were digging around for a while back there. I guess I'm unlike anything they'd ever seen before, so they wanted to take a better look."

This concerned Bawb. If they could figure out a weakness in the mechanical men's makeup, then he and his friends' entire force of cyborgs could become compromised, unable to be of further assistance. He just hoped their inner workings were beyond the skill set of their captors.

"What do you think they're doing to them, Bawb?" Tim asked, glancing at the vacant stares of the captives strapped down all around them.

"I cannot say for certain. But this does seem somewhat familiar."

"Oh?"

"Yes. But I've never seen it achieved in a rapid manner. Normally, it takes some time to properly hold sway."

"Hold sway? Over what? What are you talking about?"

"My apologies. I sometimes forget you and I are able to communicate, but our frame of reference is worlds apart," Bawb said. "What I speak of is a form of mind cleansing."

"Brainwashing?"

"Ah, so your world has something similar."

"Well, sort of. We possess the technology to manipulate minds, but it is typically used to implant new information, like training for a job, or learning a new language."

"Which you would not need if you but had a proper translation spell."

Tim flashed an amused smile. "Well, we didn't have magic on our world until you arrived," he noted. "So you can't fault us for working with what we have."

"A valid point," Bawb conceded. "But all of that aside, this still does not answer the most pressing question in regards to our fellow prisoners."

"And what is that?"

Bawb studied each of the captive's blank faces a moment, searching for something, anything that might give him an answer. But none were to be found.

"The question," he finally said, "is, what exactly are the Tslavars planning to do with them if they *do* manage to alter their minds?"

Tim looked at his new friend, then scanned the vacant stares of the other prisoners, hoping to perhaps find a clue. But just as the Wampeh had discovered, there were none to be had. Whatever the Tslavars had in mind, it would remain their secret.

CHAPTER FORTY

Being a coastal region, hyperbaric medicine had been greatly advanced in Southern California. The diving industry had seen a boom in its heyday, and with a massive naval base toward the southern tip, men and women were constantly challenging the depths of the Pacific.

Unfortunately, every so often, the ocean would win. The bends, nitrogen narcosis, pulmonary embolisms, were all infrequent, but nevertheless deadly, risks that came along with the thrill of exploration.

While the industry had died off--literally, when the war eradicated the population--the know-how was still a well-respected part of modern medicine, despite the cellular regeneration and replacement capabilities the AI medbots now possessed. But sometimes a simple, old-school treatment would do the trick better than anything so invasive.

In Charlie and Leila's case, a quick hour spent in a hyperbaric oxygen chamber breathing pure O_2 at a few times normal pressure had set them right in no time. The high concentration of oxygen permeating their cells at pressure not only relieved any residual discomfort and grogginess from their ordeal aboard the downed sub, but had also wiped away aches and pains they'd not even noticed they were sporting.

Once they had emerged, sharp and recovered, they immediately hit the debriefing room to go over what had happened with the others. Captain Watkins had wisely taken the sub's core data storage with her during the rescue, providing Cal and the other AIs an opportunity to thoroughly review the parts of the engagement they hadn't been able to properly monitor from the surface.

"What do we know about this ship?" Charlie asked, getting right to business as he and Leila sank down into the comfort of one of the command center's couches together, leaning into one another.

The ordeal had brought them near death, and now, in the brief hours afterwards, the couple had instinctively gravitated toward one another. A residual subconscious tell of just how close they had actually come to meeting their end.

"We are tracking it as best we can," Cal informed them. *"Ara had indicated that the great depths had muted even her magic, rendering the ship untrackable."*

"Well, shit."

"But it would seem the ship is now once more near the surface. She picked up the scent just an hour ago."

"Good. Because I want to kick those bastards out of the water and off our planet," Ripley said. "After we rescue Bawb, of course."

"Which is probably going to be a little bit tougher than we originally thought. They seemed to have been quite adept at blocking our weapons' fire."

"Yeah, that's going to be an issue." Rika said. "But first and foremost, we need to figure out where they're going next. Cal, you said Ara is tracking them again?"

"Yes, Rika. Traces of their craft indicate it is currently traveling beneath the surface just off the shore of Long Beach."

"Why Long Beach?" Rika asked. "I mean, I suppose if they're snatching people to experiment on, it doesn't really matter where they're getting them from, but I thought it was just a quiet little beach town."

"And you would be correct. However, in addition to the small civilian population, there is also a long-vacant munitions depot there. We have one of our AI brothers overseeing it, of course, but otherwise, the facility is mothballed."

"So, what's the big deal, then?" Charlie asked.

"It housed nuclear weapons, Charlie. And while we have slowly been tracking down and either storing, or decommissioning, these remnants around the globe, it has not been a top priority, as they were deemed safely locked away."

"Until an alien invasion landed."

"Yes, that did rather change things."

"We can't be sure they're even interested in those weapons," Leila noted. "I mean, they are from my galaxy. And despite their hostile intentions, that doesn't seem like something they would even know about. I know I had no clue about these massively destructive weapons on your world until you told me about them. And these Tslavar invaders don't have the benefit of a cooperative intelligence filling them in."

"Good point. And from what we've seen, they haven't taken anyone with an inkling about the planet's military stores," Rika noted. "More likely than not, they're just snatching convenient targets along the coastline. I'm sure after their run-in with Ara, they'll be wanting to stay as close to the water as possible."

It was a logical point. The odds of these invaders, unfamiliar as they were with the intricacies of modern Earth technology and weapons suddenly targeting the most destructive munitions on the planet were slim. But whatever their goals, they were proving to be a far more difficult opponent than anticipated. And the team would be well-served to remember that.

"Their magic is strong," Rika said. "Of course, we already

knew that, but they've got a modification of some defensive spells that seems to be able to pretty effectively block our gunfire."

"Yeah, that bit kind of sucked," Charlie agreed. "The principles are the same as stopping magic attacks that launch debris, only now they are ramped up to stop ultrasonic rounds fired from guns. And if they can block those, we're kind of left at a disadvantage."

"You could always upgrade to more modern arms," Cal noted. *"I understand the wish to use a type of projectile they were previously proven ill-equipped to defend against, but it seems they've adapted to that tactic, leaving the firearm option an inefficient one at best."*

"Nat's cannons seemed to make a dent in their defenses," Rika noted.

"Yes, but that was simply due to the sheer caliber and velocity of their rounds. And it is utterly impractical to carry anything near that size as a portable weapon. They were designed to take down airships and stop ground transport."

"So we're shit out of luck," Charlie grumbled. "Just great."

"You're not out of luck, Charlie. You just need to adapt. There are plenty of arms stored in my local munitions depot that I would wager the invaders are not yet adept at defending against."

"What kind of guns are we talking about here, Cal?"

"The pulse weapon kind. And plasma weapons."

"Pulse weapons? And plasma? Like what the cutter uses?" Rika asked.

"No, those just fire these little balls of plasma," Ripley said. "A few ships have them. And pulse rifles are pretty common. My dad takes me shooting sometimes just for fun."

"Teaching a kid to blast things with pulse rifles is fun?" Rika said with an incredulous chuckle.

"Well, yeah. Doesn't it sound fun to you?" she shot back with a healthy serving of snark.

Rika had to admit, she probably would have gotten a kick

out of it when she was a teen as well. Of course, in her case, she had been taken out and taught to fly by her father since she was big enough to reach the controls.

"So will these pulse and plasma weapons impact the magical defenses in a different enough way that they'll pass through? Like the bullets did when we first used your guns while we were fleeing the Council of Twenty?" Leila asked.

"I don't know for sure," Charlie replied. "But it beats what we have now, so I can't see the harm in trying. If not, we're going to have to resort to close-quarters combat again." He looked at Rika and nudged Leila with his elbow. "Speaking of which, I didn't tell you, but you two were pretty impressive back there. You fight well together."

The women shared a glance and a smile. "Thanks, Charlie," Rika said. "Leila's a really fast learner."

"And you're a good teacher," she replied.

"I saw it from above," Ripley chimed in. "That was pretty badass. You guys have got to teach me those moves some time."

"Speaking of teaching," Charlie interjected, "it looked a hell of a lot like you were casting a force spell down on the sea floor. When exactly did you learn magic? We weren't down there *that* long."

"Neuro-stim," Ripley said.

"Neuro what?"

"It's a bit of tech they hadn't gotten around to showing us yet, Charlie," Rika explained. "It's a sort of slow-feed learning tool, apparently designed to let space crews download useful skills while in stasis on long flights."

"Huh, clever. So they'd arrive with a new skill set already in place, eh? We should play around with this thing. Could be useful."

"You catch on quick, Charlie. And yes, it allows for the implanting of knowledge while the user is in stasis. However, I should also mention that a typical neuro-stim cycle takes months, if

not years. There are layers upon layers of safeties in place, designed to prevent damage to a user's mind."

"But Ripley had zero magic skill just the other day," Leila said. "This wasn't done over months."

"No, it was not. However, Ara provided the knowledge for only a pair of very specific spells. This allowed myself and the other AIs to focus our attentions on modifying the neuro-stim stream in a manner that implanted the skills in a greatly expedited manner. It was still somewhat dangerous, but with the relatively small size of the data packet, we felt it was manageable."

"Magic is easy?"

"Not easy, per se. But the data itself is not a terribly complex mixture of information, like learning to pilot a ship or speak a new language, for example. From what I've seen, spells—and the means to cast them—are relatively simple. Quite arcane, but otherwise straightforward."

"And it's totally kickass!" Ripley chirped. "Me and Rika, we were overlapping spells, and it was like, all, *wham!* And then the water pushed back, and we kept doing it until we reached the sub. It was so cool! I can't wait to learn more!"

Charlie looked at Ripley as she bounced gleefully in her chair with a goofy, enthused grin.

"Great. We've turned the kid into a wizard," he said with a chuckling sigh. "Her folks are gonna kill me."

CHAPTER FORTY-ONE

The fabrication facilities in several major cities were fired up and running with only a few hours' notice, thanks to their extremely competent AI systems, and small ships were trickling in, one by one.

"How's the retrofitting going, Rika?" Charlie asked.

"Cal and his AI buddies have tracked down a handful of AI-run ships they think will be capable of handling the firepower," she replied. "Not all of them were designed to fly with the recoil of a pulse cannon, of course, so those that can't handle an actual firefight are going to fly cover for us, acting as additional eyes in the sky."

"So they're getting the pulse cannons and plasma weapons installed without problems?"

"For the most part. From what I've seen, though, the AIs we have at our disposal don't really seem to be the cream of the crop, as it were," she noted. "All of the top-tier ships and their crews have been off world for months on long-range surveys. Seems to be something they do periodically."

"Yeah, Cal told me about it. Searching out other advanced races. A needle in a haystack kind of thing, really. But it has to start somewhere, I suppose. The timing sucks, though. I mean, from what we can tell, it looks like the Tslavars are gearing up to make another snatch-and-grab run any time now, and we could really use the extra firepower."

"But their crews would have been frozen," Rika noted.

"Well, of course. And that would have sucked, no doubt. But the AIs could have still flown the ships, and that's really what we need right about now. But we'll just have to make do with what we have. The cyborgs have been armed with pulse rifles, and we've got a cache of them standing by for us when we're ready."

The time was coming. The time to strike back. And hopefully this time they would succeed in not only disabling the Tslavar ship, but in rescuing their friend as well. The longer he was in their clutches, the longer they had to do who-knew-what to him.

"You good here?" Charlie asked. "I need to pow-wow with Ara and go over our plan of attack one more time."

"Yeah. I'm just finishing up coordinating with Cal. Then Leila and I were going to go fire off a few rounds to get her familiar with these new weapons."

"Should be pretty self-explanatory."

"For us, sure. And she's damn quick to learn. But still, she's from a magical world, so a little extra practice surely won't hurt."

Charlie was glad to see the two women become friends. When he'd first rescued Rika from her mind-controlled imprisonment, he had been worried Leila might have some difficulty with a friend from his former life suddenly popping back into the picture.

A *female* friend, no less, though one he had never had any relations with. Still, they had history––though she couldn't remember it––and that alone could make some less confident women uncomfortable.

It was a rather symbiotic relationship that had wound up forming between the two very different women, and they really did seem to complement each other's gaps in skills nicely. That, and it was just nice that any awkwardness was nipped in the bud. Now all they had to do was defeat an invading alien force, and maybe they could all get back to just living their lives.

Eddie had taken a quick flight to visit the Dark Side moon base at Cal's request, while Ripley was napping, catching up on a bit of sleep after the draining undersea rescue. Like Rika, she was bouncing back nicely, but unlike her new friend, she wasn't yet used to the strains that wielding magic at that level could put on the body.

And so she crashed for a few hours, during which Eddie had flown to Dark Side base and retrieved the mysterious crates from Hangar Two.

"Cal will know what to do with this," Sid had said, the moon base's resident AI fully confident in the city-sized AI's abilities.

"But what is it?" Eddie asked.

"Something special Cal wanted to add to your existing armaments."

"Better than the new pulse cannon they installed?"

"I wouldn't necessarily say *better*," Sid said. "Just a little something extra. Just in case the need should arise. I could say more, but I really should leave all of that to Cal. It was his idea, after all."

Eddie wasn't about to argue with the military AI. If Sid believed it was best to leave the explanation to Cal, then he wasn't about to voice an objection.

"Thanks, Sid," he said once the moon base's human and Chithiid crew had loaded the crates. "I hope we get this all sorted out. This magic-on-Earth thing is making it rather difficult."

"You're telling me," a gruff man with a ceramisteel replacement arm grumbled. "I was supposed to be meeting my gal for a weekend of R&R, but instead, she's frozen down there, and my leave got canceled because of these goddamn aliens."

He noted the look the seven-foot-tall Chithiid standing at his side was giving him.

"Uh, sorry, Apaari. No offense."

"You are such a dick sometimes," the alien chuckled.

"And you're getting better with slang," he shot back. "Anyway, I don't wanna wind up a human popsicle, but otherwise, I'd come along with you to the surface. All of us would. It feels wrong sitting out a fight like this."

"But you would fall victim to the spell enveloping the planet."

"Yeah, we know. Doesn't make it suck any less," he grumbled. "Anyway, you'd best be off. Got an invasion to defeat, after all."

"Yeah," the young ship replied. "And if I had fingers, I'd cross them."

"I'll cross mine for ya," the man replied.

"As shall I," the Chithiid added.

Eddie quietly lifted off and made his way clear of the base, then hurried back to Earth, where Cal's retrofit team was waiting to install whatever this new toy was.

"I hope it's something cool," he said, then plunged through the atmosphere, re-entering his native airspace in a streak of fire.

CHAPTER FORTY-TWO

The rag-tag group of modified AI ships and their cybernetic counterparts had just gathered together and run through the most preliminary of tactical plans when word came in to load up and move out. Their quarry was coming ashore, it seemed, and it was time to put a stop to their plans, whatever they were.

Unfortunately for Ripley, her ride was still mid-modification when the call came.

"But we've gotta go!"

"I'm afraid I cannot clear Eddie for flight yet," the AI fabricator unit stated.

"Bullshit. There's a fight coming, and we've gotta be there."

"Again, I apologize, but this craft is simply not flightworthy. His power systems are tied in to the modifications currently being installed. Neither will function without the process being completed," the AI said, not once slowing in its work. "You have my sympathies, and I will work as quickly as possible, but Eddie will not be able to fly for at least another forty-five minutes."

"It'll all be over by then!" Ripley said. "Come on, hurry!"

"Sorry, Rip. I guess we shoulda waited to install this stuff," Eddie said.

"It's not your fault, Eddie. We had no idea," she said, admitting not only to her AI friend, but also to herself, that it was simply shit timing. They were going to have to sit this one out, and no one was to blame.

Meanwhile, the small fleet of modified AI ships swarmed the skies above Long Beach, their cyborg troops ready for action. It seemed the Tslavars had decided to make a move on that soft target after all. And this time the defending forces––with Ara's senses leading them directly to the ship––were ready for them.

Charlie, Leila, and Rika were geared up, flying in atop the mighty Zomoki. Each was wearing powerful konuses and slaaps in addition to their blades, moderate body armor from one of Cal's armories, as well as a fully charged pulse rifle slung over each of their shoulders. This time, they were going in prepared.

"You got them?" Charlie asked his winged friend as they circled the shoreline. *"I don't see anything down there. They must've gotten their shimmer spell functional again."*

Ara dipped her wing and swooped a bit lower, breathing deeply as she did.

"Oh, yes. They're here all right. I can still smell my magic on their craft. Have the other forces deployed along the coastline where the main boulevard runs past those canals. Do you see the disturbed section of sand?"

Charlie did. There was no wet spot as before––the Tslavars had apparently learned their lesson in that regard––but the dry sand in one area had the look of being recently moved. Smoothed over and dried. No one would notice it from ground level, but from above, the pattern of the sand was different than that around it, the wind not having had enough time to blow it in line with the surrounding beach.

"Yeah, I see it. They're covering their tracks."

"Indeed. But that was their entry point, and I can definitively place the ship less than a mile inland from that point following the

main boulevard. If our troops advance from the shoreline behind them, the Tslavars will be cut off."

"And, meanwhile, we all come charging in from the other direction, driving them right back into our trap."

"Precisely."

Ara soared high, acting as if she was searching for the ship, while Charlie relayed the instructions to the other craft. The AI ships quickly looped out to the shore and dropped their payloads, wasting no time regaining the air and flying to the opposite end of town before soaring high again, keeping the illusion of their confusion intact.

But the forces of Earth were ready this time. And the Tslavars were going to pay.

"Drop me on that rooftop, Ara," Rika said. "I can take the stairs down and get in position for a crossfire without you having to touch down a street level."

Ara didn't hesitate, flapping her wings mightily as she briefly landed on the rooftop, making a show of craning her neck as if searching for the enemy, while Rika quietly slid from her back and darted into the access door. The dragon then dove off the roof and flew wide, again looping over the area.

"I have them," she said. *"Are the others ready to engage?"*

"Charlie, to Cal. We have a fix on the ship. Status of the other forces?"

"They are in position. The faster-moving among them have already taken up positions a block behind, and the modded ships are set up on both flanks."

"Great. When Ara strikes, everyone moves in."

"Affirmative," Cal said. *"Good luck."*

"Game on, Ara," he sent to his friend.

She looped then banked, diving toward the cloaked craft. *"And so it begins."*

She had just begun spouting flames, the other ships diving

in from their positions, when powerful magical attacks bombarded her from both sides.

Charlie sensed them at the last moment, shifting all of his power into his defensive spells, his reflexes the only thing keeping them from being blown from the sky as Ara was thrown sideways from the force, momentarily stunned.

"That was not from the ship!" she warned, flapping hard as she came down atop a building, her legs shaky.

"Are you okay?" Charlie asked.

"I will be. But there are more of them!"

Before Charlie could broadcast a warning to the others, a pair of Tslavar ships uncloaked, their shimmer spells briefly receding as they unleashed a barrage of magic skyward. The incoming ships didn't stand a chance.

The first wave was torn to pieces, thrown to and fro by the powerful spells. The subsequent ships were able to fire off their weapons and break away, but not without incurring damage as well.

Their shots landed, the plasma rounds and pulse blasts piercing the enemy's magical defenses. They had been prepared for a conventional projectile attack as well as Ara's magic, but this new type of weapon had caught them off guard, though the damage was still minimal. At least for the moment.

The question was whether or not the Tslavar forces would be able to modify their defenses against this new means of attack before another volley landed. The ground forces suddenly caught between their original target and the new enemy would play into that equation. They may have walked into a trap, but this time they were armed with pulse rifles.

The cyborgs fired wildly, the rounds taking down several shimmer-cloaked ground troops protecting the ground between them and the ships. A firefight between better-armed cyborgs and camouflaged Tslavars erupted into full force.

"They've got ground troops too!" Charlie yelled into his comms. "Cal, this was a setup."

"I've received the real-time feed update, Charlie. There are three vessels and unknown ground forces at your location."

"Of course," Leila growled, as she slid off of Ara's back and began sniping from the rooftop.

Amazingly, despite only a day's practice, her shots were flying true, leaving more than one Tslavar uncloaked and dying in the street below.

"Now it makes sense," she said, her next shot flying true, right into another Tslavar mercenary.

"What do you mean?" Charlie asked, taking up a position next to her.

"How they were able to cover such vast distances in so little time without being seen. It was never just one ship. That's how they did it. Multiple ships snatching people from around the globe."

"Shit," he grunted as he fired off a burst from his rifle. "And we can only track one of them."

"Allow me," an angry voice rumbled from behind them. Ara rose to her full height, magic crackling from her body. She was tapping into her core power, the deep magic of thousands of years. And she was pissed.

In a flash, she leapt into the sky, her plan of attack shifted from assisting Earth's forces to simply spraying everything with her magical flames, the power of the spell she had layered into them permeating the crafts' structures, marking them with her smell while ripping away their defenses.

The lead ship had already sustained damage from her first run-in with it, and with this attack its magical integrity failed immediately from the intensity of the hit, driving it into the ground, disabled and broken.

The other two ships had been prepared, however, and

despite the sheer power of her attack, had managed to come out relatively unscathed.

From their vantage point on the rooftop, Charlie and Leila saw a lone figure racing toward the downed Tslavar ship.

"Rika? What the hell is she doing?" Charlie said, watching his friend take down a pair of Tslavars with brutal efficiency before breaching the ship.

"She's getting our friend back," Leila replied, firing off another burst, cutting down the alien trying to follow Rika into the ship. "Now stop gawking and help me cover her back."

CHAPTER FORTY-THREE

The explosive impact that had driven the ship into the ground had broken apart a great many sections of the Tslavar craft's interior. On top of that, the sheer force of Ara's attack had ripped much of the vessel's magic asunder, leaving a terribly damaged, unflyable wreck in her wake.

Fortunately for Bawb, the holding area was designed to keep the prisoners far from escape. That meant well-insulated from the exterior areas of the ship, where the most damage had been incurred. While their compartment had been hit hard as well, it was nowhere near as bad as the rest of the ship.

"Tim, are you all right?" Bawb called out through the smoke to the cyborg prisoner.

"Still in one piece," the cybernetic man replied. "Though not for lack of trying of whoever did this."

"Ara," Bawb replied. "My friend. She struck this craft down."

"She could have killed us."

"Perhaps. But she is old, and very wise. And she undoubtedly knew, as I would have, that we were almost certainly held in a secure central area of the ship."

"Meaning?"

"Meaning we would be protected," he replied, gazing around the wrecked compartment as the smoke thinned.

Humans and Chithiid lay dead, as did several Tslavars. It seemed they had not been quite as protected as he had initially believed, though the force of the attack hadn't felt so extreme. Still, he'd lost consciousness for a moment, and the destruction in the Zomoki's wake was incontrovertible.

Bawb yanked hard on his restraints, and this time his right arm abruptly swung free, a chunk of the ship's hull tearing away, dangling at the end of his wrist restraint. He quickly undid his other bonds, then ran to his cyborg friend, freeing him as well.

"We must release the other survivors," Tim said.

Bawb noticed the magical attack seemed to have snapped them out of whatever daze they'd been in. They were not fully themselves, he could tell, but the men and women were definitely coherent enough to realize the danger of their situation and the need for a rapid egress.

"You take that side. I'll free the others," Bawb directed, then set to work releasing the prisoners' bonds.

In short order the human guinea pigs were fleeing the room, scurrying for safety like rats from a sinking ship. And that wasn't so far from the truth.

Bawb was attempting to follow, pulling the chunk of metal still dragging behind him. While he'd freed himself from his other restraints, the damaged one on his right wrist was, unfortunately, stuck shut and would take quite some time to get open. And time was something they simply did not have.

He hefted the piece of metal, cradling it in his arms as best he could.

"We need to move, Tim. Are you ready?"

"Yes. Everyone is freed," he replied as the last prisoner scurried out the chamber door. "But do you really think there are any more Tslavars aboard? Wouldn't they have abandoned ship by now?"

Why did he have to say that? Bawb silently lamented, fully expecting the mysterious entity Charlie called Murphy to make an appearance, having been offered so tempting an invitation.

"It doesn't matter, Tim. We must run. Now!" Bawb called out, bolting into the corridor.

The cyborg followed close behind as they navigated the twisted remains of the ship's interior hallways. The spell had done a number on it, no doubt, and there was no way this craft would ever submerge beneath the waves again, let alone travel aboveground.

A glint in the smoke caught Bawb's eye, and he lunged aside just as a wicked-sharp blade sliced through the air where he'd just been standing. Two more weapons joined the mix, the light reflected from them visible before the Tslavars wielding them were.

Bawb's reflexes kicked in without him even thinking about it for a nanosecond. Decades of training in the deadly arts of his sect took over despite his exhaustion and disadvantaged state. In a heartbeat, he had tangled one of the blades in his remaining restraint, wrenching it from the attacker's hand and promptly driving it through his chest.

But he didn't stop there. A blade now in hand, he flew into action, though fighting with his left rather than his right. The funny thing was, even left-handed he was a far better swordsman than most would ever be with their right.

More Tslavars pushed their way into the corridor, their blades already slick with blood. Someone had paid the highest price this day, and seeing as the entire population was frozen, that left just one option.

"They're killing the others!" Tim blurted as he tripped over the body of a slain human captive.

"I am aware, Tim," Bawb grunted as he took on a trio of attackers. "Now, defend yourself!"

The cyborg was not a combat machine, but even so, the

instinct toward self-preservation ran strong in him, as it did in all living things, organic or cybernetic. The blade flashing down toward him drew blood as it sliced through the flesh covering his arm, but the sturdy metal endoskeleton within was barely scratched.

The Tslavar's hands vibrated painfully when the sword rang out against the hard metal, causing a delay before he could pull free and move in for a killing blow. But Tim was a quick study and was on his feet in an instant, his mechanically powered hand snapping his attacker's arm, nearly wrenching it from his body.

The sword dropped to the deck as it slid from the gash in Tim's flesh. He looked across the smoky space and counted the numbers, doing the math only a machine could do so quickly.

They were outnumbered, and Bawb was fighting handicapped, his right arm nearly useless with that piece of metal dragging behind him. There was simply no way they'd win this, but he'd be damned if they'd go out without a fight.

Tim reached out and grabbed the Tslavar by the throat, squeezing and pulling as hard as he was able. The man's eyes bulged as he fought with all of his considerable strength before abruptly going limp as his windpipe was torn from his body with a wet snap.

Bawb, occupied as he was, saw what Tim had accomplished, and had to admire the cyborg's creativity and determination. They would die this day, but they would do so in the thick of battle, having made an honorable and impressive showing.

Tslavar bodies were piling up at Bawb's feet, but his weariness from captivity was finally getting the better of him. A glancing blow cut his shoulder. Nothing deep, but he knew it was the beginning of the end. It was only a matter of time before little injuries would sap him of his remaining strength.

And as he accepted his fate, his mind flashed to Hunze, and he couldn't help wonder if perhaps he'd been mistaken about the lack of an afterlife all this time. Perhaps, he thought, if he was lucky, they'd be together again one day.

A burly Tslavar was lunging toward him, and Bawb knew without a doubt, he would never be able to free his sword from the torso of the man he'd just slain in time to defend himself.

And so it ends, he thought, strangely at peace as his death raced to greet him.

Bright steel struck home and a spray of hot blood showered the Wampeh, dripping from his face and torso.

He looked down. The blood was green.

Tslavar blood.

The sword yanked free from the attacker's chest, tearing a nice hole as it did so, the man's body falling in a heap. Rika flashed a little wink at the stunned Wampeh, then spun into action, firing a strange type of rifle that seemed to emit some sort of energy pulse with one hand, while mowing down the enemy with her sword in the other. And on top of that, he could feel her magic as she deftly cast with her konus, mixing magic, firearms, and bladed combat into a singular assault of impressive intensity.

Buoyed by his reprieve, Bawb yanked his sword free and tore into the Tslavar crew with renewed vigor.

"Here!" Rika called out, tossing him a konus. "More of them than us, so even at close range, we're more likely to hit them than us."

The konus was nowhere near as powerful as his own, but the feel of magic in his hands once more was, at that moment, the second most viscerally joyful sensation he'd ever known. He slid it onto his wrist, the ferocity of his spells suddenly powered by the stored magic.

"You ready to get the hell out of here?" Rika asked, mowing down two more of their adversaries.

"Lead the way," he replied with a rejuvenated grin, diving into combat once again, the two of them leaving a wake of death the likes of which the poor cyborg following close behind would never scrub from his mind.

They rushed from the smoldering ship's hull, out into the fresh air—or semi-fresh, to be precise. The stench of burned Tslavar and newly spilled blood adding a particular tinge to the breeze.

"She's got him!" Charlie called into their comms. "Everyone, cover Rika and Bob!"

A massive layer of suppressing fire erupted from all sides as the human, Wampeh, and cyborg darted for safety behind the ranks of their comrades.

Tim noted as they ran from their former prison that every last one of the other captives had been slain. Murdered in cold blood before they could reach safety. And as foreign as the emotion was to the metal-hearted man, he suddenly knew what it meant to want revenge.

CHAPTER FORTY-FOUR

The battle had raged on for some time between the camouflaged Tslavar craft, their troops, and the rag-tag Earth forces, and had it not been for the shift in weaponry, the Tslavar gambit to take down their greatest threat might just have succeeded.

Fortunately, Ara was quick to recover, and the surprising new tech-magic wielded––albeit clumsily––by the flesh and metal forces opposing the invaders had been enough of a disruption to allow her to fly clear of the magical crossfire and recover. Had that not been the case, even the great and mighty Zomoki could very well have fallen to the three-pronged attack of so powerful and clever an enemy.

The invaders had been gauging the planet's defenses, holding back two of their craft and likely hundreds of men in reserve, letting their adversaries reveal their strengths and weaknesses as they pursued the decoy ship. And it had almost worked. The metal projectiles were easily stopped, now that their casters had the opportunity to adjust their spells accordingly. That is, with the exception of the larger rounds.

Despite their magic, the Tslavars realized quickly that the fixed auto cannons mounted at strategic positions in the cities possessed a degree of firepower that could still inconvenience them, if not cause catastrophic damage. For that reason, they opted to avoid routes that might intersect those defenses.

Today, however, the trap was set, and the Zomoki had flown right into it, but the strange new energy weapons wielded by the harassing ships and the men and women with metal skeletons beneath their flesh were punching right through the Tslavar defenses.

Their carefully adjusted spells could stop bullets, but this new attack was something different. Something that would force them to forego their planned eradication of the dragon, instead fleeing to regroup and address the beast at a later time.

She had taken the brunt of the magical attack, but it seemed the caster with her had been able to deflect much of the spells' damaging powers, leaving the dragon free to strike back. And strike she did, weaving powerful magic into her flames, spraying them across the shielded ships.

The two new additions to the fight were ready for her, however, and they had a huge amount of magic poured into their defenses for just such an eventuality. The previously damaged decoy ship, though, was simply not up to the challenge. The others saw as it fell, driven to the ground, broken, never to submerge again.

Captain Sindall had done well, though, and despite the loss of that ship, as well as the escape of all of its prisoners, his mission had been a success of sorts.

The tide having turned with the barrage of energy pulse weaponry, the remaining Tslavar ships sounded the retreat, quickly gathering their surviving troops and fleeing to the safety of the planet's deep oceans.

"Let them go," Ara called out as the ground forces attempted to pursue the escaping enemy. *"Tell them to stand down, Charlie,"* she sent to her friend. *"I landed solid hits on their ships, and despite the magic protecting them from damage, my power is solidly on them. Tracking them will not be a problem."*

"What if they go deep again?"

"I took that into consideration and modified my spell. From what I learned the last time, I believe there will be little chance of losing them this time."

Charlie relayed the message over his comms, the circling ships breaking off their pursuit and returning to retrieve their contingents of ground forces. The cyborgs, for their part, had performed admirably, making a good showing despite their lack of military training.

Some, however, had fallen to the Tslavar onslaught. The spells had been modified to address the unusual physiology the cybernetic people presented. No longer were they simply aimed at killing the flesh—which the metal-framed people could still function without. Instead, great blows, designed to shatter and incapacitate, had been woven into their magical attacks.

More than a few cyborgs had their limbs rent from their bodies, while still others had been crushed beneath debris utilized as makeshift projectiles. And then there were the humans and Chithiid who had fled the downed ship.

Bodies lay strewn near the wrecked craft, which had finally collapsed in on itself, though Charlie was pretty sure it was a scuttle spell that had finished it off, not their attack. Knowing the Tslavars, their captain had likely deemed it better to utterly destroy his own ship rather than let any intel fall into the hands of the enemy.

And that was likely also why they had slaughtered the escaping prisoners. Of all of them, only Bawb and his bleeding cyborg companion had survived. The Wampeh would heal. He always did. And the cyborg's injuries appeared to only be to his flesh covering, which, likewise, was easy to repair.

Leila rushed to their friend and wrapped him in a tight

embrace, whether the exhausted Wampeh wanted one or not, stoicism be damned.

"I'm so glad you're okay!" she said, eyes wet with emotion. "We thought, well, we didn't know what they'd done to you. If you were even still alive."

Charlie clasped his friend's hand. "Yeah, man. It's good to have you back with us."

"Thank you. Thank you all," he said, then turned to his blood-soaked savior. "And especially you, Rika."

"Hey, just glad to help out," she said, slightly uncomfortable at the attention.

"I am in your debt," the pale assassin said, the weight of his words heavy in the air.

Charlie noted his friend's tone, but held his tongue. There was plenty of time to discuss what had happened in there later, and he was sure it would be quite a tale. Bawb simply did not utter things of that nature lightly. And to have the deadliest assassin in thirty systems owe you his life? Well, it was a debt that held far more weight than your average 'I owe you one' scenario.

"You'd have done the same for me," Rika replied.

Bawb, given his nagging distrust of the woman who had so recently engaged them on the other side of the field of battle, couldn't help but wonder if he would have.

"That was amazing, what you did back there," the bloody cyborg said. "I didn't get a chance to thank you, what with all of the fighting and whatnot. But now that we're free, thank you. Thank you so much for saving us."

"Don't mention it."

"I've never seen someone fight like that. Not even in old entertainment videos from the archives," Tim continued to gush.

Bawb could not help but agree. "He is correct in his

assessment. Your wielding of magic and martial skills with both blade and this unusual tech-weapon was impressive indeed."

"Praise from the Geist? Wow, now that must've been one hell of a fight," Leila joked, patting Rika on the shoulder.

"I'll say," Charlie added. "Now, come on. Let's get you guys cleaned up and back to command. I know Cal and the others will want a full debrief. There's a lot you need to be brought up to speed on, and I'm sure you have a lot to tell us as well."

Bawb scanned the debris field of ships downed in the initial wave of the assault.

"I do not see Eddie. Were he and Ripley––?"

"No, they're fine," Leila said. "Held up getting Eddie's weapons systems modded. They missed the battle."

Bawb seemed to relax slightly at the news. Annoying as she was, the teen had welcomed them to her world with open, and enthusiastic, arms, making him and Hunze feel at home in their new abode. And despite her often-exhausting exuberance, he had quickly grown fond of her.

"Hunze? I was taken at our home. I must get to her," he said, his intent clear.

"She's fine," Charlie told him. "Relax. The booby traps you set up were more than adequate to keep her safe. And once we saw that you'd been taken, we had additional measures put in place, including round-the-clock guards camped out on the perimeter. Though I think with your spells still active, she's far safer in there than the armed men outside will ever be."

The Wampeh followed them into the belly of a waiting ship for the short flight back to LA. Ara would join them shortly, but for the time being, she was flying high in the sky, tracking the fleeing Tslavar ships beneath the waves.

"As I anticipated, the craft are far easier to locate this time."

"Good news," Charlie replied. *"We're taking Bob and his cyborg buddy back to Cal for a debrief. Once we're done, we can regroup and plan our next move."*

"I'll see you Downtown shortly," she said, gliding in the sun's healing light.

"Okay, guys. Let's get back to Cal and go over all of this madness," Charlie said as the ship's door slid shut behind him.

"Yes," Bawb said coolly. "I will postpone my visit home for now. We shall first assess our status with the AI minds and determine our next course of action."

"That's the plan," Charlie said.

"But then," Bawb continued. "*Then*, I shall return home and gather my weapons."

Charlie knew that look in his eye, and heaven help those who had drawn his wrath. Retribution was coming, and it would be swift and fierce.

CHAPTER FORTY-FIVE

Bawb had sucked down a half dozen electrolyte pouches on the flight to Los Angeles, the revitalizing liquid doing him a great deal of good, calming his nerves, while replenishing his depleted blood sugar. Apparently, he was more dehydrated than he'd anticipated. But then, going on a non-stop killing rampage against dozens of highly trained alien mercenaries could really take it out of you.

The flight was short, and the others left him to his thoughts as he processed the events of the past few days. Soon enough he would be recounting them for Cal and the other AIs. No sense making him do it twice.

"Here," Leila said, handing a towel to Rika. "You've, uh, got something..."

Rika accepted the offering, the white cloth quickly turning green as she wiped the sticky Tslavar blood from herself. "I seriously need a shower," she griped. "You sure we can't postpone this debrief long enough for a quick rinse?"

"You know better, Rika," Charlie said.

"I know. Just fuckin' with ya," she said with a chuckle.

Judging by the amount of blood and gore Rika and the two survivors were wearing, the fight must have been something to behold. Charlie had seen Bawb in all-out combat before, and had fought against Rika before her mind was freed from Malalia's spells.

Both were formidable—Bawb much more so, naturally—and the two of them would have been a formidable team in any circumstances. And with Bawb's anger piqued? No wonder it had been a seemingly literal bloodbath.

Of course, they would all be able to watch the play-by-play once they reached Cal's command center. Tim, the rescued cyborg, possessed a talent that meat people often took for granted. Namely, his electronic brain recorded and stored everything he saw or heard. With the equipment at Cal's disposal, it would be no problem tapping into those data stores and retrieving the information.

The hope was that perhaps he had seen or heard something that, while seemingly innocuous at the time, might actually prove useful in combatting the invaders.

Judging by their seeming confusion at cybernetic physiology and how it was not affected the way entirely flesh beings were, there was a good chance they'd gotten sloppy in the presence of their captive. Time would tell.

"We're touching down in two minutes," the gruff AI piloting the small ship notified his passengers. Charlie had learned that this particular craft had been a cargo hauler, a task best suited for the less-than-charming AI. However, when fighting broke out, he had been one of the first to arrive to be outfitted with new pulse cannons.

The ship landed with hardly a jolt, testament to their artificially intelligent pilot's skill. It made sense, of course. An AI tasked with transporting valuable materials would learn early on how to best keep his cargo from jostling unnecessarily.

"All right, let's get in there and see what Cal and his buddies have to say," Charlie said as they stepped out into the sunlight before heading beneath the city to Cal's command center in the city's transit hub.

Deep underground, the thick cement and steel of the loop tube stations insulated them from any sound that might have been generated above. In the old days, before the war, the constant bustle of people and machines had made it almost as busy sounding as the surface. But now, with a fraction of a fraction of the population inhabiting the city, the loop tube station system was a ghost town.

"I'm glad you made it back so soon," Cal greeted them as they mounted the stairs to his command center. *"We have much to discuss."*

Cal had the foresight to have had tasteful, yet easily washed, covers placed on the furniture before the team's arrival, knowing full well more than one of them would likely be sporting a sizable quantity of blood, and likely not their own.

Refreshments had also been laid out, along with clean clothing in the adjacent rooms, should anyone feel the need to shed their bloody attire. The massive AI had done all he could on short notice to make the debrief as comfortable as possible for the team. He knew that despite his stoic exterior, the Wampeh assassin was surely enduring an emotional tempest beneath his calm façade.

"If you'll all please make yourselves comfortable, we can begin."

With that, the debriefing began, the AI and his other brilliant artificial counterparts listening intently as each teammate recounted the experience. It had not gone as expected. They'd seen that much from the surveillance cameras on both the ships and the ground that had been monitoring the events as they unfolded.

Additionally, Sid, the AI on Dark Side base, had re-tasked a few satellites to better observe the goings-on down below from that particular vantage point. The result was a rather comprehensive video record of what occurred that day. Including the startling appearance of a new pair of alien ships.

"And no one saw signs of them on the ground?"

"Nothing," Charlie said. "They must've entered the city single-file, using the wet trail from the damaged ship to mask their own. By the time they split off and took their positions, the water had run off enough to not leave any more traces."

"So, they knew we'd be coming," Rika said. "Maybe not how many or from what direction, but they knew it."

"Yeah, looks that way," he replied.

"And they tried to take down Ara as quickly as they were able," Leila added. "Meaning they know our strengths and were trying to even the playing field by taking her out of the mix. It's just a good thing Charlie was so quick with his defensive spells."

"Not quick enough," he grumbled. "Ara still took a hit."

"Is she all right?" Cal asked, concerned.

"She's fine. It just took her a minute to shake it off. I'm sure by now, with all the direct sunlight she's soaking up, she's feeling close to one hundred percent again."

"This is disconcerting," Cal said. *"That they would feel they had a realistic shot at removing the dragon from the equation means they are confident in their strength. And using the damaged ship as a trap, well, that shows a level of cunning above most foot soldiers' pay grades."*

"Meaning there's someone of a higher rank calling the shots," Rika said.

"I only encountered a Tslavar captain aboard the ship during my captivity," Bawb noted. "And while he appeared most competent, I do not take him for a leader of armies. What was your impression, Tim? You spent more time with them than I."

All eyes turned to the bloody cyborg. His own red blood

intermingled with the green of the Tslavars. The wounds he'd received during their escape were still oozing, as was the nasty cut on his back where they'd performed exploratory vivisection on him.

"Ah, yes," he stammered. "Uh, what did I see? Well, from what I could tell, they were experimenting on the humans and Chithiid captives. They were all dazed when they would be brought back from whatever they'd had done to them, but they were no longer frozen in stasis."

"Which means a counterspell must exist that can unfreeze individuals as well as the planet's population as a whole."

"Yeah. I'll have Ara get working on that," Charlie said. "But what else, Tim?"

"Tell him what you told me," Bawb said.

"Ah, that. Right. So, the thing is, when they took me to experiment on, they activated some sort of translation device."

"It was a spell," Charlie said. "Just call it a spell, it's easier that way."

"Okay. They activated a spell and questioned me while they were digging around inside my body."

"Which must have been something of a shock to them," Rika noted. "A metal man inside a flesh body. Not something they've ever seen before."

"They *did* seem intrigued," he agreed. "Only, when they took a break from their digging and walked away, they didn't bother turning it off the translation spell."

"But how did that help you?" Leila asked, still unfamiliar with all of the nuances of cyborg anatomy.

"They didn't realize exactly how an AI mind works. Or my ears, for that matter."

Leila began to realize what he was implying. "You have enhanced hearing."

"Precisely. And I heard them talking all the time, since I first got there, really. But at that moment, I had the translator active, so I could actually understand what they were saying."

"Which was?" Charlie asked.

"That they were going to find a way to destroy the strategic mind guiding the planet's forces. Once they achieved that, the rest of the planet would be easier to conquer."

"But that is me," Cal said. *"And just how exactly did they propose doing such a thing?"*

"That part I don't know. The rest of the time I didn't have a translator, so it was just gibberish."

"But now that we are back, I can help with that," Bawb said, casting a translation spell, binding it to the cyborg's body. "There. Now you have the spell the rest of us possess."

"Oh, so I can understand now?"

"Precisely."

"Great. Then let's dig in and see what else they had to say. Cal, do you want to make a copy of my files while I replay them?"

"Yes, that would be wise. Unlock your wireless, and I will send a secure link. Accept it, and I will be able to copy as you go."

"I see it," the cyborg said. "Okay, got it. You're in."

"Excellent. Then let's begin."

Tim fast-forwarded through his memories to relevant sections where alien voices could be heard. He then slowed to real-time so the non-AIs could keep up and replayed the conversations.

Mostly they were discussing the prisoners and how weak a species they seemed to be, though the taller alien subjects did seem a bit more resilient. But it was the one called Tim's immunity to their magic that was troubling them. He was impervious, somehow.

A lengthy silence followed, until they finally came to bring him for experimentation. Initially, they activated a translation spell for him, asking questions as they opened his body. His lack

SCOTT BARON

of pain reactions disturbed them. That the metal man could disconnect from his flesh exterior's damage sensors was simply beyond their comprehension. Only when they dug deeper and found his metal endoskeleton did they realize they had something entirely new on their hands.

They called the captain, who came to the lab to examine the cyborg. By this point they had deactivated his translator spell, so he had no idea what they were about to say until the replay taking place this very moment.

"The fact that it is able to be opened up without harming the internal functions is remarkable," one of the Tslavars could be heard saying. "The other subjects would be rendered unusable with such invasive activity."

"Yes," a deeper voice replied.

"That's Captain Sindall," Bawb noted. "I know the voice well."

The Tslavar conversation faded as they walked from the chamber, returning a short while later with something in tow.

"Are you certain this will work?" the captain could be heard asking.

"Yes, Captain. Once planted inside, we will seal the wound enough to hold it in place. From what I can tell, the subject is no longer receiving pain stimuli from that area, so I believe he will not even notice it is there."

"Good," Sindall said, the smile on his face almost audible in his voice. "And once this prisoner is rescued and taken within the innermost halls of the Earth people's defenses, the device will detonate, wiping their leaders from the board and giving us the edge we need."

All eyes locked on Tim, but the cyborg was already on his feet, one hand groping around his back at the stitched-up wound his captors had inflicted upon him. "Oh no," he said, wide-eyed.

He locked gazes with Bawb, then turned and ran from the

room, darting down the hall and diving into the concrete-walled changing room Cal had provided for them should they so desire.

The blast tore him to shreds, knocking out the thinner walls of the room, sending sparks bursting through the air as a magical fireball flashed out through the facility. Charlie and Bawb instinctively combined their powers, each casting a protective spell with all of their might within the command chamber.

Leila's Magus stone flared bright as well, adding an additional layer between them and the flames that were devouring the facility around them. The walls shook and collapsed, and if not for the magic preserving the room's rough shape, they'd have been entombed beneath hundreds of tons of rubble.

The debris finally settled into a stable resting place, allowing the survivors to stop casting their spells and crawl through the gaps in the rubble until they reached the open space of the loop tube terminal.

"Holy shit," Rika gasped, looking at the sheer scale of the damage.

The destruction was massive. Whatever spell the Tslavars had managed to embed within the device hidden inside of Tim, it had destroyed indiscriminately. Cyborgs were shredded, some reduced to molten slag. Humans and Chithiid who had been frozen in place since the ordeal began were now no more than piles of blood and bone.

"There's nothing we can do for them," Charlie said, shaking off the shock as best he could. "Cal, you there?"

Nothing.

"The automatic fire suppression systems are only semi-functional," Rika noted.

"I see," Charlie replied. "We have to get to the surface."

He started for the far end of the terminal, where the damage seemed less intense. The others silently followed behind him, stunned at the sheer destruction around them and the utter miracle that they had managed to survive.

Bawb joined Charlie in prying the stairway access door free, then they all began the climb toward fresh air. They would survive this day, and they would regroup. And then there would be hell to pay.

CHAPTER FORTY-SIX

Sunlight and fresh air greeted the survivors of the magical blast as they stumbled out of the partially collapsed stair access and onto the streets. What they saw was incredible.

The ground above the terminal, while intact, had sunk—several feet, in some areas. A portion of the roadway had also buckled, forming a sinkhole where the high-pressure water pipes beneath were sheared away, blasting their contents out with great force before the backups to the backups finally sealed off the flow.

The explosion had likely caused far more damage than the Tslavars had ever hoped to achieve. And it made Bawb even more angry than he already was. Despite his blank expression, the vein in his temple was beginning to pulse visibly, and Charlie had never seen *that* kind of rage and restraint from him before. Whoever wound up on the receiving end of the Wampeh's blades, it would undoubtedly be a brutal demise. And he had an inkling that the Geist was going to make it slow and painful.

"It was all a setup," Bawb growled as he surveyed the

damage. "The whole damn thing. The crash, the escape, all of it. They *wanted* us to break free. It was the only way they could secrete that bomb into the command center."

"There was no way you could have known," Rika said. "And remember, those Tslavars damn near killed you back there."

"I am well aware. But it is also highly likely that they were not aware of the plan. More likely than not, the intention was for Tim and I to make our escape during the battle, eventually making our way back to command, where their device would detonate. But when Ara and your new weapons caused more damage to the ship than originally expected, lines were blurred, and troops meant to be on the front lines fell back to defend the ship."

"Which is why we encountered so many," Rika noted.

"Precisely. Regardless, with all the confusion, we returned to command a bit earlier than planned. It was the only thing that afforded Tim the window to do what he did."

"He saved us," Charlie said. "Sacrificed himself to save us all."

"And he will be remembered," Bawb said. "With a great deal of violence and bloodshed."

A burst of steam rose from the fissures in the sidewalks and roadway, as well as spouting out in a great plume from the stairwell.

"Looks like the fire suppression system is back online," Charlie said. "At least it'll stop any further damage. But what kind of spell was that? I mean, I've seen some pretty powerful and unique things thrown at us, but nothing like that."

"I am familiar with it," Bawb said. "Though I would never sink so low as to use its like."

"Why? What was it?"

"A tool of the weak and cowardly. A terrorist's device, designed to cause maximum damage in a completely indiscriminate manner," the pale assassin said, his distaste readily apparent. "I have killed many in my time, but a Wampeh Ghalian does not lay waste to innocents. Whoever cast this spell has no honor, and I look forward to ending them personally."

"If we can find them," Charlie added. *"Ara, you close enough to hear me?"*

A long pause hung in the air. *"Barely. What do you need, Charlie?"*

"I need you to get with the ships still in the area and form an observation network. We need to know exactly where those bastards are and be ready to strike at a moment's notice."

"You sound agitated?"

"Damn right I am. Bob's escape was a setup. They planted a massive bomb inside the cyborg we rescued along with him. The command center is destroyed, and much of the loop tube terminus is inaccessible until the fires are all out."

"How could this happen, Charlie? I felt the intensity of their magic. That was no diversion they launched at me. They were very much trying to kill me."

"I know. But that doesn't mean they didn't also want to cripple what they thought was the nervous system of the planet's defenses."

"But how?"

"If those other ships were cloaked all this time, it's very possible they've observed us coming and going long enough to have figured out where command was, and how best to get inside."

"This does not bode well."

"No, Ara, it does not."

A crackling hiss boomed out across the intersection, the static receding until it was no more than a faint background noise.

"Now I am angry," Cal said, his voice crackling over the damaged speakers.

"He's alive!" Leila exclaimed.

"Oh, yes. Very much alive, my friend," the mighty AI replied.

SCOTT BARON

"It seems our Tslavar invaders once again misunderstood the nature of this world's technology."

"I don't understand," Leila said.

"What he means is the AI computer itself—the actual machines that are Cal's brain—that is nowhere near that command center, am I right, Cal?" Rika said.

"Exactly. I merely chose to utilize that location for our base of operations out of convenience and proximity to the loop tube network. As for me, my mind is perfectly safe, and it would take quite a lot more than that attack to even scratch the walls of my processor vaults."

"And now the loop tube system is damaged," Charlie pointed out.

"Yes, but only in this location. It is easy enough to bypass, but I believe we will not have need of—" Cal abruptly fell silent.

"Cal? Everything okay? You still with us?"

"Yes, Charlie. But I have just received word from other AIs across the globe. It would seem that there have been other instances of cyborgs detonating within city walls."

"You mean there are more booby-trapped people out there?"

"It would appear that way. None were rescued as Bawb and Tim were, but there have been some reports of confused cybernetic citizens appearing after unexplained absences."

Charlie's mind raced. This wasn't just an attack on Cal. This was a global attempt to disrupt the AI network itself.

"Cal, you need to get a hold of every AI you can. Tell them to immediately quarantine any cyborg who has even the slightest abnormal behavior in a blast-resistant area until they can be evaluated. We know what to look for. Now we just have to keep them from wandering into any sensitive places and accidentally blowing themselves up."

Bawb and Rika shared a blood-thirsty look, then turned to their friend.

"Charlie?"

"Yeah, Bob?"

"We must get to my home."

"Hunze's safe, man. She's okay. Relax."

"No, you misunderstand. We must get to my home so I can retrieve my weapons," the assassin said with scary calm in his voice. "For *now*, my friend, it is *our* turn to hunt."

CHAPTER FORTY-SEVEN

The escaping ships had plunged deep beneath the waves as they sped off in a magic-powered flash. As soon as she saw them accelerate to speed, Ara realized the spells being used to power the craft were far more formidable than even she had imagined.

Much like the sonic tech-magic aboard the submersible craft Charlie had intuitively helped power, these ships were utilizing a magic-driven version of the Earth technology. Only, they used spells rather than science to achieve the effect.

"They are increasing their speed," Ara called out to the small squad of AI-piloted ships keeping pace alongside her.

The ships, possessing an intelligence of their own, were thrilled to be flying a mission with an actual dragon. It was the sort of thing they'd tell tales of for the rest of their days. That was, of course, if they survived the current endeavor long enough to tell them.

Ara pushed herself faster, the magic she cast without so much as a thought cutting the air in front of her, allowing her to reach supersonic speeds without the discomfort of a sonic boom. "Soon I may be unable to match their pace," she said into the buffeting winds. "Without exiting the atmosphere, I cannot fly much faster."

Far below, her quarry moved at likewise impossible speed, deep beneath the waves.

It was a true feat of highly specialized magical skill that the Tslavar craft were able to move at such a velocity underwater. Whoever had funded this invasion had spared no expense, for there were but a handful of power users alive who possessed the skill to craft such a spell. And this was confirmation of a sort that the ships were only the first stage of a much larger plan.

Ara knew no one would pour such resources into a mere scouting mission. Something far larger was afoot. And it looked like they'd be finding out what it was sooner than later.

Eddie had been the first to arrive in Downtown after the destruction of Cal's command center. He and Ripley had only just left the retrofitting facility a short flight to the east when the event occurred and had immediately diverted their course to the city center.

Ripley raced out the door as soon as they touched down. "Oh my God! What happened?" she blurted as she took in the destruction—that which was visible above ground, that is.

"The Tslavars planted a magic bomb inside one of the captured cyborgs," Charlie informed her. "When we brought him to command, he detonated."

Ripley's eyes went wide. "But Uncle Cal? Oh, no!"

"I'm fine, Ripley. And thank you for your concern," a scratchy voice said over the damaged speakers.

"You're okay!"

"Of course I am. You know my core systems don't reside in this place."

"Well, yeah. But it was a *magic* attack, so who knows what they might be able to do."

"A fair point," he conceded. *"In any case, I am unharmed. However, I cannot say the same for the dozens who were within the terminus when the device went off."*

Bawb walked straight for the ship, determination in his stride. "Come. We must retrieve our gear and prepare."

It was only once the initial shock of the destruction on the ground wore off that Bawb and Rika's appearance sink in. They were still green-tinted with the residual aftermath of their battle.

"Uh, is that alien blood?" she asked as the team boarded her ship.

"Yeah," Rika said. "It was a tough one. You don't want to know."

"Oh, it's not that," she replied. "I was just thinking I should get some towels to put on the seats."

Charlie couldn't help but laugh at her resilience in the face of alien carnage. "Yeah, I hear ya, kid. I'm sure it's a real pain, scrubbing alien blood out of the upholstery."

"Hey, I'm serious. We just got Eddie detailed," she shot back with a wry grin.

"And how did that go? Did you finally get your upgrades, Eddie?" Leila asked as she took a seat.

"I sure did," the ship replied. "Though we didn't get to do a full firing cycle assessment, what with the battle we were missing."

"I'm sure you saw the feeds," Charlie interjected. "They had additional forces waiting for us. We lost several ships in that first wave. So maybe it was better you were held up in the workshop."

"I'm not looking to avoid a fight," the AI said.

"Me either," his teenage pilot agreed.

"And no one is asking you to. All I'm saying is, you may have dodged a bullet there. And now you have a proper weapons system, right?"

"Well..."

"Well, what?"

"We didn't get a chance to do any tests at the targeting range," Eddie admitted. "But hey, it all looks to be in working order. I'm confident it'll do the job."

"Less chatter, more flying," Bawb said as he politely accepted the towel Ripley offered him and laid it out on his seat. "Time is of the essence. We do not know when they will strike next. Or where, for that matter. And as we so recently discovered, there is far more to this plan than we originally realized."

"Okay, hang on," Eddie said, lifting off into the sky. "I'll have you home in a couple of minutes."

"Can you please patch Cal in?" Charlie requested.

"He's on."

"Hey, Cal. I was wondering, has Sid noticed any unusual anomalies in orbit? Anything that might be a shimmer-cloaked craft?" He turned to Bawb. "That's possible, right? In space, I mean."

"It could be done, but there are too many ways to detect such a craft, as most shimmer magic does not function terribly well in the vacuum of space. It simply requires too much magic for most casters to maintain."

"Ah, gotcha."

"In any case, Sid has not observed anything out of the ordinary in orbit. But as a precaution, he has already deployed the few scouts who have returned from the nearby systems but were forced to stay out of Earth's atmosphere to serve as additional eyes in the sky."

"Great. We need all the help we can get, even if they can't risk passing through the atmosphere."

"And an additional bonus is they are all well-armed and more than capable of extra-orbital combat."

"Meaning?"

"Meaning there is a small but deadly force ready to shoot down any hostile ships, be they entering the atmosphere or exiting it," Cal said. *"And they are quite good at it."*

Charlie liked the sound of that. The orbiting ships couldn't help the people fighting down on the planet's surface, but at least there was something of a backstop lurking high above. It wasn't a lot, but it was a start.

"Please stand by. I'm receiving a transmission from one of the smaller craft flying the tracking pattern with Ara."

"Good," Charlie said. "I can't reach her, so wherever they are, they've got to be pretty far away by now."

Cal assessed the information the little ship had to offer, then conferred with the other AIs that were monitoring comms and satellite tracking. All confirmed the AI ship's report.

"It would appear the hostile craft are still submerged and traveling together, heading south at a blistering pace."

"If they are together, then they are moving on to the next stage of their plan. Whatever that may be," Bawb noted. "They wish to subjugate the population of this planet. The question remains, how will they do so with so few resources at their disposal?"

"I'm not sure, Bob. But I think your plan's the best start for the moment. Get home, gear up, and take to the sky."

"And pause to wash off the Tslavar blood," Rika suggested. "I don't know about you, Bawb, but I could really use some dry, non-bloody clothes right about now."

Despite the nature of their plight, the Wampeh cracked a little grin.

"Hey, I've got clean clothes that'll fit you at our place," Leila offered. "Eddie, can you drop us there after we stop at Bawb's?"

"Of course. It's just a tiny hop."

"Thanks."

"It would seem the fleeing ships are indeed heading south."

"How far south?"

"Likely all the way. Based on what has been observed of their path, the Tslavar craft aim to round Cape Horn and proceed into the Atlantic."

"Which means they could be going anywhere," Charlie groaned. "Okay, keep an eye on them. We'll gear up and get ready as fast as we can."

"And then we bring the fight to them," Rika said.

"Hell yes we will," Charlie replied. "And this time, we'll be ready."

CHAPTER FORTY-EIGHT

"Wait, there's what, now?" Charlie repeated, the confused tone of his voice matching the look on his face.

"I said there is activity at the Asbrú's landing site," Cal repeated. *"We cannot tell for certain, and none of the drones Vic has sent to survey the area have sent back any useful data. But something has happened."*

"How can you be so sure?" Bawb asked as he dug through the large duffle bag retrieved from his home, now resting at his feet at the armory of their temporary command center.

He pulled out his familiar pair of armlets, fully charged with magical power. A look of comforted relief flashed across his face for an instant as their weight embraced his flesh.

"Because of this," Cal said.

The display screen in the makeshift command center the AI had rerouted his feeds to blinked on, the data stream from across the globe flashing an image of the downed ship.

"Looks like the *Asbrú*, all right," Charlie said. "But I don't see how––"

"I'll zoom in for you."

The image quintupled in size, fixing on an area of leaves and grass to the ship's starboard side. There was nothing to see there. But that was the point.

"Hang on. Play that again," Charlie said.

"So you saw it, then?"

"I'm pretty sure we all did, Cal."

"I didn't," Ripley grumbled. "What did I miss?"

"There, near the tree stump."

"There's a lot of tree stumps out there, Charlie."

"The one at the bottom of the screen. Snapped at a sharp angle. You see it?"

"Yeah."

"Okay, now watch the ground just to the left of it."

Cal replayed the frames again on a loop.

"You see it?"

"I don't know. Was it the—oh! Oh, shit! There's a footprint there now, and it wasn't there a minute ago!"

"Precisely," Cal said. *"We were receiving some odd readings from the area, but the ships tracking the progress of the undersea vessels confirmed both ships were still together."*

"But that doesn't mean they didn't already leave a contingent of troops on the ground," Bawb noted. "And if they are there, camouflaged by shimmers all this time, preparing for their next steps, then that's where they will be regrouping. Right back where this all started."

Charlie leapt to his feet. "Come on! We've finally got the upper hand."

"But their ships are untouchable," Leila said.

"Sure, but this time we know where they're going. And we can get there before them. There's a likely path they'll take to come ashore, and they'll probably stick close to the water this time."

Bawb smiled as he continued to gear up. His form-fitting armored vest slid easily into place, the lining of Ootaki hair from Hunze hidden from view but providing him an enormously powerful wellspring to draw on. His time for revenge was drawing closer, and the anticipation was delicious.

"Possessing all of this information ahead of time, we can position forces beyond the area of the crashed ship. They won't be party to the initial engagement, but they'll be standing ready to cut them off should they attempt a seaward escape. I like this plan, Charlie. I like it a lot."

"There are still many details to work out," Cal noted. *"And it will take some time to get the necessary pieces deployed and in place."*

"Then get started while we're en route," Charlie said. "Bob, you have your shimmer cloak?"

"Of course."

"So you can get in close. Think you might be able to take a few of them out? Maybe snatch their shimmer cloaks while you're at it?"

The assassin gave him an amused look.

"Yeah, I thought so," Charlie said. "So, if you can snatch us a few shimmers, then we'll be on even footing. We can get close and have the cyborgs stay out of sight until we're good to go. And when the cavalry arrives, they'll look like the main attack, but we'll already be in position to strike."

It was an audacious plan, but with this group at his side, Charlie actually thought the crazy plan just might work.

"What are we waiting for?" Rika asked, bouncing on her feet. "Come on. Let's get moving, already. Time's a-wasting."

"Wait," Bawb said, placing his hand on her shoulder. "First, we must outfit you in a manner becoming a woman of your abilities."

"I'm good," she replied, waving her slaap in the air.

Bawb smiled at her, then drew a much more ornate slaap from his bag. It wasn't too much larger than the one she already possessed, but even without sliding it on, she could feel the power it contained.

She took the offered device, the metal warm in her hands as she traced her fingertips over the seamless design. The scrollwork and details were exquisite, the work of a true artisan. This was no ordinary slaap. It was the tool of a master assassin, and a lot of coin had undoubtedly gone into its forging.

"I can't take this," she said, offering it back to the Wampeh. "You'll need it."

He chuckled as he slid his wand into the specialized holster he had crafted for it, protecting it from the harms of combat, while allowing easy access from its position on his hip. "I am more than adequately armed, my friend," he said with a smile.

"Well... okay," she finally relented, sliding the device onto her hand.

The magic it contained was even greater than she'd anticipated, and only now that it was hers to control could she feel the slaap's true potential. It was a tool of great power, and in the right hands, it would spell the end of many.

"I'll get it back to you in one piece," she said. "Promise."

Again, the Wampeh grinned. "This is not a loan."

"What? No. There's no way I could possibly––"

"A warrior deserves a warrior's tools. And you are most certainly a warrior," he said warmly. "Now, come. Let's get you familiar with it while we are still on distant shores, where our enemy will not sense its use."

Rika looked at Charlie, realizing just what a big deal this was. For a Wampeh Ghalian to part with one of his weapons in this manner was unheard of. Her friend gave her a little nod, accompanied by a happy grin. Leila was smiling as well. Rika, it seemed, had––at long last––gained Bawb's approval. And more than that, she'd gained his trust.

"Well, if you insist," she relented.

As she said the words, Bawb uttered an incantation under his breath. Something very old, and very arcane. Rika felt the power from the device latch onto her viscerally, bonding the slaap to her and her alone.

"What did you just do?"

"A particular weapon, that one," he replied. "A warrior's tool. Powerful. Deadly. And it would not do to have your own weapon used against you, would it?"

"You bonded it to me?"

"Yes. And while it would possibly still respond to me as its original master of so many years, this slaap is now linked to you alone. And should another attempt to wield it against you, great harm will befall them by their own hand."

Charlie grinned. "It's like the *gallen* spell I had on my weapons when I was a pirate."

Bawb nodded. "Yes, it is similar in the most basic of ways. Though this is specialized, striking down any who wield it besides its owner, whereas a *gallen* merely prevents one from harming one's comrades with their weapon."

"Right. So you don't have any 'same side' problems," Ripley said. "Friendly fire, though I still don't get how they call it that. Shit's anything but friendly, if you ask me."

Rika laughed at their young friend. "I'm with you on that," she said. "But come on. I want to try this thing out."

The group followed her outside, a noticeable spring in her step.

"You did good, man. I haven't seen her this happy since we got here."

"Yes, she does approve of the gift," Bawb replied. "Though it was more to prepare her for the impending combat than to simply lift her spirits."

Rika called up one of the most basic force spells and cast at a thick oak tree nearby in an overgrown park. She expected to perhaps knock a small branch from the sturdy tree. Or maybe even one of the thicker ones.

The tree exploded in a blast of force, reduced to pieces no larger than toothpicks.

"Hooooly..." She gasped, looking at the weapon on her hand in disbelief.

Bawb chuckled. "It may take a bit of getting used to," he noted. "And this is why I wanted you to try it out now, when we are not in the thick of battle."

"Holy shit, Bawb. It's so powerful!"

"Yes, it is. That slaap will never disappoint you with a lack of power. However, learning to control that power and rein it in will be the challenge for you. At first, that is. I have no doubts you will master this tool quickly."

Rika held up the slaap, admiring its lines once more, feeling the power flowing through it. "*Kika rahm,*" she cast, knocking a small branch from a nearby tree with precision.

"As I said," the Wampeh said with great pleasure. "You will indeed master this quickly."

"She's good with that thing," Charlie said with admiration.

"Yes, she is," Rika laughed. "Now, come on. Let's go kick some alien ass!" She smiled playfully at Bawb. "No offense."

CHAPTER FORTY-NINE

Getting a force ready on UK soil was far easier than Charlie had anticipated. For one, there had been plenty of lead time from the initial attack to the present retaliation. Additionally, the people of that isle had always had a bit of a fearsome bent—something that had been reflected in the AIs inhabiting the region.

When the attack had first occurred, it had been the UK cyborgs who had immediately volunteered to go and kick the arse of whoever it was that needed kicking. They'd been talked down by Vic and the other AIs in the region, as they simply had no idea who was to blame. Also lacking was a convenient address at which to deliver said arse-kicking.

But now, with a full-fledged engagement being planned, it was with great joy that the cybernetic men and women armed themselves with pulse rifles and prepared to have it out with their planet's invaders.

"No bagpipes?" a particularly zealous cybernetic man named Connor grumbled. "Och, what's the point if ye cannae march ta war with yer pipes?"

He'd been a regional tourism assistant back before the Great

War, and his programming had included some of the more colorful aspects of Northern life, from the brogue down to a love of the shrill wind instrument of the region.

"The point is stealth, Connor," Charlie had told him for the umpteenth time as they gathered their forces and went over the plan of action.

The advance team of Bawb, Charlie, Leila, and Rika, would sneak to the perimeter of the suspected zone of alien activity. From there, Bawb would stalk and eliminate three of the Tslavar troops, hiding the bodies and commandeering their shimmer cloaks. Once he'd provided them to the others, the four of them would then take up a position close to the downed ship.

The cyborgs, meanwhile, would split into three groups. The main body would take up positions just in from the shoreline, where the most likely route for the arriving ships would be. They'd then do what machines could do so much better than humans. They'd sit perfectly still.

With their flesh coverings providing them all the camouflage they needed, they would blend in with the other immobile people in the area by simply freezing in place. Once the Tslavar ships had passed and the coast was clear, they would then set up their heavy weapons to intercept the ships when they tried to escape.

The final group would set up for an assault on the ground forces guarding the *Asbrú*, providing a distraction, while the small, shimmer-cloaked team located the leaders of the Tslavar forces and eliminated them.

It wasn't pretty, and they'd likely fall under some pretty heavy fire, but the cyborgs were game for an attempt nonetheless. Charlie and his friends were heartened by the show of confidence, their own rising to meet that of their new comrades.

"You ready for this?" Charlie asked as they quietly trekked

close to their starting point, having been dropped off by Eddie well away from range of his being spotted.

"I shall forge ahead," Bawb said.

"Great. We'll keep an eye out for you."

"You need not," he grinned. "You will never see me coming."

With that, he slid the hood of his shimmer cloak over his head and vanished.

"How does he do that?" Connor the cyborg asked, amazed at the disappearing trick.

"Just a thing he does," Charlie replied as the rest of his small group started creeping forward. "Okay, you guys, stay back and fall into position. When we signal, start the assault."

"Got it," Connor said with an excited look in his eye.

"Is he carrying an axe?" Rika asked.

"Yeah, that he is," Charlie replied.

Something tells me we might have to keep an eye on this guy, Charlie mused with a little chuckle as they set off.

The trio covered the distance to the area the *Asbrú* had landed in good time, despite the extra precautions they were forced to take to prevent accidental discovery. They stayed well off the rabbit-established trails, instead, sticking to the rabbit tracks that wove between the trees, staying low as they made their approach.

"We're getting close," Rika said, pointing to the broken treetops that signaled they had arrived at the area of the ship's final descent.

Charlie and Leila had noted the same thing, crouching even lower than previously as they strained their ears for the slightest sound of their stealthy adversaries.

"You'll be wanting these," Bawb said, sliding his shimmer hood off as he stepped away from a tree he'd been perfectly camouflaged against.

In his hands were three shimmer cloaks. And he'd even been so polite as to have wiped the traces of blood off of them.

"Already?" Charlie said with an appreciative look.

The deadly Wampeh just smiled and handed them each a shimmer cloak.

"Damn, he *is* good," Rika said with admiration.

"Don't tell him that. It'll go to his already enormous head," Charlie joked.

"I can hear you both, you know," the assassin said, amused. "Now, don your cloaks and follow my lead. I shall drag a small thread in my wake that you may see my path."

"How many Tslavars are there, Bob?"

"I couldn't tell for certain. But, Charlie, it would appear there are far more than we originally anticipated. And there's something going on close to your ship."

"I don't like the sound of that, Bob. Something like what?"

"I cannot say for certain. I procured the cloaks and doubled back as quickly as I was able. But I am certain whatever they are doing is of consequence."

"Then we need to get in close and find out what it is," Leila said. "Right, Charlie?"

He was both proud and amused by his queen's enthusiasm for the dangerous mission. Of the four of them, she was by far the least trained, but she was holding her own, and making a good showing of it in the process.

"Yeah, that sounds like the logical next step," Charlie agreed. "Lead on, Bob. We'll be right behind you."

"I will take us in a pattern that avoids their cloaked troops. I could teach you to spot them yourselves, but with the quality of these shimmers, it would simply take too much time."

"Later, then," Rika said. "For now, at least, lead the way."

The four of them crept silently ahead, Bawb taking point, the finest of threads dragging from beneath his shimmer cloak, allowing the others to follow a few paces behind.

SCOTT BARON

Charlie, Leila, and Rika were moving as a unit, one hand on the person in front of them on their lower back, the contact keeping them in a tight formation but also preventing them from tripping over one another and blowing their cover.

"What the hell are they doing?" Rika gasped when the clearing beside the ship came into view.

What appeared to be a powerful caster—possibly even an emmik or minor visla—was standing beside the *Asbrú*, chanting a steady stream of magic words, drawing power from themselves, as well as the rays of the planet's sun and pouring it into the casting. The ship seemed to even be glowing a little from all the magic in the air.

"Oh, shit," Charlie hissed as he realized what was going on.

"What is it?" Leila asked in a hushed voice.

"That guy isn't generating a new spell. He's adding to the ones already on the ship. Remember all of the Ootaki hair woven throughout the entire hull?"

"I fear Charlie is correct," Bawb said. "And given the sheer quantity they possess, this changes things rather drastically."

"Meaning?" Rika asked.

"Meaning we must stop whatever they are doing, and immediately," he replied.

Charlie agreed, and given their element of surprise, plus the sheer power of the weapons they had at their disposal, he thought they actually stood a good chance. If only Ara were with them, it would be even better.

Then he sensed her, just on the periphery of his mind, but growing stronger by the second.

"They're here," he said. "Fuck. I can sense Ara. That means the Tslavar ships are going to make landfall any minute."

"Then there is no time to waste. If they reinforce their ranks, we may not have another opportunity," Bawb said.

"It's not the plan," Rika pointed out.

"No, it isn't. But if they have another high-level caster aboard those ships, we won't be able to stop them," Charlie said, activating his comms bud in his ear. "Attention, all forces. Change of plans. There is an urgent situation. The Tslavar craft are almost here, and a situation has arisen. All forces engage immediately. Draw the enemy from the ship."

Charlie's command was met not with vocal affirmation, but rather, the heart-warming sound of pulse rifle fire as the cybernetic forces charged from their positions. The Tslavar troops, despite their camouflage, were taken by surprise. They'd made the mistake of complacency, believing themselves unobserved and secure. The first of them to fall informed the rest of the error of their thinking in the form of an explosion of green gore from the hole in his chest.

A battle broke out into full force, the magic-wielding aliens rushing into the tree line to engage the hostile natives. It was a blender of pulse blasts, magic, and the occasional plasma burst rained down from above as the smaller ships made strafing runs on the alien ground forces.

"Yeah!" Charlie exclaimed quietly as he observed from beneath his cloak.

The Tslavar mercenaries were driven back momentarily by the sheer force of the unexpected attack, but then they regrouped, pushing back with surprising resilience. And much to Charlie's horror, he realized the other two ships had arrived and were already dumping their forces from their holds and onto the battlefield.

The ships above continued to fire, but the Tslavar casters had adapted yet again. Apparently, they'd managed to revise their defenses since the battle in Long Beach, and they were now passing the new spell through the ranks.

Within minutes, the pulse rifles were nearly as useless as the conventional ones had become, and the plasma bursts from the air were likewise being batted aside with relative ease.

"We're here," Ara called out to her friend.

"I noticed. Where are you?"

"Just a minute behind them. They were moving faster than I could fly within the atmosphere. It was all I could do to keep them close enough to track."

"Well, they've got a new trick," Charlie said. "They can block the pulse and plasma weapons now."

"This does not bode well."

"No, it doesn't. Do you think they're still susceptible to your flames?"

A familiar shadow flashed overhead. "Only one way to find out."

"Just remember, steer clear of the Asbrú. With their fail-safe, any hit to the ship might cause it to go off."

Ara did not hesitate, dropping into a dive right at the Tslavar ships. Flames erupted from her mouth, engulfing the craft. But while her attack had landed squarely on the two vessels, both seemed to have remained unscathed. Their magical defenses had been shifted against her particular type of magic as well.

"Oh, this is not good," Charlie said. "This is not good at all."

CHAPTER FIFTY

Bawb and Charlie cast together, the Wampeh leading the human in the very specific spell. "Rika, Leila, come join us," he urged. "We need more power."

The two women quickly ran to their friends, took in the words to the spell and their function, and joined in the casting. Their addition was not perfect by any means––they hadn't the time to practice and perfect the spell––but the additional power was enough for Bawb's purposes.

Previously, Ara had incinerated every scrap of the invaders and their tools, but now, having captured several of the invaders' shimmer cloaks intact, the Wampeh was in possession of precisely what he needed to work a counterspell. He knew the shape of their magic.

It would make the wearers *mostly* visible, while not alerting them to the fall of their camouflage. So long as you wore the shimmer, you would not notice your own comrades around you. Only in shedding it would they realize their clever defense had been defeated.

The spell burst out, the wave of power catching the attention of a few of those mercenaries more attuned to such things, but with no visible effect. They ignored it and kept fighting.

To the small squad and their cyborg forces, however, it was suddenly a target-rich environment. One at which they began firing with great accuracy.

Unfortunately, and much to their surprise, the majority of their targets were unfazed by the barrage.

"Why are the plasma rounds suddenly not working?" Leila shouted out over the increasing din of battle as she fired off a futile shot at the Tslavar in front of her before discarding the rifle for the sword on her back.

"They have adapted," Bawb said, plainly as they charged into the fray. "And so shall we."

He then did something a bit unexpected, heaving his useless pulse rifle toward the powerful man casting his spell, ramping up the magic within the downed *Asbrú*, while safely ensconced in his magical protections.

"Give me your rifles," he told the others, snatching them up and throwing them along with the others.

Being a lobbed projectile, each had merely bounced off of the man's magical shielding, the way a metal bullet would have been, but at a much lower velocity. The effect was that each of the weapons had landed at the exact same place when the magic stopped them and dropped them to the ground.

"Perfect," Bawb said with a smile.

"What about the emmik?" Charlie asked as he disarmed—literally—a charging Tslavar whose shimmer had been disrupted. "His spell won't even let us get close."

"We do not have to," Bawb replied. "Oh, and this is a visla," he added. "A lower-tier one, I believe. In any case, a potent power user."

Charlie saw the look in his friend's eye. They'd kill the man if they had to, but not before he sucked his power from him, if he could. Doing so would allow the Wampeh to use the incredibly rare talent he bore, that of draining another's power by drinking their blood. It would not only provide Bawb with an incredible amount of power to tap into, in addition to his Ootaki-powered armor, but would also leave the visla weak enough to be contained. That was, *if* they could somehow reach the man.

The visla, for his part, seemed unconcerned by the goings-on around him, focusing all of his attention at ramping up the spell already underway. Whatever he was up to, Charlie had a very bad feeling in his gut about it.

The two other Tslavar ships swung in, flanking the cyborg forces and dropping low, spewing out dozens of additional troops into the battle while simultaneously launching powerful spells into the sky, knocking the smaller ships from the air when the magical attacks flew true.

"Whatever you're going to do, do it quickly," Charlie shouted to the Wampeh.

"You'd best duck," Bawb told his friends as he slid a particularly sleek slaap onto his hand.

Charlie had seen him use this one before. It was a device used for longer-range attacks, capable of focusing a spell with pinpoint accuracy rather than the usual wide-reaching blast of power from a regular slaap.

Bawb blurted a single word under his breath––he had not quite mastered Ara's manner of silent casting yet––blasting forth a very specific spell. But rather than targeting the visla casting within his little shell of power, he landed a direct hit upon the pile of pulse rifles. The *fully charged* pulse rifles, to be precise.

The explosion of all four of them going up as their power cells were simultaneously overloaded despite the layers of safeties built into the devices was substantial. More importantly, it was a type of energy the invaders' shielding spells had not been designed to repel, and thus, were not entirely efficient at dissipating.

The visla was blown from his feet as the impact tore through the rear of his spell. The frontal portion managed to contain nearly all of the residual blast, keeping it from reaching the *Asbrú*'s hull. All around them, the Tslavars nearest the blast had been thrown like toy dolls.

"The path is clear," Bawb said with a satisfied grin as he pulled his wand from its holster. It was already beginning to glow with the brutal disabling spells on the tip of its owner's tongue. "Cover me. I shall incapacitate the caster while he is stunned."

He took off at a full sprint, Tslavar limbs and heads flying as he dispatched the dazed enemy mid-stride as he raced toward the visla before he could recover. The other mercenaries turned their attentions rearward, no longer focusing on the cyborgs, but rather the lone man at the rear of their lines.

"Leila, get on defensive spells with me!" Charlie called out. "Rika, throw them something nasty while we cover Bob's six!"

Rika already had the new slaap on her hand, its power begging to be unleashed. And unleash it she would, but this time, she was in control. A brutal wave of power attacks flashed out from the human, an attack the Tslavars had not been expecting. Quickly, they shifted to magical defenses, but not before several had been thrown through the air by the battering power unleashed into their midst.

Meanwhile, Leila and Charlie cast together, weaving their power as only connected beings were capable, feeding into each other's spells, blocking everything the mercenary forces threw their way.

Leila had always been a quick study, and it was defensive spells Charlie and Bawb had first drilled into her with mind-numbing repetition. And now that repetition paid off as she effortlessly shifted from one spell to the next, varying her defenses as needed to buy their friend the time he required.

Suddenly, a massive surge of magic hit their defensive shield, knocking Rika from her feet and forcing Charlie and Leila to their knees with its intensity. Another player was on the board, and they'd turned their attentions to the magic-wielding trio.

"That was massive," Charlie said, tasting blood in his mouth where he'd bitten his cheek. "A visla for sure."

Leila locked eyes with him, still casting as best as she could. But she knew as well as he did. They couldn't stop another visla in the middle of this battle. They'd be overwhelmed. And if *both* of the Tslavar ships possessed casters of this power, they were doomed.

The front hatch of the nearest Tslavar craft opened, its shimmer disrupted as well by the spell they'd cast. A tall, thin man stepped into the doorway, an air of power crackling around him.

So this is it, Charlie thought as he watched the visla pull power to him, focusing for his coup de grâce that would end their attempts once and for all.

Then, without warning, the man exploded into a mist of bone and blood. The rest of his ship, likewise, torn to pieces as holes silently appeared in its hull. Only a few seconds later did the sound waves of the projectiles reach them with a series of loud booms.

A moment later, the ship erupted in flames, engulfing the troops nearest, while the force of the blast knocked down those farther away.

"What the hell?" Charlie gasped in amazement. "Was that a freakin' rail gun?"

"If I didn't know any better, I'd swear that it was," Rika said, brushing a strand of sweaty hair from her eyes.

"Those weren't even fully functional in our time. And now? It's all pulse weapons. Where'd that come from? And who's shooting it?"

The other Tslavar ship didn't care *what* the attack was, only that it got the hell out of there, and fast. The power signature around the vessel surged as it spun on its axis and set off at top speed for the waterline. As fast as it was moving, and with its defenses tuned to pulse weapons, the waiting cyborgs on the shore would stand no chance of stopping it.

Eddie flashed down from above, his shiny new rail gun hurling hypersonic rounds into the remains of the downed ship for good measure.

"Hey, guys!" Ripley's excited voice called out over their comms. "Did you see that? How cool, right?"

"Rip, where'd you get a rail gun?" Rika asked as she fired a series of disabling spells at the remaining Tslavar mercenaries, giving the cyborgs a window in which to physically engage them.

"Uncle Cal had it pulled from mothballs for us. You know how those military guys are. They never seem to get rid of anything. So when all the weapons systems shifted to pulse and plasma tech, this baby just went into cold storage up on the moon."

"And now Eddie's sporting a freakin' rail gun," Charlie said with a grin. "Holy hell, that's fantastic."

"The other ship!" Leila called out. "It's at the shoreline."

"Shit. It's already underwater by now," Charlie groaned.

"Don't worry," Eddie said. "Ara lit it up again as it was fleeing, and her flames are still burning underwater for the moment, so I can target it. Unless it dives really deep really fast, I'm pretty sure my sabots will have no problem with a few hundred feet of water. Not at Mach six-plus."

The ship darted toward the coastline, and the sound of a volley of hypersonic rounds being launched into the water soon echoed from the shore. After a several-second pause, a great explosion followed, the sea churning from the blast.

"Got it," Ripley called out merrily over their comms.

With the destruction of both of their ships, the Tslavar mercenaries' spirit was broken. They would not be taken without a fight, though, and for the next twenty minutes, the battle continued as the cyborgs slowly mopped up the remaining invaders.

Though quarter was offered, none would accept defeat, opting instead to fight to the death. And so it was, the remains of the alien invasion ended at the hands of the denizens of Earth.

CHAPTER FIFTY-ONE

The man lying at Bawb's feet was an orangish hue, his hair likewise veering toward the red scale of the spectrum, but something closer to the color of old bricks. He was of indeterminate age, and was well muscled within his finery. A man of action, it seemed. And one of great power as well.

Ara had laid a heavy restraining spell upon the unconscious man when Bawb, lips still red with fresh blood, had carried him from the battlefield.

"How was he?" Charlie asked. He was not inquiring about the man's physical state.

"Powerful," Bawb said, licking his lips, the stolen power heavy in his veins. "*Very* powerful. Even as I was draining him, he fought back and nearly bested me."

"I didn't think people could do that once you got your teeth into them."

"Normally, they cannot. Only the most powerful of beings are able to resist my kind's natural effect and resist even as we take their power. He is exceptionally strong, Charlie. And dangerous."

"Obviously. I think all of their casters are. Or *were*, I should say."

"Yes, I saw the aftermath of the new weapon our AI friend is carrying," the assassin said with an approving grin. "The sheer velocity of those projectiles overpowered even the most heavily layered defensive spells as if they were but paper walls trying to shield their ship from the onslaught."

"Rail gun tech," Rika chimed in. "Hypersonic sabots that travel at many times the speed of sound. The rounds themselves aren't explosive, but the shockwave generated by their impact and path as they tear through a target causes a rather catastrophic reaction, as you saw."

"We need more weapons like that," Leila said. "Do they make them smaller? Like, a size we could carry?"

"I don't know. Charlie, any insights?"

"Beats the hell out of me. But we'll ask Eddie when he and Rip get back from their mop-up flight with the others. From what I gathered, this was a one-off, but maybe Cal can work up something for us now that we know how effective it was."

The bound man at their feet shifted position.

"Our guest is regaining consciousness," Bawb said.

"Shouldn't we gag him?" Rika asked. "I mean, a caster as powerful as that, right here in our midst could be a very bad thing."

Bawb was unconcerned. "I have drained his power, Rika. Despite his best efforts, he should not be able to cast." He turned his attention to the enormous red dragon crouched beside them, observing the orange-skinned man. "Ara, do keep a close eye on him, though, would you, please?"

"Of course, Geist," she replied with a toothy grin.

"Geist?" their captive said. "Funny, you should take your moniker from such a legendary assassin. You should consider yourself fortunate he has been dead for nearly a thousand years, or he might take umbrage at your use of his name."

"Oh, didn't he tell you?" Charlie said, leaning in close, but not *too* close. "This *is* the Geist."

"Impossible. Even a Wampeh of his abilities has his limitations. The Geist is long dead."

"Yeah, well, time travel's a funny thing like that. So what you've got here isn't a thousand-year-old remnant of the man, but rather, the real deal, deadliest assassin in thirty systems, in his prime."

"Thirty?" their captive said with an amused grin. "Far more than that, I assure you."

Bawb turned to Charlie and shrugged. "I told you so."

"Oh, shut up, Bob. You know what I meant." Charlie turned his attention back to the orange visla. "So, you seem to know my friend here. Then I'm sure you've also heard of our friend Aranzgrgghmunatharrgle, here, as well."

Their captive, despite his best efforts at maintaining an aloof and indifferent expression, nevertheless betrayed a look of shock at the name. Once, he might have commented that the great Aranzgrgghmunatharrgle had died over a millennia ago, but given the revelations of this day on the battlefield, he felt it wise to hold his tongue.

The Zomoki was the right kind, and her coloring matched that of legend. And if she had indeed survived so much longer than any believed, her size, and power, would logically have increased. And she was a big girl, for sure. And now that he recognized the origin of the power weighing down upon him, he realized the true might of the creature casually looming over him.

He glanced at Leila and Rika, the weakest of the group, magically speaking, and uttered a short, guttural phrase. The magical restraints surged around him, snuffing out his feeble attempt.

"What was that, Ara?"

"A killing spell," she replied. "Incredibly weak. My restraints dissipated it before it reached its target, though given his weakened state, I doubt the spell would have done any real harm."

"Fascinating," Bawb said. "Even after my draining him of his power, he still retains the ability to cast. I must admit, I am impressed. You are a truly powerful being, my friend. Perhaps I should have gagged you after all," he said with a wry grin. "But that is of no matter now. What is of interest is, what are you doing here on this planet? Why have you come, and to what end are you freezing the planet's populace?"

The visla looked at his captors, his shoulders drawing back as he rose to his full height, head held high. There was no fear in his eyes, only defiance. "If you think for one moment I am going to––"

A moment later, he lay dead on the ground.

"What the hell just happened, Bob? We needed to question him! What did you do?"

"I did nothing, Charlie. You were standing right here with me."

"Well, he was alive just a minute ago. So what killed him?"

Ara bent down, sniffing the air near the visla's body. "Kill switch," she said with a disgusted sort. "An automatically activating suicide spell."

"Of course," Bawb said. "Now it makes sense."

"Uh, guys? What makes sense?"

"His reaction to us. And why he was focused on just one task while a full battle raged around him," Bawb said. "We didn't have the time to discern if he was an actual leader of these forces, or merely a tool."

"Someone that powerful? I'd bet he'd be nobody's tool," Charlie noted.

"Unless that someone was even more powerful that he," Bawb posited. "And I would wager this man was not even aware he had been saddled with a kill-switch spell. More likely, it was quietly placed upon him by whoever is *really* running this show. And the ability to do that means they are a caster of rare abilities." He turned his gaze on the body at his feet. "But in any case, there will be no questioning this one. Which was likely the point of the spell."

Charlie looked at the staring eyes of the man now dead on the ground. He had been so cocky. So sure of himself. And now, someone even more powerful than he had snuffed his lights out in an instant. And all to keep him from talking.

"What was he doing?" he wondered aloud.

"He was tapping into the Ootaki hair woven within the structure of the ship. That much we are certain of," Bawb said.

"Yeah, I know. But I mean, to what end? Like, the entire population is already frozen, right?"

"Yes," Bawb agreed.

"And they've shown absolutely no sign of thawing out, or whatever you call it when the spell wears off, right?"

"Correct again," Ara said. "I think I see where you are going with this, Charlie."

"I figured you would. It seems obvious that something bigger is at play here. Something that needs the Ootaki hair bound to the *Asbrú*'s frame to be at full-power. And that's what this guy was doing. He wasn't casting a new spell, or reinforcing the one that's already here. Hell, even depleted, the hair was more than capable of maintaining the stasis hold on everyone on the planet. So what was he doing?"

The implications were staggering. Charlie was right. The power pulled from the Ootaki hair and fueling the spell was a drop in the bucket of the golden locks' potential, now that the original spell had been cast. But the bulk of their massive power had been spent getting the *Asbrú* there in the first place. Ripping a hole in space to deposit it in Earth's atmosphere.

"Oh, this is not good," Ara said, shifting her weight and rushing to the downed ship.

She sniffed deeply, picking apart the scents of the layers of spells tied to the ship's hidden magical power source. She recognized several, having encountered variants over the previous few days, but there was something else there. Something more. Something growing rapidly stronger as the Ootaki hair greedily sucked in the planet's sun's energy.

"He used his own power to spark a reaction within the Ootaki hair," the mighty Zomoki gasped. "And now there is no stopping its absorption of your sun's power."

"Right, we know the sun here supercharges Ootaki hair— and you too, for that matter."

"No, Charlie. This is different. The visla used himself to make the process jump into a rapid cascade of power."

Suddenly it was clear to the human. "He kickstarted the process with his own power. Sonofa... Okay, what does this mean, Ara? That's gonna be an utterly massive amount of magic this thing eventually releases. Do you know what it's for?"

"Unfortunately, I do," she replied. "The smell of this magic, I knew it was familiar. It just took me a while to remember."

"Remember what, exactly?"

"Why I know it," she replied. "This magic smells almost identical to the forces that brought us here as we fled the Council of Twenty. They're using this ship to create a portal to my galaxy."

"Oh, shit," Charlie said. "But is that even possible? I mean, it is, obviously, but what good is a tiny gateway? Why send a handful of ships to scout out a planet this size?"

"Because, thanks to your sun's unusual powers, with this much Ootaki hair, supercharged with power as this visla has done to it, the result will be a self-sustaining power source, replenishing itself instantly from your sun's rays."

"So there will be no depletion of power?" Leila asked.

"No. Or minimal, at most," Ara replied.

A very bad feeling settled into Charlie's stomach. He knew

what the Tslavars had been doing. What they planned to do. He turned to his friends, a horrified look on his face.

"Guys, I know what they're doing."

"What, Charlie?" Rika asked.

"They're not preparing for a scouting mission. They're preparing for a full-fledged invasion."

CHAPTER FIFTY-TWO

"How long?" Charlie asked, his face ashen. "It's got to need time to fully charge, right?"

Ara sniffed the air, weighing the forces at work. "A few weeks at most. Likely less."

"Fuck." He sat there silently for a long moment. "Is there anything we can do?"

"I'm afraid not. The portal powered by the Ootaki hair will open, and there is nothing we can do about it. And this is no small thing."

"What do you mean?" Charlie asked, his concern growing.

"I mean, this portal spell is massive in power. If it successfully opens, craft far larger than the *Asbrú* could easily pass through it. And the sun is giving it all the energy it needs."

Leila began pacing. "There has to be something. Can't we mute the power somehow?"

"Believe me, Leila, I wish it were not so, but this craft has layers upon layers of fail-safes guarding it. Complex, deadly spells designed by powerful casters. Vislas, all of them, from what I can sense. And the power being directed to the spell freezing the population is massive. And that is dwarfed by the portal spell being created."

"But every spell has a means to be countered. To be undone," Leila said.

"Of course. But we simply do not have the time to pick through all of the layers, especially with these booby-trap spells peppered throughout the casting. For something of this complexity and power it could take us months, which is likely how long it took to create this amalgam of power in the first place. And we simply do not have that long."

Bawb walked to the *Asbrú* and ran his hand along the smooth metal of its hull. "All of that effort, yet the spells have not restricted us from access to the vessel, it would seem. Most curious."

"There was no need," Ara replied. "With the magic already in place, the craft is perfectly safe from meddling. So long as no one tampers with the Ootaki hair, and the spells it is feeding, those fail-safes will remain dormant. Any attempt to disrupt them, however, and the results could range from damaging to catastrophic."

"But we *can* board it. Move it. Do whatever we want, for the most part. But if we touch the magic layers we're screwed," Rika said.

"More or less," Ara said.

Rika looked long and hard at her former ship. The craft she'd been second-in-command of before they were sucked through a wormhole, starting them off on their unlikely path that led them to this moment.

"Can it be contained?" she finally asked. "The fail-safe spell, I mean."

"No. I'm afraid it is far too powerful. And so far as I can tell, even if it were possible to negate the destructive forces of the fail-safe spell and somehow keep the planet's atmosphere from being destroyed, the act of doing so would still cause a fatal surge in one of the *other* spells. The one freezing the population. I cannot be certain, but it appears quite likely they would all perish in an instant."

"You mean in addition to the whole losing-the-atmosphere thing," Rika grumbled. "Sonofa––"

Bawb's jaw flexed as he thought of Hunze, still frozen in their home. He desperately wanted a physical course of action. Something he could do to further their cause. But instead, he was powerless, just like the others.

Charlie circled the *Asbrú*, taking his time as he made his way around the massive craft. It was odd, seeing something he'd spent so much time focused on, then forgotten as his life took a U-turn, only to find it in front of him once again. He walked to the doorway leading into the ship's hull, where he paused, his hand resting lightly on the doorframe.

"Where ya going?" Rika asked.

"I'm not really sure. But I'm out of ideas here, and I don't know. Maybe this will jolt my brain into a flash of brilliance. Who knows, right?"

Rika chuckled. "Yeah, a walk down memory lane and you'll suddenly become mega brain Charlie, huh?"

"Beats standing around. Anyway, I'll be back soon," he said, then stepped into the ship he was instrumental in building all those years ago. Leila watched him go, wanting to accompany him, to help soothe his agitated mind, but she knew him well enough by now to know he needed some space. Some time to think.

Charlie inhaled deeply, the dusty smell of a craft long-abandoned in the harsh wasteland still in the air, despite the recent inhabitants who had walked these buckled hallways.

Judging by the damage, the invading forces hadn't done anything further to the interior of the ship since it had first landed––at least, not so far as he could tell. There were muddy bootprints, but aside from that, it all seemed the same as when they first surveyed the scene.

Except for the buzzing feel of magic all around him, of course. That was new, but he was well aware it was the secret power store running within the ship's walls that was giving off the trace magic.

Charlie walked deeper into the craft, passing the remnants of the old command center, and even making a loop through the cargo bay that had once held Rika's mech, now long abandoned to the sands of the Balamar wasteland.

The ship was still as much a wreck as it had been when he had left it on those barren sands in a distant galaxy so long ago. Sure, the Tslavar force had rebuilt the exterior and made the ship more or less sound, but they hadn't made even a cursory attempt at restoring the ship's systems.

Not that the tech-ignorant aliens could have done so if they'd wanted. Theirs was a magic-based system, and the *Asbrú* was not of their worlds. They couldn't fix her, and she'd never fly again. At least, not by her own power.

Instead, Ootaki hair––now highly charged Ootaki hair, at that––was woven throughout the ship's hull, magically powering the craft from tip to tail. It was incredible, the amount of power that quantity of the magic-storing hair could channel into the craft.

And with the Earth's sun providing a steady stream of magical energy, renewing the power of the hair with every ray, it was very likely that there would be no way to break the cycle. To break the link.

"Hang on a minute," Charlie said as a realization dawned on him. His voice sounding strange to his ears in the eerie silence of the dead ship's walls. "Why the failsafe? Why threaten to destroy Earth if they already had the power to do so?" Gears were turning in his head as things became clearer.

Charlie raced through the wrecked ship, careful not to fall

through the weakened areas of flooring where the metal was still weak. He darted out into the fresh air, a wild look in his eye.

"What is it?" Leila asked, a flash of concern crossing her face. "Is everything okay?"

Charlie was beside himself with his revelation. "Look, I was thinking. If this really is an invasion, then they have no desire to destroy the planet. So why the freezing spell?"

"Because they needed to neutralize the locals. To keep the fighting to a minimum," Rika said.

"But they could neutralize them by killing them, right? But they didn't. They froze everyone and just left them there."

"Ah, I see what Charlie is getting at," Bawb said. "And a valid point."

"Which is?" Rika asked.

"That they are planning on subjugating the populace, not killing them."

"Exactly!" Charlie agreed emphatically. "And if they really are coming here to conquer the planet, then they are planning on using the population as assets. Slaves or servants. But whatever it will be, that means there has to be a way to shut it off. It would be the only way they could use these people."

"Hmm, a very interesting take on things," Ara said as she considered his points. She fixed her gaze squarely upon her friend. "Are you thinking what I'm thinking?"

"You know it," Charlie replied with a grin. "We need to talk to Cal."

CHAPTER FIFTY-THREE

"I suppose it could work," Cal said over Eddie's external speakers, making it possible for Ara to participate in the discussion––the giant dragon could certainly not fit inside his passenger compartment. Nor would she want to.

"And your other AI counterparts?" Ara asked. "What is their opinion on this plan? We wish to unfreeze just one victim, but we will not proceed without the full agreement of the parties overseeing the planet's well-being. And that would be you and your friends."

"Which is greatly appreciated, Ara. However, even if there were a dissenting member, I think we can all agree that these are extenuating circumstances and extreme measures must be risked if there is any possibility they can make a difference."

"What Ara is proposing should not be risky," Bawb noted. "At least, not if we manage to craft the right counterspell."

"How does that even work?" Ripley asked, bouncing impatiently on her toes. "I thought you said you couldn't cast anything against the spell already being pumped out by the hair-filled ship."

"Yes and no," Bawb replied. "You see, we cannot directly

attack that spell with anything overtly hostile. That would cause either the fail-safe to engage and destroy the planet's atmosphere––"

"Which would be bad," Charlie noted.

"*Or*, it would cause the frozen people to either perish or become trapped in their state of stasis permanently."

"Also bad," Rika added, throwing Charlie an amused wink.

Even Bawb chuckled slightly. "In any case, we now possess something of an advantage, stemming from my experience aboard the Tslavar ship. There was residual magic from the un-freezing process. I could faintly smell it on the dazed prisoners––though how best we can utilize that observation I was not entirely certain. But from what Ara has told me, we may have an option, Cal. Is that correct?"

"*Yes. I've been looking into the way your magic casting functions, after the successful neuro-stim transfer of a spell from Ara to Rika and Ripley. The sending out of the information to the recipients was straightforward enough, though novel at the time. The downloading and parsing of the spells themselves, however...well, that was the more difficult aspect.*"

"Wait, do you mean you can actually pull traces of someone else's magic from Bob's memories?" Charlie asked. "Something we can use to crack this spell? Is that even possible?"

"*We do not know for certain, Charlie. However, with Ara's help, I believe there is a decent possibility she may be able to aid our AI collective in identifying the precise portion of the memory that would be of use in this instance. Then, if I am not mistaken, she could re-work the spell, taking the fragments from Bawb's memory and restoring it with her own knowledge of these arcane skills. But only if the casting was going on nearby.*"

"But the booby traps––"

"Not if we are using their own magic against them, Charlie," Ara said. "Obviously, I cannot recreate their actual spell this way, but I can get a good *feel* for the magic behind its creation. With that, I can then cast a spell that their safeguards would sense as non-threatening. While it would not be entirely of their origin, I think enough of a similar magic woven into my spell *should* keep their defenses from activating."

"Should?"

"Well, nothing is one hundred percent in this sort of thing. But I am fairly confident we can make it work."

"Hang on a minute," Leila interrupted. "You're talking about casting a complex spell from a trace of one tucked away in a memory. But what if there was something more tangible you could use as well?"

"By tangible, what exactly are you talking about, Leila?" Ara asked with curiosity.

"The slain prisoners. The ones cut down by the Tslavars during Bawb's escape have been sitting in a cooling facility to be stored and eventually studied. They may be dead, and the rest of us do not possess any skills that might allow us to glean any additional information from them. But you're different, Ara. You can sniff out magic."

Ripley saw where her olive-skinned friend was going with that. "Oh my God, yes! I totally get it! Wouldn't those bodies still retain the distinctive smell of the magic that was used to release them from their stasis spell?"

Ara sat up a bit straighter. It *was* a clever idea, and in conjunction with the audacious plan she, Cal, and Bawb had devised, that might just be the thing that put them over the top. That is, if the bodies still retained traces of that particular bit of the Tslavar magic.

In any case, it was worth a try. And with their adversaries routed and sent to their makers, they at least possessed the one thing lacking in the past several frantic days.

Time.

"I will fly to Los Angeles immediately," Ara said. "But I will require Bawb to accompany me. Cal's facilities are already prepared for the linkage, and I feel confident, based on my previous experience with the machine, that I can help him and the other AIs pinpoint the information locked in Bawb's memory. And once we have that, we can prepare for the next step."

"You mean turning this thing off?" Ripley said.

"Oh, nothing so hasty," Ara said. "First we must make certain the reversal spell even works. And for that, we will need a test subject."

"Plenty of those lying around," Charlie said.

He looked at Bawb. The conflict in his friend was plain to see. Here he was, trying to reverse the very magic that was keeping Hunze trapped, and they were going to need a guinea pig to test it on. Of course the urge to free his golden-haired love was fierce, but Bawb was also practical, no matter how much it hurt.

"There is risk," Bawb said as plainly as though nothing was troubling him. "I suggest we first attempt the process on a prisoner."

"We do not experiment on our prisoners, Bawb. And besides, after the Great War, the focus has been on rehabilitation and return to society."

"Be that as it may, surely there are some who would be more suitable for this test than valued citizens?"

Cal was silent a long moment.

"Perhaps there is someone who fits your criteria."

CHAPTER FIFTY-FOUR

Eddie and Rip provided Bawb a much-needed lift back to Los Angeles, where he and Ara would immediately get working on their plan. He'd have just as soon flown there on his giant red friend's back, but without his space suit, the ballistic orbit of her flight would have been rather uncomfortable. As in, freeze-to-death uncomfortable.

So it was that he bummed a ride with an overly curious and exuberant teen, and her wet-behind-the-ears ship. It made for an interesting flight, but one that, fortunately, did not last too long.

"Oh, we're here already?" Ripley said, taking a breath from her incessant chatter.

"Yes, it would appear so," Bawb replied, anxious to get off the ship and get started having the AIs poke around in his head.

It would undoubtedly be more relaxing than listening to all of the teen's theories about Tslavars and magic and space travel. Ever since she had received her neuro-stim upload of magical casting ability, her mind had been racing with the what-if's and how-about's of her new knowledge.

And it was exhausting.

"I greatly appreciate the ride," Bawb said as he disembarked.

"Oh, yeah. No problem!" Ripley replied. "You know, if you want, I bet I could help Uncle Cal with some of the––"

"But don't you need to visit the fabrication labs to have your weapons assessed and reloaded? I thought that was first on your list, was it not, Eddie?"

"Yeah, he's right, Rip. We really should get over there and get that taken care of ASAP. Wouldn't want to have to miss out on *another* battle because we're in dry dock."

"Shit, you're right. Thanks, Bawb. Good lookin' out."

"It is my pleasure, Ripley. And thanks again to you both for bringing me to Los Angeles. It is greatly appreciated."

"No worries, dude," she chirped. "Okay, Eddie. You ready to get that new toy tuned up and reloaded?"

"You know it, Rip. See you later, Bawb."

"Safe travels, Eddie," the Wampeh said as he watched the ship lurch skyward.

"She can be a bit much at times," Cal said when Eddie was out of sight. *"But she's a good kid, and she and Eddie have proven their worth on more than one occasion."*

"Yes, they are valued members of our team, no doubt. Now, where do you need me to go, Cal? I understand you have already rigged up a device suitable for Ara."

"Indeed. We made a modified neuro-stim band that would not only fit her head, but also accommodate her most unusual brainwaves."

"She is a Zomoki. One of the oldest. It is only logical that she would function a bit outside of your normal parameters, I'd think," Bawb said with a little grin. "But as for this much smaller being now standing before you, where exactly would you like me to go?"

Cal directed him to a nearby building, where they had set up a feed running from Ara's outdoor setup to the massively modified neuro device that would attempt to allow her access to the Wampeh's memories.

It would be far too dangerous to let her go traipsing willy-nilly through Bawb's mind, and the damage it could cause to both of them was a very real possibility. But with the help of the massive AI network channeling all of their spare processing power to this one task, the ancient dragon would be able to pick her way through a minute or so of her friend's memories without much risk.

Bawb slipped the neuro-stim band onto his head and leaned back in the reclining chair. "What do I do?"

"Just close your eyes and try to focus on the times when you were in closest proximity to the recently unfrozen captives. We will be relaying rough data to Ara throughout the process, and when a particular memory shows promise, we will focus in on it, allowing her to access that snippet in time."

There wasn't much more to worry about. It would work, or it wouldn't, so Bawb did as he was asked, closing his eyes and letting the strange tech-magic machine reach into his thoughts and memories. It took but an instant for him to feel the strange sensation of technology probing in his mind.

Normally, the process wouldn't have even been noticeable by the neuro wearer. But in Bawb's case, he had just absorbed an utterly massive amount of magical power from their captured visla, and that power afforded him an unusual experience within the device itself.

Ara's presence was there on the periphery. He could almost smell it, a musky magic just beyond sight.

So, this is what she means by smelling magic, he mused as he marveled at the merging of tech and magic.

As it turned out, the additional power he now had flowing in his veins worked both ways, and Ara was startled at just how clearly she could sense her friend's mind. His memories were clearer than she'd expected, as were the sights and smells contained therein.

"There! That one!" Ara called to the AIs monitoring the process. "Their caster was boosting their spell. That's the one we're looking for," she informed them, pinpointing the section of memory containing the magical signature she required.

It was far more complete than she expected it to be, Bawb's newfound power making the memory far sharper than anticipated. And with it, the smell of the spell that had freed the prisoners. It was there, dancing at the tip of her nose, almost familiar in its smoky aroma.

Cal and the others turned the full processing power of their combined systems to the lone task of isolating the identified data stream. What was a tangible memory to the Zomoki and Wampeh was perceived as pure data to the machines. Whatever the case, in a matter of seconds they had copied it and secured it to their storage facilities.

"We have what you needed," Cal informed them both. *"We have refined and cleaned the signal and are sending the information to you now, Ara."*

Bawb opened his eyes and removed the band from his head. The last thing he had felt while they had been in the shared neuro space was the effort it was taking for her to absorb the data. It was simply never designed to implant information in a brain of her nature, and the strain was palpable.

The Wampeh rose from his seat and took to the stairs, taking them two at a time as he rushed to the low building's rooftop where his friend lay, quietly working to assimilate the new spell.

He watched his Zomoki friend, her brow furrowed, eyes closed, as the band resting on her massive head struggled to transfer the data. Her own magic was crackling in the air, an instinctive reaction to her internal fight. She was dangerous to all around her without meaning to be, and if something went wrong, she could cause a lot of damage in an instant.

Bawb took a deep breath and concentrated, pulling up the stolen visla's magic from within. It was such a massive amount of power, he almost lost himself in it for a moment, overwhelmed by the sheer potency. But he was a Wampeh Ghalian, and in short order, he had his newfound power under control.

Focused. Harnessed. Standing by at the ready to help his friend, or protect the others. Whichever case arose, he would be prepared. He just hoped neither eventuality would come to pass.

Finally, several long minutes later, the weary dragon opened her golden eyes.

"Got it."

CHAPTER FIFTY-FIVE

The sight of an alien space vampire flying atop a giant red space dragon might not have been such an unusual occurrence in both of their distant galaxy, but for the cyborgs of London who were helping prepare their test subject, it was enough to cause their entirely electronic speech centers to stutter for a moment.

"That's a–that's a–that's a dragon!" the poor fellow guarding the street outside the Tower of London managed to stammer.

"Yes, Terry, that's a dragon," Charlie said with a little laugh. "And yes, that's a space vampire on her back," he added, sharing an amused look with Leila.

His queen had been practicing spells with Rika ever since they arrived in London. While both were tired from battle, a bit of casual magic work was both a soothing as well as bonding experience for them. Some women went on spa dates. These women devised new ways to wield their magic and toss people to-and-fro.

"You two okay?" Charlie asked. "Need anything?"

"We're good," Leila called back. "Just let us know when you're ready to begin."

"Will do," Charlie replied as he walked to meet his returning

SCOTT BARON

friends. "Hey, guys, Vic said things went okay in LA." He sized up his Zomoki friend. Ara looked a tiny bit tired, but the sun's rays had been replenishing her energy as she flew high above the cloud cover, popping into low orbit as she returned to the UK.

Bawb climbed down from her back, taking off the helmet to his space suit, conveniently retrieved while they were back in LA. The brief stopover had also given him a moment to check in on Hunze.

The golden-haired woman lay exactly where he'd left her. Untouched, unbothered, and unwaking. She was safe, which was his primary concern, but she was frozen in stasis as well.

"I see you have our test subject nearly ready," Bawb noted as he began unfastening the space suit closures. "Big one, isn't he?"

"Yeah. Apparently, he was one of the leaders of the Chithiid loyalist sect that fought against the humans and AIs in the Great War. Cal was telling me about it the other day."

"We have all heard the stories," Bawb replied.

"Well, yeah. But he was finally getting into some of the details. Everyone lives together in peace now that the war is over, but they teach this stuff to every Earth-born kid in school so they never forget. I mean, this wasn't all that long ago."

"Of course. It is why the older generation all have metal limbs and replacement parts."

"Exactly. The first generation of entirely organic kids is finally growing up, mod and oppression-free, and their parents want to make damn sure they stay that way."

The two men walked over to better examine the test subject. He was like the other Chithiid in that he was roughly seven feet tall, had four muscular arms, and a second set of eyes toward the back of his head. His skin was a grayish hue, and thick callouses could clearly be seen on his wrists, where years of wearing restraints had caused them to build up.

On his right shoulder was an unusual symbol. And from what Bawb could tell, it had been branded there.

"This appears to be some sort of tribal marking," he noted.

"A sign of the loyalists," Terry the cyborg said, having regained his composure. "Not all of them wore it, though. In fact, many hid in the ranks of the regular Chithiid, kind of like spies. But the higher-up ones usually had this burned into their skin."

"And they sided with your enemies?" Bawb asked, a note of disgust in his voice.

"They did. They helped wipe out pretty much everyone on the planet," Terry said. "Of course, you know all of that now, with Cal filling you in."

"Yes. It sounds to have been a war for the ages, indeed. And this one was part of the forces responsible for the genocide. A perfect test subject, then," Bawb said.

It wasn't even his species that had nearly been made extinct, but Bawb was nevertheless angered at the acts of the traitorous alien. Plus, Charlie was his friend, and *he* was one of those people. Had he been on Earth at the time of the war, he would almost certainly have been wiped out along with the rest of humanity.

Bawb looked at Charlie, who read the thought in his friend's mind even without the benefit of a silent link like he shared with Ara. Charlie nodded once.

"Very well," Bawb said. "Bring him, and restrain him."

The cyborgs carting the frozen Chithiid rolled him out to the middle of the intersection, which had been cleared of all people and conveyances for this attempt. They then drove long metal spikes into the ground, securing the alien traitor's chains, despite his being frozen in place.

If Ara was successful in her attempt, he would not remain frozen much longer. And they had no intentions of allowing this particular loyalist to run free.

·　·　·

Ara had been absorbing the warm energy of the sun's rays while the test subject was procured and moved into position. Unlike many, she was a predator at heart, despite her demeanor toward her friends. A dragon, and one who had killed and eaten all manner of man and beast over her incredibly long life.

If this test subject should perish, it would be unfortunate, but his demise itself would not weigh on her conscience one bit. In fact, she might even get a free meal out of it, though she thought the others might object.

"I'm ready whenever you are," she silently informed Charlie.

"Cool. You sure about this? I mean, it's the first time they've ever tried to use their neuro-stim devices to implant knowledge into a Zomoki, after all."

"And a... fascinating' process it was," she noted. *"But it appears to have been a success. At least so far as I can tell. The spell is in my mind, as clear as if I'd been casting it all my life."*

"Okay, then. I guess it's time we try this." Charlie turned to the others. "Y'all better step back a ways. Ara's ready to give it a go."

The cyborg tenders took the lead from his friends and made sure to stand way back, giving the dragon plenty of room to work her magic. Once they were clear, she turned her attention to the Chithiid restrained before her.

Poor dude, Charlie mused. *If this works, the first thing he's gonna see upon waking up is a giant dragon looming over him.*

He glanced over at Leila, and judging by the slightly amused look in her eye, she'd just been thinking the same thing. They locked eyes a moment, sharing a warm smile, then turned their attention back to the spell their friend was beginning to cast.

Magic crackled in the air as she focused her energy on the single frozen individual in front of her. It was a spell she was perfectly comfortable casting, thanks to the neuro-stim, but nevertheless, they'd been forced to make a few little adaptations as they filled in the blanks where they had been unable to fully retrieve the magical memory from Bawb's mind.

The Chithiid remained completely motionless, locked in place in a deep stasis. Then, slowly, he began to move. Not with intent—not yet, at least—but his body was freed from its imprisonment, finally able to move freely once more.

A moment later all four of the Chithiid's eyes snapped into focus, darting around the faces of his captors. Then the gray man turned a paler shade as he looked up at the impossible sight towering above.

Ara smiled, but all he saw was a mouth full of massive teeth. Teeth that could rend him to pieces without so much as an effort. It was a good thing his bowels were still somewhat frozen in place, or he'd undoubtedly have loosed them at that moment.

"What is that thing?" he managed to say.

"Huh, that's odd," Terry said. "This one refuses to speak anything but Chithiid normally."

"Ah, that is my doing," Bawb noted. "I have made a habit of it these days. Wherever we go, my friends and I bear with us a translation spell, and it typically extends to those in our immediate vicinity if we are adequately powered. At first, when we arrived in this time and place, this Chithiid language was unable to be properly translated. But that was quickly rectified, and now that tongue is understood as readily as the others."

"Wait, so he's speaking Chithiid?"

"Yes."

"Fascinating," Terry said, turning to the prisoner. "You hear that? Even if you only speak Chithiid, we all understand you now. Though, to be fair, we've all had the Chithiid language upgrade for years, now, so I don't know why you're still so stubborn about it."

The Chithiid loyalist rose to his full height. If he was to be devoured by a beast at the hands of his enemies, at least he would face his fate like a man. "I speak the language of my people, not yours. And one day, my masters will return and lay waste to this place once again."

"You know that's not happening, right?" Terry said. "You know you lost the war."

"So you keep saying."

"It is of no consequence," Bawb interjected. "The spell worked. We have no further use for this man. Do with him as you wish."

"You hear that?" Terry said, gesturing to Ara. "Lucky for you, our new friend here isn't hungry."

"I actually could do with a bite," she silently told Charlie. *"I am feeling a bit peckish."*

"We'll grab you a cow or something in a minute," he replied, amused at the cyborg's mind game with his prisoner.

Terry and the others pulled up the chains tethering the Chithiid in place and led him back toward his cell in the tower. As they walked away, Charlie could hear him working on the prisoner's spirits a little more.

"Your former masters are nothing compared with the power our dragon friend wields, you know," he said to the Chithiid. "And if they ever were to make a reappearance, they wouldn't stand a chance."

"He's really enjoying this, isn't he?" Leila said as she leaned against her king.

"Yeah," Charlie replied. "But I suppose it's only natural. I mean, if the guy's been a pain in their ass all these years, it must feel pretty nice finally getting a rise out of him."

The group moved in close again and gathered around Ara.

"So, it works," Rika said. "And it didn't cause a reaction from the fail-safes on the ship."

"No, it did not," Ara replied. "I would definitely have noticed if it had. And this is a very good sign."

"Do you think you will be able to unfreeze the others?" Bawb asked expectantly.

"One at a time, I might eventually be able to do so. But I don't know if you noticed, but the test subject, while alert, was still moving slowly. He's not fully unfrozen, and I do not know what long-term effects there may be from this underpowered process."

"But you can possibly do other individuals?"

"Bawb, I know what you are asking, but I would not risk causing Hunze harm. And this is larger than just our friends. Even if I could free her, there's still the issue of the whole planet at once. I am afraid I would need a lot more power than what I possess. Even with your Ootaki hair adding to the spell, I still don't know if it would be enough to negate the spell worldwide."

It was true. Bawb had a massive amount of power stored in the locks Hunze had gifted him, but even that might not be enough for a spell of this sheer enormity.

Suddenly, a smile broke out on Charlie's face.

"What is it, Charlie?" Ara asked.

"Guys. I have a plan."

CHAPTER FIFTY-SIX

"I'm sorry. How much lead?" Cal asked, sounding a bit confused, which for a super-powerful AI was really saying something. *"Are you sure about those numbers?"*

"I'm the engineer who built her, Cal. Trust me, I know what it'll take to fully entomb the *Asbrú*. And yes, it *is* a shit-ton of lead, but I've tried it out small scale with a bit of Hunze's hair, and my theory played out. The lead does seem to keep the sun from powering it up, at least for the most part."

"But once the ship grows closer to the sun, even the lead won't stop all of the energy from reaching it."

"I know. And that's why Ara has already begun casting a cascade of spells, all of which will combine into one larger blast of magic when she triggers them. By the time we've prepared a container for the *Asbrú* and have her loaded inside, there should be thousands of smaller spells already stacked and ready to go."

"And I currently possess the power of a visla, in addition to that of Hunze's locks," Bawb said. "If you can devise the means to provide me with the counterspell, as you have for the Wise One, then I too can begin casting to help buttress her spells."

"I believe that with our mapping of your physiology, while

extracting the specific memory that created the spell, that should be doable."

"Then, please, let us perform the procedure as soon as you are able."

"Visit my facility in two hours. I believe we should be able to adjust the system to accommodate your request by then. And as for your project, Charlie, it may take a little time to source that quantity of lead and set up a fabrication facility to build an encasement for the ship."

"It doesn't have to be anything fancy, Cal. Just so long as we can seal it around the *Asbrú*, we should be good."

"But how are you going to launch it into space if it's wrapped in lead?" Rika asked. "I mean, it's already a heavy ship, and with all that lead? It's going to be impossible."

"Not necessarily," he replied. "Cal, those massive ships you guys captured from the invaders during the war. They don't have AI control, right?"

"That is correct. The Ra'az systems were entirely manual."

"So trashing one of them wouldn't be costing anyone their life. An AI, I mean. So all we need is to find one big enough to carry the *Asbrú* in its hold, and from what I saw when Rip was showing us around, it looked like at least a few of their old captured ships would be big enough to fit her inside—if we stripped them out, that is."

"It would be possible, yes. At least as far as raw capacity is concerned. Many of the Ra'az ships we captured were originally used as transport vessels for the Chithiid work force. With a minimal amount of work, the interior of one of those could be retrofitted to accommodate the Asbrú. *But it will take us weeks, if not months, to get the engines on those craft modified to be able to break the incredible mass of that ship—especially once it is encased in lead— out of the atmosphere."*

"But they can fly, right?"

"Yes, they have the capacity for flight."

"And they're sturdy enough to survive flight in space, right?"

"That as well, yes. But as I have mentioned, their thrusters are simply too weak in their current condition to exit the atmosphere, and by the time we are able to retrofit them with modifications capable of providing the extra thrust, it will already be too late."

Charlie sighed. It was a good idea, and if they could get the *Asbrú* contained in a lead casing, then it might buy them some additional time. But Cal was right. They simply couldn't afford to wait a month until the ship was modified enough to do what they required.

"A question," Bawb said.

"Yeah?"

"Cal said that this craft you wish to utilize is already capable of flight, correct?"

"Yes. But its engines don't have the lift we need to––"

"I'm getting to that," Bawb interrupted. "As I see it, if this ship is indeed able to fly close to the upper reaches of the atmosphere, then all it really needs is a boost of sorts to get it to the gravity-free environs of outer space. Once there, the ship should be able to fly as normal."

"Right, but like Cal said, it can't break atmosphere."

"Not on its own, no."

"What are you getting at, Bob?"

"What I am trying to say is I possess a powerful Drookonus. And Ara and I both have substantial additional power at our disposal. What if we were to use our combined magic to give the ship a little push?"

Charlie looked at Rika. She knew flying better than he did, and from the look on her face, she thought the plan might actually work.

"So you'd basically take an already-flying ship and nudge it the rest of the way out of the atmosphere, is that what you're saying?" she asked, intrigued.

"Yes, basically," Bawb replied.

She turned to Charlie. "You know, it might actually work. I mean, a huge ship like that, there's no way magic alone could lift it. But if it's already in flight like Bawb said, then a little magical push might be just enough to get it into space."

"And if it falls?" Charlie asked. "It's the end of the world, you know."

"So we don't let it fall," Rika replied. "And if we don't make this work, the aliens will invade and overrun Earth, which is basically the end of the world anyway. So I say let's go out swinging if we're going to go at all."

Charlie paused, thinking about the variables that might come into play. At the end of the day, though, Rika was right. There simply wasn't enough time for anything else. And she was right about something else. It was indeed better to go out on your feet, giving it your best shot.

"Okay," he finally said. "Let's make this happen."

CHAPTER FIFTY-SEVEN

Sourcing the quantity of lead Charlie had requested might have been a simple affair in the days of a bustling human civilization, but after the war, there was simply no demand for any ore––or smelting of any sizable amount, for that matter. What they required to rebuild would simply be drawn from the wreckage of the planet's former inhabitants, as well as that of the vanquished invaders.

It would take at least a week with all of the available cyborgs and AI robotic systems around the globe to acquire the amount needed to build the sealed tomb for the *Asbrú*. It was cutting it close, from what Ara could tell, but they really didn't have any other choice.

In the meantime, however, the great minds of Earth's AI network leapt to action with their fabrication bots making quick work patching the damage to the rather large Ra'az ship they had determined to be the best candidate to carry the sheer mass of the encased craft in its hold.

There was a great deal of cutting away of the interior walls and storage, but not the load-bearing or structural walls and reinforcements. But rather than scrapping all of the metal removed with the portable plasma cutters, much of the material was repurposed into a reinforced structure to hold the *Asbrú*.

That portion of the project was surprisingly quick work—the facilities for ship maintenance were already up and online, unlike those for smelting the uncommon metal Charlie required. The result was a cradle of salvaged parts, all locked into place and ready to hold the *Asbrú* fast, while still allowing the construction bots ample access to install the lead paneling as the pieces became available.

The smaller ship was loaded into place with great care, Ara standing by to monitor the magical signature emanating from the craft, ensuring they didn't accidentally trigger the fail-safe spell.

With Ara, Bawb, and even Charlie's growing power guiding the process, the magic-wielders worked hand in hand with the AI workforce to slowly, and *carefully* transfer the *Asbrú* to the shipworks and nestle it into the waiting receptacle.

It had taken every bit of that week to ready the space for it, but given the nature of their task, that was an incredible feat for the bots hard at work twenty-four-seven. And to Charlie's eyes, the sheer speed and precision of technology in his future was almost magic in its own way.

"You know, it took *years* to build the *Asbrú*," he commented as he watched the AI machinery fly through their carefully planned motions.

At the end of that week, the smelting of the initial scraps of salvaged lead had just begun in the makeshift facilities so hastily cobbled together. Within only a day, the first several massively heavy panels of the thick metal had been delivered to the waiting fabricators, the still-warm metal passed up into the ship's hold, where the waiting *Asbrú* was slowly being encased in a lead cocoon of sorts.

But when its chrysalis occurred, something far deadlier than a butterfly would emerge. The hope was to delay that until their plan was complete.

At the end of the process, nearly three weeks had passed. It was cutting it incredibly close, but the invaders' portal had not opened yet, likely delayed by the thick lead dampening the Ootaki hair's absorption of the sun's energy.

Ara had sensed a change in the magic after just the first few lead panels were hauled into place and secured.

"There has been a shift in power," she noted. "It is slowing. Only slightly, for now, but I believe this is going to work."

She and Bawb had been casting their layers upon layers of the counterspell the entire time, and even Charlie had learned it—albeit naturally, and without use of a neuro-stim. After what had happened to Rika's mind at the hands of the Tslavars, he was reticent to have anything tamper with his own gray matter.

Fortunately, his blood tie to Ara had helped him home in on the correct *feel* of the spell. The *intent* behind it. Within two days, he was helping them cast, adding his own power to the mix. They worked at a relaxed pace, not to the point of exhausting their own power, but in a calm but continuous manner that would lead to a far greater spell potential than just a single casting.

It was much like the strength of a palm tree in a storm. Made of thousands of individual strands of grass-like fiber as opposed to the singular nature of a piece of wood. One would snap under a storm's pressure, while the other would merely flex with the load. Their hope was that the layered spells would be equally robust.

And so it went, the trio casting as the AI members of their team worked tirelessly around the clock, as only machines could. At the end of three weeks, the *Asbrú* was entirely encased in its lead shell, and the hull of the Ra'az ship had been sealed, reinforced, and made space-ready.

They should have already passed the trigger date for the

portal spell by that point, by Ara's reckoning, but Charlie's plan had been successful so far. The lead was thick, and it had done a far-greater job of blocking the Ootaki hair from soaking in the radiant power of the Earth's sun than he'd expected. A pleasant surprise, and a much-needed win for his team.

The spell within the walls of the ship was still ramping up, however. But so far as Ara could sense, they still had at least a few days before it would reach critical mass.

"Well done," she said. "This was a good plan, Charlie."

"Indeed. Without it, the portal would have opened by now, and the invaders would have likely already succeeded in overthrowing this planet and claiming the system as their own," Bawb added.

"Aww, shucks. Thanks, guys," Charlie said. "But it ain't over yet. Hell, the hardest part is still ahead. We've gotta get this thing out of the atmosphere, somehow. And that's not going to be an easy trick."

CHAPTER FIFTY-EIGHT

Charlie was once again in the comfortable familiarity of his space suit's embrace, his most powerful konuses worn inside the material, resting directly against his skin. Strapped to the outside of his suit were the slaaps and konuses of a much larger man—big enough to fit over the suit's arms and hands if need be.

Leila pulled him close, resting her forehead on his.

"Come back in one piece."

"That's my plan."

"And we know how your plans sometimes go," she joked, but the look in her eye was one of concern rather than cheerful mirth.

Charlie knew it was difficult for her to sit by and merely play passenger while the others did the heavy lifting. And equally frustrating was the knowledge that the Magus stone hanging around her neck was likely one of the most powerful ever recorded. At least Bawb and Ara thought so, given the way it had flared up, protecting her and her friends—though likely by mere proximity.

But she had no means to tap into its power. It was

frustrating, having so much potential resting against her skin but being unable to use it.

"It saved your life, babe," Charlie had told her. "Hell, it saved all of us."

"But you can cast with your power. So can Bawb, with what he's taken, I mean."

"You can still use your konus."

"I know, but it's not the same."

He knew she was right, of course. Ever since his internal power had begun to grow, his reliance on his konus had begun to diminish as the Zomoki blood in his veins continued to strengthen. To be reliant on only a konus at this point would leave him feeling somewhat helpless. And he imagined that was somewhat how Leila felt.

"Look, you may not be able to control it, but that stone is tied to you, and you alone. And we'd all be dead or worse without you. So be annoyed, sure, but also remember we all owe you our lives."

A little smile tickled the corner of her lips, which she pressed to his warmly. "Thanks, Charlie. You're the best."

"You know it," he said with a loving grin.

"I'm sorry to interrupt, but are you ready?" Bawb asked as he strode up to his friends.

"Damn, Bob. Way to make the rest of us look like we're hobos," Charlie joked.

The Wampeh chuckled. He *did* look rather impressive, clad not only in his space suit—which also contained myriad magical devices on his person within—but also wrapped in a thick rope-like braid of Hunze's magical hair. He'd kept it in full sun, charging to its greatest capacity possible in the weeks they had been preparing. And now it was time to use that power. Power which, like Leila's Magus stone, was bound to him and him alone.

Unlike the hair of any other species, Ootaki hair stored

massive amounts of magic within each strand. Additionally, their locks were exceptionally strong, able to withstand the harsh environs of space with ease where other materials might fall to pieces. And now it was going to be put to the test.

"Ara is ready to go when you are," the Wampeh said. "And Ripley and Eddie insist on accompanying us, in case you hadn't heard."

"Oh yeah, we had a little chat about that," he replied.

Leila chuckled. "I can imagine how that went."

"Yeah. No way I was talking her out of it. And even Cal was okay with her coming along. He liked the idea of her and Eddie flying as a backup to the backup, just in case something should go wrong."

The backup in this case was Rika, manually flying a ship she'd had fine-tuned to her preferences over the last couple of weeks. It had been years since she sat in a pilot's seat, but she'd always been exceptional, and despite the damage and healing to her mind, that, at least, was one of the muscle-memory things that had remained intact.

She was also wearing a konus, as well as her powerful new slaap, and a space suit on top of that, just in case. She didn't intend to lose cabin pressure, but she was also well aware that their mission was going to put all of their craft under a lot of strain. Losing pressure was simply too great a risk to ignore.

Her small ship had been docked atop the massive freighter that would carry their lead-ensconced payload into space. The controls of the Ra'az ship had been reworked to function via a hardlined link to the smaller one, riding atop like a remora on a shark. She could steer it on its way, then cut free when the time came.

Leila would be flying with her, ready to assist in whatever way she could if needed. But if all went according to plan, she and Rika would merely be there as a safety. A backstop, just in case. With a dragon leading the way, though, they were pretty confident their help wouldn't be required.

Charlie and Bawb walked to their winged friend and climbed atop her towering back. Leila joined them for the quick hop over to the launch site, not needing a space suit for the low-level atmospheric flight.

When they touched down, they saw that Ripley and Eddie were standing by, ready and eager to take off. Rika, likewise, was set to go, her ship securely resting atop the massive craft waiting to be pushed into space.

"Comms check, one, two," Charlie said into his earpiece.

"All comms are good on this end," Cal said.

"And localized comms are good here too," Eddie noted. "We're ready when you are."

Charlie took one more look at the massive ship, then donned his helmet. "Well, then. I guess let's get this show on the road."

Eddie gave Rika and Leila a quick lift to her waiting craft atop the freighter, then took up his standby position a safe distance from the ship. In case they were required to use excessive magic to help nudge it into space, it was decided he and Ripley should stay well clear, just in case there was any blowback from the Ootaki-fueled device in the *Asbrú*'s hull.

"Lifting off," Rika called out. She turned to the woman at her side and gave her a reassuring smile. "You ready for this?"

"As ready as any of us will be," Leila said. "Just don't crash us, okay?"

Rika let out a laugh. "Yeah, definitely not on my checklist today. Okay, hang on, here we go."

She powered up the ship's drive systems slowly, ensuring everything was functioning properly. Then she feathered the throttle, and with a low rumble, the craft slowly pulled from its terrestrial bonds, rising into the sky.

"*Icarus* is airborne," she said over the comms.

"Copy that," Charlie replied. "Reading you five-by-five." It was just like old times, their old training coming back to them as if it were just yesterday they crewed a flight team together. "Looking good from here. How are the power readings from the main drive systems?"

"Green across the board," she replied. "She's a beast, but she flies all right."

"Copy that," Charlie said. "And *Icarus*?"

"I thought it was a fitting name. Why, you don't like it?"

"No, it's fine. Just, that story didn't exactly have a happy ending."

"Not all stories do," she replied as the ship powered higher and higher into the sky. "Hang on. I've got a yellow light on the board. You seeing any smoke? I might have lost one of the stabilizing jets."

"Ara, can you swing closer? She thinks something might be wrong with a stabilizer."

"Of course," the dragon replied, gently banking, bringing them much closer to the ship.

"Yeah, I see it," Charlie said. "Looks like your number four flamed out. Nothing we can do about it now. How are the rest?"

"They seem to be okay, but this thing is getting sluggish as hell. There's no way it's going to make it without a nudge. You guys ready to give a girl a hand?"

"You good, Bob?"

"I am awaiting your word, Charlie."

"How about you, Ara? You ready to give this massive boat a little push?"

"Whenever you say," she replied.

"Okay, we're all ready and standing by," Charlie said. "Just say the word."

"Well, then, *word*. Hurry up and do it now, before I start losing altitude."

"Copy that. Bawb, you heard her. Start casting. I'll tell Ara."

The Wampeh began drawing from his Drookonus, utilizing the very specific type of magic stored in it to help power the enormous ship toward the atmospheric shell encompassing the Earth.

"It's time, Ara."

The mighty Zomoki began casting as well, her power providing further force to the energy driving the ship toward space. Charlie then tapped into his own power, providing the final boost to push Rika's rumbling load to its zero-g goal.

"Almost there," Rika said. "Keep it up just a minute longer."

The magical trio continued their assistance, the massive ship's hull vibrating as the edge of the atmosphere drew close. Then it abruptly stopped, easing into the silent smoothness of space.

"Clear. You can back down," Rika called out.

"Copy that. Easing off," Charlie said. The three casters ceased their magical assist. "Nice flying, Rika."

"Thanks."

"Yeah, that was pretty kickass," Ripley chimed in. "From where we were watching, it looked like you might not clear the exosphere for a minute there."

"I had to modify the trajectory slightly to compensate," Rika replied.

"It was an impressive on-the-fly adaptation to an unexpected variable," Eddie noted. "Very good flying, for a non-AI."

"Gee, thanks."

"No, that's a compliment," Rip said. "I mean, we couldn't kill an AI flying the ship, but you did it almost as well as one of them could. That's impressive, for reals."

"Well, thanks, then."

"And it's even more impressive using a Ra'az ship. I mean, our stuff is pretty intuitive, but theirs is a different kind of tech altogether."

"I noticed. But we got it to work."

"Good thing, too. It would have really sucked to have to burn up one of our own ships. I mean, warp engines are hard to come by, you know."

Charlie had been listening to the two banter, but that last bit caught his attention. "Hang on a minute. Did you say *warp?*"

"Oh, yeah. You know, using a warp drive system to power the ships," Ripley said as if it were as normal as breathing.

"You have *warp* drives?" Rika said, joining Charlie in his astonishment. "You can warp?"

"Well, yeah. I thought you knew that."

"No one ever mentioned that to me," Rika said. "Charlie?"

"Nope. First I've heard of it."

"My apologies," Cal said. *"It was simply not something I'd thought to bring up. As Ripley said, it is a well-known means of interstellar travel, though we are still somewhat limited in which craft possess the technology. I am sorry for not briefing you on it."*

"It's okay, Cal," Charlie said, still reeling at the news. "I suppose there's a lot I still need to learn about this future of mine. And if we succeed in this, I look forward to picking your electronic brain for all kinds of things we just don't know yet."

"I would be glad to help in any way I can, of course."

"Thanks, Cal, I appreciate it."

"Hey, don't forget about me," Rika interjected. "I want in on this tech lesson too."

Charlie chuckled. "Of course you do. But for now, we've got work to do."

"Already on course," Rika said. "Now it's just a matter of time. And hoping we don't burn, freeze, decompress, or blow up in the process."

"Such an optimist," Charlie said. "All right, then. Let's do it. Let's fly this thing into the sun."

CHAPTER FIFTY-NINE

Ara flew well ahead of the ship—fittingly deemed *Icarus* by its amused pilot—double-checking the way was free of debris, ensuring there were no unforeseen obstacles in their path.

All was clear, as anticipated, and as they drew close to the massive ball of burning plasma, the proximity of the sun's rays affected Ara and the Ootaki hair worn over Bawb's space suit even more than expected.

"This is amazing," Ara said.

The feeling of her words, shared between her and Charlie alone with their silent, visceral link, was one colored with intense satisfaction. She was becoming supercharged with power. It was part of the plan, of course, but the sheer intensity of the magic surging though her body was so much more than she'd ever experienced. More than they'd ever expected to be possible.

Bawb, likewise, felt the massive surge in power build in the Ootaki hair wrapped around his space suit. Hunze's gift was already of incredible potency, but this was something entirely new. Massive. Powerful. Nearly overwhelming. The power he now possessed dwarfed any he'd felt before.

"Charlie, can you feel this?" he asked.

Charlie did, though more through his link with Ara than its direct effect on the Zomoki blood flowing in his own veins. "Yeah, man. It's incredible."

The trio pushed ahead at a faster clip, flying closer and closer to the sun, leaving Rika and the massive freighter far in their wake. And as they did, the balance of power slowly began to tilt in their favor.

"Ara, can you feel the spell at this distance?"

"Yes. My senses are greatly heightened with this influx of energy," she replied. *"And so far as I can tell, the spell is gaining in power, but far slower than we are. The lead shielding is doing its job, it would seem."*

"So the dual layer of the ship around it on top of the lead we built is slowing the rays."

"Yes. And I can feel the magic potential of Hunze's hair increasing by the minute, just as my own powers are increasing."

"And our spell? We have a few thousand smaller layers cast by now, but this is the lynchpin. If this casting fails, the whole thing does. Will we have enough?"

"It will be close, but I believe we just might succeed in overpowering their spell. So long as the shielding continues to block their Ootaki hair from buttressing their spell further."

The plan was, so far, proceeding as they hoped. But Charlie was quite familiar with Murphy and his unexpected alterations to people's best laid plans.

"I'm going to have to break away pretty soon, guys," Rika said from her perch atop the massive freighter. "The shielding on this ship is going to start giving way soon. I'll stick with it as long as I can, but I'm going to run out of tricks in just another minute or two."

"Copy that," Charlie replied. "It looks like we're closing in on the tipping point. Ara and Bob are pretty much supercharged from all of this direct exposure."

"And you? You're human, Charlie. Even with Zomoki blood in you, you're still susceptible to radiation. And heat, for that matter."

"Believe me, I'm well aware. And trust me, I've been casting *multiple* protection spells since we pulled ahead of you guys. Bob too. We're in a cozy little bubble here."

"Good," Leila said, coming on comms. "Come back to me in one piece, please."

"Don't worry, babe. I'd rather not roast to a crisp. And you know how Wampeh are about their complexions."

Ripley crackled over the comms. "We can pick you up if you want. Eddie's got some super top-end shielding. Just say the word."

"No, we're good, Rip. But thanks for the offer. We're going to start casting any minute now, so stay a good ways back. And Rika, if you haven't cut her loose yet, when I give the word, gun the engines one last time, then get out of there. And be sure to fly well clear of the ship. We don't know how it'll react."

"Copy that. Don't have to tell me twice."

The massive Ra'az ship shuddered slightly, the vibrations rattling the much smaller craft mounted atop its bulk.

"I think we're going to have to disengage sooner than later, though. So hurry, okay?"

Charlie turned his attention to the magic building all around him. The sun's energy, while deadly, was also fueling the magic keeping him safe. And the closer they got, the stronger both became.

If he was right, the same would happen to the Ootaki hair within the *Asbrú*'s walls. But by then, they'd either be successful, or dead. He was sincerely hoping for the former.

"Ara? Cutting it a little close here."

"I think we're ready, Charlie."

"I'll tell Bob."

"No need," Ara replied. *"He is linked with us both through my*

spell. And with all of this power we are absorbing, I believe he is party to this conversation now, aren't you, Geist?"

A new voice joined the silent conversation. "That is correct, Wise One," Bawb replied, a hint of the awe flooding through him coloring his voice. "And I am honored and humbled by this act."

"It's merely a side-effect of the sun's power ramping up our enjoined magic," she replied. "It will fade as we distance ourselves from its rays once again."

"This communication, yes. But you are sharing your power, and I am humbled by the act."

Ara chuckled warmly. "A necessity of the situation at hand, Geist," she said, turning her head to look at the man on her back. "But even were it not a dire need, know that you are one of the very few I would ever consider sharing it with. You're a good man, Bawb. One I am glad to call friend."

For just a moment, the three of them flew silently, feeling the bond of friendship and power flowing between them.

"Okay, guys. I think it's time to do this before the shielding around the Asbrú starts to fail. If that Ootaki hair gets a blast of this much power, we'll never be able to break that spell."

"I agree. We are as ready as possible," Ara said. "Tell Rika and Leila to break free and take up a position far off. Once she is clear, we shall begin."

Charlie relayed the instructions over his comms.

"About freakin' time," Rika said. "Our shields are just about at their limit, here."

"Cut free. We'll circle back when it's done," Charlie replied.

"Already on it. I'm setting the engines to engage at maximum as soon as we release, so start casting now. We'll be long gone and well clear by the time your spell hits."

"Copy that."

"And, Charlie, good luck."

"Thanks."

With that, the three casters began intermingling their power, drawing upon their internal stores as well as the additional boost of the magical devices worn by the human and Wampeh.

This was their one shot, so they poured all the power into it they could. Either it would work, overriding the global freeze spell, or it would fail spectacularly, likely killing them in the process, as well as the entire population of Earth.

Rika, true to her word, punched it and cut free, sending the *Icarus* flying straight for the sun at great speed. Her small ship shuddered with the force of her sharp bank away from the much larger craft, the full brunt of the sun's energy buffeting the ship now that it was no longer protected by the mass of the freighter.

"Hang on, Leila," she grunted as she struggled with the controls.

The ship bucked and rolled, tossed about as its engines strained to put as much distance between them and the sun as possible. Minus the restraining mass of the much larger ship, however, the nimble craft was able to increase speed nearly instantly. In just a few moments, they were free of the turbulence, well on their way clear of the impending casting.

"They're clear," Charlie sent. *"Now or never."*

Ara and Bawb immediately responded, beginning the final stage of the massive casting, all three of them compounding their magic, resulting in a spell far more powerful than any of them could possibly cast individually. It wasn't the same as powerful vislas casting for months, creating the original stasis spell, but it would have to suffice. With the sun's help, it just might.

"Now!" Ara signaled, the trio setting their magic loose, directly targeting the magic being reinforced by the ship now rapidly catching up to them.

The spell flew true, making the stasis spell waver in its strength. But it was not enough to stop it. Not on its own. But the thousands of smaller spells set in place for precisely this reason

began to cascade, each of them chipping away at the larger spell
that had the populace under its power.

"*It's starting to fall!*" Charlie exclaimed.

And indeed, it was. Like waves crashing on the shore, the
onslaught of spells were wearing down the alien attack. And
then, with a sudden release of power, the spell broke, like a
rubber band stretched to its limit.

"*It was a success!*" Cal transmitted several seconds later,
thanks to the signal delay so far from Earth. "*The spell is broken.
Everyone has been released.*"

Silence.

"*Charlie? Do you copy?*"

"Sorry, Cal. A bit knackered from that," he replied over
comms.

"When did you pick up the UK slang?" Rika chimed in.

"Well, we did spend a lot of time there these past few weeks,"
he replied with a chuckle. "Anyway, we're okay. Just need a
minute to catch our breath."

"Do you need us to pick you up?" Ripley asked.

"No, we're fine. Head back to LA. We'll meet you down
there."

The pair of ships plotted a course for the now-freed planet,
leaving the dragon, the Wampeh, and the human to drift in the
sun's restoring rays as they regained their energy.

Bawb was silent a long time. He knew his communication
with Ara would soon return to normal, requiring speech rather
than direct thought. But after what had just occurred, after the
power the three of them had shared, with the Zomoki opening
up her power to him, and the Wampeh sharing his Ootaki
power right back—which should have been impossible with the
power being tied to him and him alone—a connection of a new
order had been formed.

It was indescribable. Visceral. The power the three had
created while linked together would soon fade, but even so, the

effect would remain. And the deadly assassin would from that day forward be––in some ways, at least––a changed man.

"You guys can feel it, right? The other spells are still in place," Charlie said.

"Yes," Ara replied. *"Despite the lead shell, the portal spell is rapidly increasing in power as the ship nears the sun, and the fail-safe is still intact. There is no way to negate it without triggering the destruction of the planet."*

Charlie watched the huge freighter hurtling toward the sun. *"Good thing we have a plan, then, isn't it?"*

CHAPTER SIXTY

Ara flew a quick loop around the Ra'az freighter as it flew closer and closer to the sun. Having spent the energy she had been saving for their joint spell, she was now free to redirect her power to protecting herself and her friends from the heat of the sun.

Charlie had also cast his own spell to shield himself from the radiation that his friends were basking in. Unlike the others, he would quite simply fry, if not for the magical protection from the rays.

Ara, on the other hand, absorbed it with great pleasure, the energy replenishing what she had expended when they cast their joint spell. And Bawb was simultaneously collecting the energy, and also being protected from its damaging potential by his Ootaki hair wrappings, which, much like the Zomoki he rode, greedily soaked up the immense power of the sun.

Charlie sensed something beginning to change in the ebb and pull of magic around them. A shift that meant only one thing. Their moment of grace was passing.

The freighter, though managing to stay intact for such a demanding flight, had finally started to superheat despite the protective spells they'd placed on it prior to launch. Inside, however, the *Asbrú* would suffer no such damage.

It had been an inspired idea on Bawb's part as he walked through the craft while it was being slowly covered with its lead covering. He had convened with Ara to confirm his theory, and sure enough, it seemed that once they had pinpointed the spell that linked to the stasis spell generated from the ship, they would be able to gently tap into the Ootaki hair woven throughout its structure.

Essentially, they could use their enemy's weapon against them, in a sense. It would be subtle, like a parasite leeching nutrients from its host. But it would work.

The new spell he had devised was gently eased into place around the *Asbrú*. It would stay with the ship, bound to it, recharging and renewing with the sun's rays as it protected the craft from any harm from the molten ball of plasma.

If it worked as planned, the *Asbrú* would remain perfectly safe in its continuously powered shielding spell, courtesy of Bawb and Ara, the pair having spent many hours together refining the spell to ensure there was no chance of it failing. It would be safe, and in the center of the sun.

And as far as they could tell, the spell would be a success, keeping the ship in perfect condition, safe from harm indefinitely by the very Ootaki hair simultaneously powering their enemy's spells. Anything around it, however, would not be so fortunate.

A flash of light caught all of their attention as it beamed out between the cracks that had formed in the freighter.

"Shit, it's starting!" Charlie blurted as he saw the crackling glow of a portal begin to break through the hull of the nearly destroyed ship.

At this point, it was really just the remnants of their magic that was holding the outer craft together, and the lead covering of its precious cargo was already beginning to melt away.

And as soon as the first burst of the sun's rays broke through the dense metal covering, the spell previously contained within, held back to no more than a slow build, would burst forth, super-powered by the energy of the sun as the Ootaki hair sucked it in like a sponge.

"It's not close enough," Charlie said. *"We're going to have to give it a push. Bob, do you think your Drookonus—?"*

"Already casting," the Wampeh replied silently as his magic leapt out across the vacuum to the speeding ship.

"I shall assist," Ara said, pouring her power on top of his, giving the failing craft a final push toward its fiery destination.

Charlie, though less powered than either of his friends, drew deep from within and added what additional magic he could to their casting.

The crumbling ship suddenly leapt forward as if hit from behind with a massive blow. Given the hasty nature of the spells they had cast, that wasn't too far from the truth.

Magic flashed and pulsed from the *Asbrú* as the *Icarus* finally broke to pieces, burning up at the edge of the sun's blazing reach. The lead shell around the smaller ship contained within turned molten and blew off into space in seconds, the *Asbrú* blazing with a flash of such magical brightness that even Ara had to turn away.

The light was so intense that Charlie felt like he could still see it through closed eyes, a tinted visor, magical protections, and the back of his head, since he, like his friends, was facing the other direction, shielding his eyes. Finally, after a series of additional flashes that left spots before his closed lids, the light diminished to a far more comfortable glow.

The trio turned their gaze back upon the glowing ship just as it submerged within the body of the sun itself. They caught a quick glimpse of the enormous portal being generated by the craft before it vanished within the flames.

"Holy shit. It's huge," Charlie had managed to gasp before the glowing ring submerged into the sun.

It was far larger than they'd anticipated. Large enough for a sizable ship to pass through. And the portal would remain open now, and there was nothing they could do about that. At least not at the moment. But their planet was safe.

Anyone foolish enough to brave the magical transit would find themselves turned to ash the moment they passed through, courtesy of the Earth's sun. It wasn't a perfect solution, Charlie had mused when they came up with the plan, but it would suffice.

Of course, it was entirely possible that, eventually, whoever was on the other side would possibly devise some way to protect themselves. To survive the molten core of the sun.

But magic of that scale would take a long, long time to amass. No one had that quantity of Ootaki hair. And given what had already been sent their way within the *Asbrú*'s hull, whoever had planned this attack had already expended their entire bounty. And that had to be several lifetime's worth, collected from all corners of their galaxy.

It was an impossibly large amount that had been used to power the attack, and the odds of that quantity being amassed again before they could devise a solution to the problem was slim.

That many Ootaki didn't even exist, and he knew of no other power source that could manage the feat the attackers had pulled off with the Trojan Horse trick using his old ship. Not again. Not for a long, long time.

So it was that Charlie felt that, for now, they could rest secure in the knowledge that no one could pass through the portal. The invasion had been stopped.

Earth was safe once more.

CHAPTER SIXTY-ONE

Ara, supercharged with the sun's power once more, decided to make a little jump from the sun to the moon. The distance required only a minimal expenditure on her part, and the use of her magic felt really good, all the way to her bones.

After that burst of travel magic she hadn't used in a long, long time, she then took Charlie and Bawb on a little detour, taking her time flying back to Earth.

First, she made a loop around the moon. Then she flew closer and put on a little show for the men and women living on the moon, dropping in low as they passed Dark Side base.

They could see the crew of the facility through the windows, excitedly pressed up against them as they watched the fly-by. Judging by the enthusiasm they could see through the thick glass, there was quite a celebration already underway inside.

But they had other places to be, and festivities of their own to get started.

The mighty Zomoki lifted from the moon's dusty surface and soared through the void, her magic strong in her body as she easily crossed the space between the moon and Earth, re-entering the planet's atmosphere with a simple grace.

Once they'd reached a breathable altitude, Charlie cracked the visor on his helmet just a bit, the quick flash of fresh, but cold, air sending his spirits even higher. In a strange way, he supposed, it was a smell of victory. Of his home world, free and secure.

Swinging low over Southern California as they made their approach home, the humans and Chithiid alike stared up at the still-new sight of the massive red dragon soaring through the skies. And this time, it appeared, she had passengers atop her back.

"They don't even know what just happened," Charlie said to his friends. *"To them it's only been a minute."*

"True," Ara agreed. *"They were maintained in a perfect stasis spell."* A little chuckle vibrated in Charlie and Bawb's heads. *"I think a few may wonder how the weather so abruptly changed. And where they are, for that matter."*

"Ah, yes. The ones moved for their own protection. There will be a bit of explaining required," Bawb added. *"But tell me, Wise One, how is it I am still linked with you and Charlie like this? The spell has been cast, and the power expended."*

"It is curious," she agreed. *"But I believe there is more at work than merely a residual link from our efforts."*

"You mean Bob's part of the talk-without-moving-your-lips club now? Like, permanently?"

"It would seem that may very well be the case, Charlie."

The space-suited human slapped his friend cheerfully on the shoulder. *"Awesome, dude. We're like blood brothers now."*

"You might not be too far from the truth," Ara said. *"We shared our power on a far more intimate level than merely casting with one another. And with the sheer strength of the Ootaki hair Bawb is wielding, I believe a new bond has indeed been formed, similar to what you and I share, Charlie."*

Bawb was silent a long time as they flew closer to home. His suit's visor was down, so he couldn't blame it on the wind, but if

SCOTT BARON

anyone could see through the tinted material, they'd have
noticed his eyes gleaming with unexpected wetness.

*"I would very much appreciate it if you would take me to my
home,"* he said, clearing his throat as emotion welled.

"Of course," Ara replied, knowing full well his motives even
without their new connection.

"Yeah, man. We'll go do the debrief with Cal. You check in on her,"
Charlie added. *"And when you two feel like company, Leila and I
want you guys to come over for a dinner. A proper* family *dinner."*

Again, the assassin felt that strange flush of warmth in his
chest. Family. A word he'd found so foreign since his youth. A
thing of the past. But, he realized, after all the years that had
passed, that was the case no more.

"I would like that, Charlie. I would like that very much."

Even Ara seemed a little choked up with the moment, but
she said nothing, merely bee-lining straight for Bawb's home.
She touched down softly, her wings making the cyborgs
guarding the property turn away from the gust.

"Thank you, Ara," he said as he quickly slid to the ground. *"I
shall contact you all later. I first have some things—"*

"Just go see her, Bob!" Charlie ordered with a happy grin.

Bawb nodded to his friends and stepped through his layers
of spells and into the waiting arms of his love.

"There you are," she said happily as he unwrapped the
length of her hair from his suit and stepped unencumbered into
her embrace. The glistening drops from his eyes finally broke
free as he held her tight, not wanting to ever let go again.

"Hey, are you okay?" she asked, concerned. He was the Geist.
Assassin. Man of action. And he simply did not cry.

"I'm fine," he said, wiping his eyes. "I am simply pleased to
see you."

"Cal called while you were away," she said, eyeing the thick
braid of her magical hair he had been wearing, pulling its power

320

in hopes of saving her, as well as the rest of the planet. "He told me what happened."

"It's over now," he said, the pained look in his eye speaking more clearly than his words.

"I'm okay, Bawb. *We're* okay," she said, pulling him close once more.

And with the tiniest of sighs, he felt the last bits of stress flee his body and knew she was right.

CHAPTER SIXTY-TWO

"It is bound to happen at some point, and we must be prepared for it," Cal said.

"And we will be. But for now, I think we can all just take a little breather and enjoy the moment. We won, Cal. We deserve a break."

"Obviously, Charlie. But once you return from your respite, we really must discuss this new situation."

"We will," Leila interjected. "But he's right. For now, we need some quiet time, if you don't mind. It's been an exhausting ordeal."

"Of course. I was simply thinking of the inevitable. It is no longer a question of if, but rather, when. A portal has been opened between our galaxies, and we will have to plan for the eventual contact."

Charlie leaned back in his seat in the makeshift outdoor command area Cal had set up. This was one thing he was actually *not* stressing about.

"The thing is, on their end, anyone who's foolish enough to try to pass through the portal is going to have a very hot, and

322

very short, trip. And no one will be going through from our end until we're damn well ready."

"About that. How does this spell you mentioned function, exactly?"

"Shall I?" Ara asked.

"All you."

"Very well, then," she said. "When we cast our spells pushing the *Asbrú* into the sun, we left a magical tether spell linked to the Ootaki hair actively charging within the craft itself. By tapping into it, the spell will remain in power in perpetuity. But as it is *our* spell, the invaders have no means to utilize it for their purposes."

Rika leaned in, grabbing an electrolyte pouch from the low table before her. "And that means we can pull the ship back out of the sun from a safe distance when we finally *are* ready to make contact. On *our* terms, that is."

"Exactly," Charlie said. "But for now, we'll just leave it parked where it is. Smack dab in the middle of the sun. You guys can still study the phenomenon, though, right, Cal?"

"Yes. The sun should not interfere with our scans. The forces it produces, while apparently quite potent to magic users, are nevertheless a different type of energy signature."

"Fantastic," Charlie said, rising to his feet. "And on that note, I propose we table any further discussion for the time being. I could really use a hot shower and a cold drink right about now. You guys good with that?"

"Yes, please. Take a shower––you stink!" Rika said with a grin.

"Don't worry, I'll get him cleaned up," Leila said with a chuckle. "All right, Charlie. Let's go home."

They separated, Rika opting to first take her new ship for a little spin around the planet. She'd only just gotten it, after all, and it needed a proper breaking in. Something besides a near-suicide mission to the sun, that is.

She took to the skies, the familiar feel of a ship's controls lulling her into a state of aerial contentment. With a quick loop over her friends and a wag of her wings, she was gone, off to enjoy the skies of her home.

Ripley had also made a quick run for it, Cal having cut her free before the debriefing. Eddie took the teen straight home, and despite her professing the contrary on any other day, she really had missed her parents, and immediately ran into their arms as soon as she'd stepped in her front door.

And her parents, having just learned their daughter had played a role in saving the world, decided they'd overlook her exuberant canine friend's muddy paws when Baloo came padding into their home for a visit shortly thereafter.

"Baloo!" she squealed, wrapping her arms tightly around the massive animal's neck, burying her face in the fluffy warmth. "Come on! Let's go for a ride!"

She jumped atop his back, the huge beast easily able to carry her weight. He turned to her, licking her face clean of those tasty, salty tears, then trotted off into the hills with his friend.

Not far from there, Charlie and Leila rinsed clean of the day's exertion, then grabbed a blanket and walked out to the bluffs overlooking the ocean. Curled up together, taking in the glorious sunset over the glistening water, they realized that despite being on the wrong world for one of them, and in the wrong time for them both, they were home.

They'd fought for it. Bled for it. Sweated for it. This was their Earth now, and they'd be damned if they'd let anything happen to it.

They sat like that until the sun finally sank below the distant horizon on the exceptionally clear eve. And when it did finally pass from sight, the curvature of the earth refracted the light, just right, making it flash green for an instant.

"Did you see it?" Leila asked.

"Yeah, babe. I did," Charlie replied. "Magic."

EPILOGUE

Millions of light years away, an angry visla watched from the command center of their ship as their advancing fleet burned up in the span of mere moments. The portal spell they had been waiting for weeks to activate finally did just that, but in a manner they had in no way anticipated. Had the visla's ship not been positioned toward the rear of the attack force, it too would almost certainly have succumbed to the sun's heat, just as the other ships had, despite the spell-casters aboard.

As it was, they had still only barely managed to avoid the same fate as the rest of the fleet.

There had been a delay. Maybe something in the spell wasn't quite perfect, despite the time and effort spent casting it. But when the portal finally did open—a good week behind schedule—there was but a moment of clear space showing through the opening.

The lead pair of experimental shimmer ships—the most advanced ever made—sped through the glowing ring immediately, entering the magical portal just before a blast of burning plasma from the core of a yellow star spewed out and engulfed the remainder of the fleet.

But those two had entered the ring before the fire tore through the ships. It was a long-shot, given the destruction wrought by the flames, but if they had somehow survived the journey, then someday, somehow, their crews would find a way back. A way to re-open the portal. A means to connect the two galaxies as the visla intended.

For now, however, it was a defeat, and one of extraordinary scale.

The visla fumed with rage, a cold iciness crackling in the air in the command center of the ship as raw emotion melded with powerful magic.

"It is confirmed, Visla," the captain reported, fighting to keep his voice from wavering. "Over ninety-percent of the fleet has been reduced to ash."

The mighty power user nodded once, fighting to keep the churning fury within them in check before finally speaking.

"This has cost me dearly. But it is of no matter. Not in the grander scheme of things. War will come regardless. All we need is time."

BUT WAIT, THERE'S MORE!

Follow Charlie on his continuing adventures in the fifth book of
the Dragon Mage series:
Star Fighter Charlie

ALSO BY SCOTT BARON

Standalone Novels

Living the Good Death

The Clockwork Chimera Series

Daisy's Run

Pushing Daisy

Daisy's Gambit

Chasing Daisy

Daisy's War

The Dragon Mage Series

Bad Luck Charlie

Space Pirate Charlie

Dragon King Charlie

Magic Man Charlie

Star Fighter Charlie

Odd and Unusual Short Stories:

The Best Laid Plans of Mice: An Anthology

Snow White's Walk of Shame

The Tin Foil Hat Club

Lawyers vs. Demons

The Queen of the Nutters

Lost & Found

ABOUT THE AUTHOR

A native Californian, Scott Baron was born in Hollywood, which he claims may be the reason for his rather off-kilter sense of humor.

Before taking up residence in Venice Beach, Scott first spent a few years abroad in Florence, Italy before returning home to Los Angeles and settling into the film and television industry, where he has worked as an on-set medic for many years.

Aside from mending boo-boos and owies, and penning books and screenplays, Scott is also involved in indie film and theater scene both in the U.S. and abroad.

Made in United States
North Haven, CT
10 October 2024

58627145R00203